GRACIE

GRACIE

by

Marie Maxwell

Magna Large Print Books
Long Preston, North Yorkshire,
BD23 4ND, England.

British Library Cataloguing in Publication Data.

Maxwell, Marie
    Gracie.

    A catalogue record of this book is
    available from the British Library

    ISBN 978-0-7505-3824-4

First published in Great Britain by Avon
a division of HarperCollins*Publishers* 2013

Published in Large Print 2013 by arrangement with
HarperCollins Publishers

Magna Large Print is an imprint of Library Magna Books Ltd.

Printed and bound in Great Britain by
T.J. (International) Ltd., Cornwall, PL28 8RW

PROLOGUE

'Hello little one...' the young woman said quietly as she stared at the baby she was meeting for the first time. 'I'm your mummy...'

Reaching out her hand, she touched her fingers on the clear wall of the incubator, willing the tiny person inside to know she was there with her and fighting for her. As she spoke the words, she could feel her heart beating so hard inside her chest she thought it might explode with the toxic mixture of love and fear that was racing through her whole body.

'Touch and go' was what they had said when they'd grouped around her bed to talk about the health of the child. 'Touch and go' – because they simply couldn't say if the child was going to live or die.

She ran her hands back and forth across the machine that was imprisoning the premature baby in order to save her life and tried not to cry again. It had been nearly forty-eight hours since she had given birth and apart from the fact that her baby was alive she knew nothing, except that it was 'touch and go.' Forty-eight long hours, enduring mental anguish and physical pain, before she'd been allowed to make the short journey from the maternity ward to the premature baby unit to see her daughter for the first time.

'Can I touch her?' She asked the nurse who was

standing behind her with her hands on the wheel-chair that was a condition of her visit.

'I'm sorry my dear but you can't, not yet.'

'What do you think? She looks so small...'

'She is small, but I've seen far smaller, that's for sure. We just have to wait. She's still with us at the moment and where there's life, there's hope.'

The woman continued to stare at the incu-bator, taking in every detail of her daughter. She was perfect from head to toe and she was certain she was alert and aware, unlike how she had imagined she would be when they had given her the news of her condition.

The tiny baby moved her head and her eyelids flickered.

'She's looking at me, I can see her eyes...' her mother said, her hope rising.

'I'm sure she is, she senses you're here,' the nurse said as she moved around the wheelchair and then turned it slightly. Her expression was serious as she looked down at her patient.

'Now, I have to talk to you. I don't want you to get upset again but we think it would be a good idea for her to be baptised. Just in case. Your priest came to visit while you were still groggy from the operation so you may not remember the conversation...'

'Baptised?'

'Yes, as I said, just in case. He'll baptise her as soon as you say the word; I can ring him for you. Have you chosen a name yet?'

'Yes, but...'

As she tried to interpret the meaning behind the words, the nurse jumped forward and looked closely at the baby in the incubator. The little girl's chest was heaving up and down as she struggled for breath.

'I don't like the look of this, something's wrong. I'm going to get the doctor...'

With those words, the young nurse was away out of the door.

All that the woman could do was stare at her tiny child in the incubator and pray.

Please don't let my baby die.

Please don't take another one away from me...

ONE

New Years' Eve 1953/1954

The young couple in the middle of the crowded dance-floor clapped and shouted excitedly along with everyone else, as the countdown to New Year was dramatically broadcast across the room by the band leader.

'...Five, four, three, two, one...' he bellowed into the microphone and then, as the chimes rang out across the ballroom a loud roar went up, and streamers were thrown out over the heads of the revellers, who all quickly formed into circles, linked hands and started singing 'Auld Lang Syne'.

At the height of the excitement, the young man leaned over and spoke to the woman beside him.

'I can't hear you...' she mouthed back before cupping her ear at him. 'It's so noisy.'

'I said, will you marry me?' he shouted at the top of his voice.

Gracie McCabe stopped still and stared at her boyfriend. 'Pardon?'

Across the ballroom all the hands dropped as the music stopped and the singing slowly faded away. Some couples fell into each other's arms and kissed, while others stood awkwardly, not sure what to do at that very special moment.

'Last chance, McCabe. Will you marry me?' Sean

Donnelly repeated as loud as he could, this time with his arms spread wide and a big smile on his face.

'Oh flipping hell, Sean, I don't know what to say!' Gracie McCabe laughed and put her hand up to her mouth.

'Last chance...'

'I suppose I might just marry you Sean Donnelly, but you have to do it properly; propose I mean, so as I know you really mean it, that it's not just the beer talking. You've had more than a few tonight!' she pulled a face and giggled. 'Mind you I'm not one to talk, I've gone a bit overboard on the port and lemon meself.'

Laughing, he grabbed her hand and pulled her through the mass of people, over to the side of the dancefloor where it was less crowded. Turning to face her, Sean went down on one knee and took a red leather ring box out of his jacket pocket. He flipped the lid and held it out to her.

'Gracie McCabe ... for the very last time, will you marry me?'

Caught up in the excitement of the moment, Gracie jumped up and down on the spot. 'Yes, yes, of course I will, yes...'

He took a delicate diamond ring from the box and slipped it onto her finger.

'Do you like it?' he asked.

Gracie held her left hand up in the air and waved it around. 'Oh Sean, it's beautiful and it fits just perfect...'

Beaming, she spun round on the spot, making the full skirt of her black and white polka dot frock flare out and show a lot more of her petticoats and legs than she anticipated. Gracie stopped and pulled a face.

'Oh God, I'm making a fool of myself again ... but I love it, Sean, I love it.'

She looked down at the ring and studied it for a moment. It was a classic engagement ring, pretty and dainty with a small diamond mounted high on the shoulders, which were diamond chips set in gold.

'And I love you,' he said, as a round of applause broke out around them. 'Let's tie the knot as quick as we can, I don't want us to be having to wait a second longer than we have to. I want us to be married; I want us to be together forever.'

As Sean stood up, she flung her arms around his neck and kissed him.

'I'm so happy, thanks for asking me, especially tonight. We can start the New Year as a proper engaged couple,' Gracie said emotionally; she blinked hard as the tears prickled at the back of her eyes.

The band started playing again but the pace of the music had slowed right down, and the atmosphere in the ballroom changed from celebratory to romantic as the Last Waltz was played. Sean took Gracie's hand and pulled her towards the dancefloor. 'Come on, we have to dance to this tune and remember it forever. It will be our song, we can play it at our wedding and on our anniversaries...'

The sprung dancefloor moved as a swarm of couples took to the floor for the last dance in the glittering ballroom that was filled to capacity with couples of all ages dressed in their finery for the occasion.

As the lights dimmed and the music of Glenn Miller echoed around the walls Gracie smiled and followed her new fiancé onto the floor. She'd often fantasised about being married and having a home and family of her own. It was what she wanted most, and in one instant it had all become a reality; Gracie McCabe was going to be married. She was to marry Sean Donnelly, the hotel chef she had known and worked with for so long.

She hadn't initially been that attracted to him, even though she liked him as a friend and occasionally went out with him, but he'd been persistent over the years and slowly but surely he'd grown on her. Gradually, she had become comfortable with him. It had only been in the previous few months that Sean had become more intense and Gracie had started to take him seriously. She could imagine him as a good husband and father, providing well for his family, and that was what she wanted, all she had ever wanted.

Everything that had gone before was suddenly irrelevant. The past that could easily have destroyed her had in fact made her stronger and she was ready to move forward in her life with Sean Donnelly.

Sean had to be at work early the next day, so as soon as the music stopped and the lights went up in the ballroom again they grabbed their coats from the cloakroom and ran out ahead of most of the partygoers. They turned onto the seafront and headed to Thorpe Bay, quickly walking arm-in-arm along to the hotel where Gracie lived and worked. The seafront was quiet and dark bar the moonlight and even though they couldn't really see it, there was the sound of the high tide lapping up against the tide-line. They talked as they walked and kissed on the doorstep but then Sean turned round and walked back the way they'd just come. He returned to the Palace Hotel at the top of the hill, opposite Southend Pier, where he worked as a chef and also lived-in.

Gracie stood at the gate of the Thamesview Hotel and waved until Sean was out of sight before walking round to the back and quietly letting herself in. Taking the stairs two at a time, she raced up the three flights to the self-contained flat at the top which she shared with her friend Ruby Blakeley, who also owned the hotel. But instead of creeping quietly into her own room as she would usually have done, she flung Ruby's bedroom door wide open and switched the light on.

'Ruby, Ruby, wake up and look at this. Look, look, look! Sean proposed to me tonight, properly proposed. Look at my engagement ring, Ruby. I'm going to be married at bloody long last! I'm not going to stay sitting on that sodding shelf forever...'

Bewildered for a moment, Ruby Blakeley opened her eyes and looked at the alarm clock, before blinking hard and trying to focus on her friend.

'Oh that's lovely, Gracie, I'm pleased for you...' she groaned, her voice thick with sleep.

'Pleased for me? Come on Ruby Rubes, you can come up with something better than that! I'm getting married, I'm going to be Mrs Donnelly...'

Gracie sat on the edge of the bed and bounced up and down like a child on Christmas day.

'I will, I promise, but do you mind if I run round the room with you in the morning? I've got to be up and working downstairs in a couple of hours and it's just me, myself and I because you have the morning off, and there are guests who want breakfast really early.'

'Oh sod the guests! Just take one little peek at the ring and then I'll leave you alone, I promise.' She shook Ruby's shoulder and laughed.

Bleary-eyed, Ruby peered at the hand in front of her face. 'That's very pretty and well chosen, lovely...'

She smiled again at her friend and blew a kiss before tugging the eiderdown right up over her head.

'Okay, I'll leave you to your beauty sleep, you miserable cow, but in the morning we'll dance round the room and celebrate – whether you like it or not!' Gracie laughed as she switched the light off again and skipped out of the room.

Still smiling, she went through into the living room, kicked her high heels off and curled up on the sofa. She stared down at the small but perfect twinkling diamond ring on her finger and sighed. Gracie had often imagined the moment she would be proposed to, but she hadn't expected that Sean Donnelly, the young man she'd known for so long, would go down on one knee in the middle of the ballroom at midnight on New Year's Eve. She had thought they were just out together to celebrate the New Year.

She thought about that moment again, the

special moment when she had realised that Sean was asking her to be his wife and smiled to herself. The proposal had certainly been romantic and he had timed it to perfection. How could she possibly not want to marry a man like that? Gracie reached a hand out, pulled a cushion over from the chair opposite, put it under her head and started mentally planning her new life. By the time she dozed off she had already chosen her wedding dress, picked a honeymoon destination, fantasised about her first proper home and named her first baby, boy or girl. Her life was finally going in the direction she had always wanted it to and she was more than content with it. She was content with the thought of being married to Sean Donnelly and happy at the thought of having his children. He had said he loved her and wanted to spend the rest of his life with her, and that was all she had ever wanted from a man.

Several hours later she awoke to find Ruby standing at the end of the sofa, holding a tray that was formally laid out for morning tea with a lace tray cloth, the best china and a selection of fancy biscuits.

'Just look at you,' Ruby laughed, 'sleeping on the sofa, with your new dress screwed up like a dishrag. Good job Aunt Leonora can't see you looking like that; she'd have a pink fit.'

She put the tray down on the table in front of the sofa and sat down alongside her friend. 'And this, Miss McCabe, is to celebrate your engagement in the way of Leonora Blakeley; it's in her honour. This morning we're going to be ladylike and take formal morning tea.'

Gracie looked at the tray and laughed. 'Oh that is so nice of you! Leonora would be so proud of you. I think she might even have overlooked my dishrag dress because she'd be so pleased I'm going to be respectable at last; mind you, she mightn't have been impressed with lipstick on the cushions. Sorry, Rubes! I was just so excited I couldn't sleep properly. I kept dozing off then waking up and wondering if I'd dreamt it.'

'You are overexcited! Why don't you go to bed now?' Ruby smiled. 'It's only nine o'clock; I've just come up for a quick break to see how you are, and to look at your ring in daylight. There's not so much to do now with only two guests left. The others have checked out, Henry's just driven them to the station.'

'I feel guilty leaving you down there on your own...'

'Well don't, it was your morning off anyway. I can manage perfectly well for today. I've got Henry to help, bless his little cotton socks. He may be getting on a bit but he mucks in. But now, the ring, please!'

'Okay, here it is...' Gracie held her hand up and waved it around. 'Isn't it lovely? And it fits perfectly.'

'It is lovely, Gracie, it must have taken him ages to save up for it. Did you know he was planning the grand proposal?'

'God no, it was such a shock! I mean I knew he liked going out with me but a marriage proposal and a ring? I'm still stunned, especially as he must have been planning it to have the ring ready.'

Ruby looked at Gracie thoughtfully as she chose

her words. 'I don't want to be like Aunt Leonora, really I don't, but are you sure this is what you really want, to spend the rest of your life with Sean Donnelly? I know you like him – but marriage? That's forever, missy.'

'Oh look, I know now that Prince Charming isn't going to appear on the doorstep and carry me off to his castle; there just isn't one of them out there for me. Sean loves me, he's good to me. I know you think he's a bit boring but he's no wide boy either, is he?' Gracie shrugged her shoulders and smiled. 'We both know he's not exactly the life and soul of the party and he's definitely no screen idol but he works hard and he'll look after me, I'm sure.'

'Are you sure you're not getting carried away on the proposal? Is he the right one?' Ruby asked with an edge to her tone. 'The right one you've been dreaming about?'

'Well, he's the nearest to the right one that I'm going to get!' Gracie laughed. 'Anyway, I like him a lot – and look where that stupid hearts and flowers fantasy got me last time. Look where it got me *and* you... I know you've sort of worked your life out and you and Johnnie are going to be together forever. You've got *your* right one, but me?' Gracie shook her head. 'No, Sean is my chance. I'm nearly twenty-eight and I don't want to end up like Leonora, forever looking out to sea and wishing for something that just ain't ever going to happen. Life isn't like it is in the cinema, is it?'

Gracie smiled to take the edge off her words; she understood exactly what Ruby was trying to say. Over the years she'd known and been going out with Sean, Gracie had always joked that she was waiting for the right one to come along and whisk her off on a white charger. It had become a standing joke when they watched the people walking along the promenade.

'Is he the right one?' Ruby would ask. 'Nope, not the right one...' Gracie would smile. 'But I'll know him when I see him!'

Ruby reached out and touched her hand. 'I'm sorry – you're old enough to know what you're doing. So if you're sure then we have to arrange an engagement party ... and then the wedding! Oh, this is going to be such fun! What sort of wedding do you want?'

'Can't afford an engagement party and a small and cheap wedding with none of my bleedin' family there to wreck it would be just about right for me!' Gracie said, only half-joking.

'You can have the wedding reception here. And an engagement party as well. If you want to, that is, and if Sean wants to, of course,' Ruby said warmly.

'Oh, a wedding reception at Thamesview would be fantastic, Rubes. I'd love to have it here, my favourite place in the world!'

The two young women blinked back tears as they hugged each other tight, aware that a big change was ahead for both of them.

Ruby stood up. 'Right, tea break over... Back to work I go; any plans for later?'

'Sean's coming round after his shift finishes at tea time, if that's okay with you. We've got a lot to talk about. I only need an hour or so while he's here.'

'Of course it's okay; this is your home as much as mine, silly. I'll stay out of the way and give you some time together. Oh, and I hereby give you the whole day off in honour of your new status of engaged woman. Can't have you slaving over a hot desk this afternoon, can we?'

As Ruby turned to leave the room Gracie called her back. 'Rubes? I nearly forgot, will you be my number one bridesmaid?'

'Cheeky moo, I thought you'd never ask!'

'You fibber, you knew I'd ask you! I wouldn't want anyone else. Apart from Maggie, of course. I have to have Maggie.'

'She'll love that.'

As Ruby closed the door, Gracie grinned again and swung her legs back onto the sofa. She leaned back, closed her eyes and thought back over her enduring friendship with Ruby.

When Gracie McCabe and Ruby Blakeley had first met on the maternity ward in Rochford Hospital in 1946, they were just two teenage girls who had naively got themselves into trouble and then had to give up their illegitimate babies. The two distressed girls had quickly bonded on the ward but had then gone their separate ways to restart their lives; they'd promised to keep in touch, but at the same time they had both really wanted to pretend the previous few months of their lives had never happened. Although Gracie at nineteen was three years older than Ruby, she hadn't known that at the time because as far as everyone in the hospital knew, Ruby was a young war widow having a legitimate baby.

In their separate miseries, neither of them could have foreseen that their chance meeting was actually going to be the start of a close and enduring friendship; one in which their lives would be so entwined they would become closer than sisters.

It had been a few weeks after leaving the hospital when Gracie had, on the spur of the moment gone to see Ruby and, away from the constraints of the maternity ward they had quickly developed their friendship; from then on, despite the circumstances of their initial meeting, they had both constantly thought themselves lucky to have met each other.

Ruby had been fortunate in that her baby girl Maggie was adopted by George and Babs Wheaton, the couple with whom she had been billeted when she was evacuated from London during the war, and she saw her often. Gracie had not been so lucky. She'd been sent to a mother and baby home, where she was constantly reminded of her sins and from where her baby, an unnamed little boy, was adopted by total strangers and lost to her forever. She had put on a brave face after the event; the wound was hidden from sight but the pain was still there. It was a constant ache in her heart that never really went away.

TWO

'Happy?' Sean asked that afternoon when they were both sitting on the sofa in front of the gas fire, arms entwined, unable to stop smiling. Gracie had spent the morning catching up on her sleep and getting ready for her new fiancé to arrive after his shift at work was over.

'Oh yes,' she said. 'And you? Mind, you'd better be. You can't change your mind now! I've got the ring on my finger and I've said YES. You're committed now, no jilting allowed...' Gracie jabbed her elbow in his side and laughed.

'Of course I'm happy and you're right, we can't be changing our minds now. Neither of us. It's official – you're going to be Mrs Sean Donnelly, you're going to be my wife! But we need to let our families know, to make it truly official. Will your parents mind that I didn't ask your father first? I should have done that, shouldn't I?'

'No, I've told you before; they really don't give a monkeys what I do. It's been a long time since I was part of the family. Anyway, I'm a grown woman. I don't need to tell them what I'm doing.'

Gracie's tone was casual as she tried to shut the conversation down but she was suddenly on edge. She didn't want to think about her family at that moment and she certainly didn't give any thought to their potential role in the engagement yet she sensed that now they were going to be married,

25

Sean would want to know more about the rift between them than she was comfortable with.

'But getting wed's something special, so maybe now's the time to be putting all that right. We'll go and visit together so I can meet your parents and your sisters. All this time us knowing each other and then going out and I've not met any of them, not a single one...' he paused and looked straight into her eyes. 'I'm just wondering, you're not ashamed of me, are you?'

Gracie smiled quizzically, unsure if he was joking or serious. 'Why would I be ashamed of you? It's more likely to be the other way round, you being a good God-fearing Irishman and me a lazy old lapsed who only goes to church for weddings and funerals. I bet your family will hate you marrying an English girl...'

'Oh Gracie, my lovely girl, they're going to welcome you with open arms. I'm the golden boy of the family, don't you know, the only boy with four big sisters who all adore their baby brother. I can get away with anything – even marrying a naughty English girl who doesn't go to mass anymore. Or confession. I'm betting you don't go to confession either...'

He laughed and pulled her into him. 'We're going to have to change that, you have to confess all your wrong-doings.'

'I don't need to go to confession, I never do anything wrong. You know, we should tell your family about the engagement right now. Let's write to them...'

Gracie jumped up and crossed the room to the small bureau, hoping she'd distracted him away from asking any more about her family.

'Okay now, here's what I think,' Sean said. 'We'll write to my parents in Ireland as you say and tell them the news, and then on my day off next week we'll go and visit with your family and break it to them together. They live out by the airport now, don't they? Right on the bus route.'

Gracie could feel the guilty panic rising as memories of the past came to the forefront of her mind.

She knew her easy-going father would be no problem, but her mother was a different kettle of fish. Gracie wasn't sure she could trust her not to sabotage the engagement by either deliberately or accidentally revealing her secret to Sean.

All Gracie had wanted from her parents was for the past to be buried and forgotten but her mother had never been able to forgive her for the shame she had visited on the family.

On the few occasions when they saw each other the woman couldn't resist sniping away over her daughter's illegitimate pregnancy. She simply couldn't forgive her, regardless of the passage of time, and it was the reason Gracie had had so little to do with her parents. It was easier to forget about her long-lost baby when she wasn't constantly confronted by her mother bringing it up.

'I know, instead of writing, let's go to Ireland!' Gracie blurted out, her voice gradually getting higher and faster. 'Let's go to Ireland and surprise them. I want to meet your family; we could take a small holiday. I've never been to Ireland, I've never been anywhere apart from London and Melton with Ruby. I know Ruby won't mind if I'm away from the hotel for a few days...'

Sean frowned slightly as he looked hard at her. 'A grand idea, I'm sure, but do I get the feeling you're not wanting me to meet your family? In fact, I'm now really thinking you're ashamed of me, Gracie. Do you think I'm not good enough for them? Not good enough for you yourself?'

'That's so daft and you know it,' Gracie replied. 'It's just as I said, I don't have much to do with them any more so telling them isn't that important.' She took a deep breath. 'But you're right and of course we'll go and tell them... Soon. After we tell yours.'

After a few moments of uncomfortable silence from Sean where Gracie was unsure what to say, he stood up and walked over to the French windows that opened out onto the balcony.

'Is it too cold to go out there, do you think?' Sean asked, with his hand on the ornate wrought-iron handle.

'Too bloody cold for me, that's for sure,' Gracie laughed, 'but you're welcome to go and freeze your ears off if you must.'

Sean shrugged his jacket on and stood the collar up round his ears before opening the full-length window and going outside. He quickly pulled it closed behind him, leaving Gracie rubbing her hands together in front of the fire and feeling as if her euphoria had been snatched away. She'd been so caught up in the dreamy planning, she'd stupidly not given a thought to Sean wanting to involve their respective families. With all his relatives being in Ireland and hers all but estranged they had never been part of their relationship and she

28

had subconsciously excluded them all, but now she found herself wondering about Sean's family and worrying about her own.

In Gracie's mind, Ruby Blakeley was her family, the Thamesview Hotel was her home and she hadn't thought much further than that.

As her new fiancé stood on the balcony, looking out into the darkness with his back to her, Gracie looked at his shadowy outline through the glass. He was standing perfectly still with his shoulders hunched up to his ears and his hands in his pockets.

At first glance Sean Donnelly looked very average and he didn't stand out at all from the crowd. He was about five foot eight in his socks, with coarse black hair that already had a few premature stray white hairs, pale Celtic skin that glowed in the sun and the beginnings of a paunch – but he also had green eyes that twinkled when he laughed, an easy-going personality and he worked hard. His Irish accent had lessened over the years he'd been in England but it was still there in the background and Gracie loved listening to him when he was in full flow, telling embellished stories of happenings in the Palace Hotel where he worked. She had seen him grumpy, tired and occasionally fed-up but she'd never seen him lose his temper or get roaring drunk and he'd never been nasty to her, even when they occasionally bickered.

As she studied him, lost in her thoughts, he turned round and smiled at her. Gracie smiled back. Sean was a nice young man, perfect husband material in her eyes, and she was going to be his wife and the mother of his children. She wasn't going to let anything spoil that for her.

Especially not her oft-regretted past and her unforgiving mother.

Grabbing her coat and scarf Gracie followed Sean outside into the cold winter air.

'It's not that bad for January, is it? I'm guessing the over-hang of the roof protects the balcony from the worst of it,' he said as she stepped alongside him. 'There's a bit of a nip in the air but we can keep each other warm.'

Sean put his arm around her shoulder and together they leaned on the balcony railing and peered out into the silent winter darkness that engulfed the estuary. As they looked ahead Gracie adjusted her eyes. The water was dark and the night clear, with a sprinkling of stars in the sky and a few random lights on the water from the fishing boats out in the deep water. It was so beautiful she wanted to cry.

'Leonora used to be out here every spare moment you know, rain or shine, watching for passing boats and ships. I once saw her sweep several inches of snow off her chair so she could sit with her binoculars. She was such a secret romantic and she loved it out here; she just wanted to be on one of the big passenger liners heading off to the great unknown.'

Gracie opened her eyes wide as she felt the tears welling up; not just at the thought of Leonora Blakeley's lost dreams, but at everything. Her heightened emotions on this special day were making her reminisce too much. She raised a hand to her eye and surreptitiously wiped a big fat tear away, hoping that Sean wouldn't notice.

'Well, it's a grand place to be, that's for sure,' he said. 'Right on the seafront like this. Ruby's a lucky girl to own this hotel at such a young age; it must be worth a fortune. She was so fortunate to inherit it too, especially with her and Leonora not even being related.'

'Oh, she knows she's lucky but she's worked really hard as well. That was why Leonora left it to her, she knew she'd take care of it; and I'm better off too because of her...' Gracie opened her eyes wide again. 'I mean, I'm living here and I've got a blinking good job as well! Rube's been good to me, same as Leonora was in her own way. I'm so lucky!'

'Ah maybe, but it's a two-way street. Ruby would have been up the creek with no paddle without you beside her after that Leonora woman passed on. Don't you go thinking you owe her any more than she owes you. If anything, you should be entitled to more than you have from her.'

'I don't think about it like that,' Gracie said firmly, wanting to shut down the conversation. 'I'm just so pleased I met Ruby and that we're friends. More than friends in fact; we're probably closer than sisters.'

She knew Sean was making a clumsy attempt to be supportive but she didn't like hearing him use that almost jealous tone when he spoke about Ruby Blakeley, her friend. In the beginning she'd dismissed it as natural envy of Ruby's lucky circumstance but sometimes his comments went just that bit too far for her to be comfortable.

'How did that happen by the way?' Sean asked,

oblivious to the tightening of Gracie's shoulders under his hand. 'I don't think I've ever known how the two of you met. Ruby was from London, wasn't she? Apart from during the war?'

It was now or never; but Gracie hesitated. She would either have to tell him the whole sorry tale or stay silent forever. If she was going to marry Sean, she would have to tell him that she and Ruby had met as unmarried mothers on the maternity ward. Be honest, she told herself, tell the truth and shame the devil.

'At the Kursaal. We met at the Kursaal just after the war when Ruby came to live down here. We were both young and daft, and we clicked. We became friends, almost immediately.'

The decision was made. Without even thinking about it consciously the words were out, the lie was told and Gracie knew there could be no going back. She sighed with relief that she had made her choice, even if it been an instant reaction rather than a well-thought out and measured decision. Now though, she knew she couldn't ever tell Sean her shameful secret.

The flat where Gracie lived was on the top floor of the Thamesview Hotel, a long established 'ladies only' hotel on the outskirts of Southend, on the Essex coast. Leonora Wheaton had set it up before the war as a quiet and select establishment where widows and single women could go for a holiday at the seaside on their own without risk to their reputation. It was genteel and quaint and although there had been some recent upgrading, the essence of it had stayed. A few of the guests had been visiting for years. Sometimes they were accompanied by sisters, daughters, even maids, but no men were allowed to stay under any circumstances. They were allowed into the lobby or the small guest lounge by invitation but the foot of a male visitor could never be placed on the stairs that led up to the accommodation.

Leonora Wheaton had enforced that rule rigidly and Ruby was following suit because it was a formula that worked for the business.

The terraced property was just three storeys high, with a basement that was used for staff accommodation, a tiny annexe flat at the rear and a comfortable self-contained flat on the top floor, where Gracie and Ruby lived. The guest accommodation was basic but it was always clean and tidy and the service was as impeccable as it had always been when Leonora had been the owner.

The decoration in the flat was not in the style that either of the young women who lived there would have chosen, but Ruby wasn't yet ready to fully modernise it. Not only did she feel it would be disrespectful to Leonora but she had also had to concentrate her time and money on the renovations of the hotel itself, which had become outdated and tired during the war years.

Despite her young age Ruby Blakeley had been bequeathed it nearly two years before in 1952, and Gracie, who had previously helped out there in between her own shifts at the Palace Hotel, now worked alongside her as manageress and general dogsbody, doing the job that Ruby herself used to do. But because it was a small hotel with few staff they both did anything and everything that needed doing around the hotel; they worked

33

hard and had long hours but they both loved what they did and worked together well.

The Thamesview Hotel was not only Gracie's workplace, it was also her home and she loved it there.

'Where shall we live when we're married?' Sean suddenly asked, still looking ahead into the dark distance of the Thames Estuary.

'Dunno. We'll have to start looking for somewhere but it'll have to be somewhere near to both hotels. There are some nice small flats around the back here...' Gracie felt a slight feeling of anxiety rise within her. She really couldn't imagine leaving the hotel and Ruby; it was another thing she hadn't given enough thought to when she had excitedly accepted Sean's proposal.

'Mind, you won't be working here for long after we're wed. You're to be my wife and then, please God, the babies will come along. We're going to need to look in Southend itself, near the Palace, near to where I work. My job has to come first, especially now I'm to get another promotion.' Sean paused and smiled reassuringly before leaning over and kissing his new fiancée lightly on the lips.

'It'll be grand having our own lives, you'll see. Maybe Ruby will see you right for everything you've done for her. As I said, a big bonus payment for services over and above. You're entitled, you know, and we'll need all the money we can get.'

Gracie smiled back, but said nothing. She knew Sean simply didn't realise what a wrench it was going to be for her to move out.

That night as Gracie lay in her bed wide awake and deep in thought, she tried to envisage her new life with Sean in their own home, hopefully with a baby. It was all she had dreamed about, ever since the day she had had to give up her firstborn baby son forever. Gracie was excited at the prospect of making a home and a family with Sean, but she also felt nervous at the thought of such a complete change in her life. The euphoria of the day had been tinged with regret and while she wanted everything Sean was offering her, she also didn't want to give up what she had.

Gracie went to sleep that night on the horns of a dilemma that she hoped would quickly resolve itself.

THREE

Feeling apprehensive, she stood on the edge of the pavement on the other side of the road and watched for a few moments, bracing herself to take the next step. As always, her stomach churned nervously; she wanted to turn and walk away as she had done on the previous occasion.

But this time Gracie knew she had to follow through so she stood perfectly still and gathered her emotions. As she breathed deeply she studied the man directly opposite her who was kneeling on a rolled-up newspaper, methodically tending the flower bed that edged a neat bungalow.

He was noticeably older and rounder, and his hair was thinner than when she'd last seen him, but there was no disputing who he was. Just looking at him nurturing his plants with his pipe sticking out of the corner of his mouth, she could tell he was still a gentle soul. She felt immense guilt at the fact that she rarely saw him or any of her family any more, but she found it just too hard to be confronted with things from the past that she wanted to bury.

She crossed the road and stopped at the edge of the tiny front garden.

'Hello Dad,' Gracie said quietly. 'How are you?'

Fred McCabe looked up from his gardening and smiled up at his daughter, his obvious pleasure at the sight of her increasing her guilt at having left it so long.

'Gracie! Hello my dear,' he said with joy in his voice as he stood up. 'It's so nice to see you. I thought you'd forgotten about your old dad, it's been so long...'

Gracie looked sheepish. 'I know, I'm sorry, but...' she paused. 'Well, you know what it's like, it's just easier to stay away and let things lie. I'm a bit of a coward under fire.'

'I know what you mean dear, but it probably makes things worse,' he said kindly. 'Maybe if we didn't only see you once in a blue moon your mother would have come round a bit more.'

'I tried that...' Gracie started.

'I know but I don't think you appreciate how hard it was for your mother. But no one knows about it here so perhaps there's hope.'

'But no one knew about it where we were before, she just thought they did,' Gracie felt compelled to reply.

'I know,' Fred McCabe said with a gentle smile. 'But your mother has always worried about the neighbours, and *her* mother before her; it's the way of her side of the family. My way is live and let live. Let he who is without sin cast the first stone and all that.'

'You could have come to see me; you know where I live, you all know where I live. It was hard at the Palace, I grant you, but the Thamesview is different.' Gracie paused, suddenly aware that she was being defensive again. 'Sorry, I shouldn't go on, I know! But it's nice to see you now and I've got something to tell you, some good news...'

'All in good time, Gracie, all in good time.'

37

Fred McCabe interrupted her quickly. 'Your mother's inside but your sisters are both out gallivanting, what with it being the weekend. You are coming in, aren't you? Not just passing by?'

'If you want me to ... if Mum won't mind. I want to talk to you.'

'When we get inside. Mustn't leave your mother out, eh?' Fred smiled at his eldest daughter and patted her shoulder affectionately.

'It's nice round here, all peaceful and homely,' Gracie said, putting off the moment she would have to face her mother once again. She looked around at the small, neat estate of pre-fabricated bungalows that had been erected just after the war to house many of the local residents who had been bombed out of their own homes. The small properties were all identical in design and colour but most showed their inhabitants' identity via the lace curtains at the windows and flowers in the postage stamp-sized front gardens.

'It's really handy for everything,' Gracie continued. 'Blimey, you've got the buses on the doorstep and shops round the corner; and the airport within spitting distance for you.'

'We were lucky to get housed here, what with me working at the airport. Now I walk over the road and there I am. I can even pop home for lunch if the mood takes me, and the pub is just down the road for when I need it.'

He laughed and Gracie joined in conspiratorially, even though she knew her father had never touched a drop of alcohol in his life. His only vice was the familiar old brown pipe that was either clamped between his teeth or in his hand being emptied and refilled almost ritualistically. At night it was always placed upside down in the large chipped glass ashtray that lived on the draining board. Gracie wondered nostalgically if it was still there in the new place or if her mother had succeeded in banishing it outside.

'And I have a shed! It's not big enough to turn round in but I've always wanted one,' her dad said, grinning.

'That's good, Dad. You deserve it.'

'I don't know about deserve it but it's nice to have my own little hidey-hole after a lifetime of living with all you girls,' he laughed.

'How are the twins?' Gracie asked. 'I saw Jenny some time back – I bumped into her in the high street. She looked really nice but she was as shy as ever, chalk and cheese that pair,' she added, referring to the twin sisters who were four years her junior.

'Jenny said she saw you, that you were doing well at that hotel with your friend. I was pleased to hear it. We'll soon be on our own here; the twins are both engaged and planning a double wedding in a couple of years' time. That should save me a few bob, two for the price of one. They both seem like nice lads...'

'Oh, Jenny never said a word about it to me...' Gracie smiled sadly. 'I suppose I'm not invited then. Me being the black sheep and all.'

Her father put his arm around her waist and gently edged her to the front door, which was ajar. 'Now, that's not like you to be self-pitying. You're jumping to conclusions again, they haven't even set the date yet! And to be fair, we've lived here for nigh on eighteen months now and you haven't come to visit us.'

'I know. I really do know, and I'm sorry but...' Gracie began.

'Come on,' Fred McCabe said quietly. 'Let's go inside and break the ice.' He put his head inside the door and called out. 'Dot? Are you there, Dot? We've got a visitor...'

Pushing the door right back he slipped his muddy boots off, hung his coat on the hook on the back of the door and stood back to let his daughter pass. Following his nudge, she turned through into the neat sitting room, at the same time as her mother appeared in the doorway opposite that led through to the kitchenette. Both women stopped in their tracks on different sides of the room.

Rather than meet her mother's eye immediately, Gracie scanned the room.

There was very little there that was familiar to her, apart from a couple of ornaments on the shelf over the gas fire, the large wooden mantle-clock that had belonged to her grandparents, and the lace tray-cloth that had pride of place on the sideboard. The furniture was noticeably second-hand but it was in good condition and the room was immaculately clean and tidy. However, it was as if she was in a stranger's home, and Gracie felt a wave of sadness engulf her.

There was no disputing that Dot McCabe was Gracie's mother. Both were tall and slender with brown hair, matching brown eyes, full lips and obvious cheekbones, but whereas Gracie was a naturally happy soul with a ready smile, her mother definitely wasn't. It showed in the frown lines etched across her forehead and around her permanently downturned mouth.

She was dressed in top-to-toe dark grey with a faded navy blue apron tied around her waist and lisle stockings rolled down to her ankles. Dot McCabe's whole persona shouted misery and Gracie could feel it sucking her in from across the room.

'Well, well... Look what the cat's dragged in, the prodigal daughter...' her mother said, without changing her expression.

Although she forced a smile Gracie could feel the familiar griping ache in the pit of her stomach. Despite her hoping otherwise, nothing had changed.

'Nice to see you too, Mum...' Gracie said as she stared at her mother, her expression neutral. 'I like the new place, real cosy isn't it? And so con-venient for Dad's work.'

'Is that why you're here? To have a good nosey round?' Dot held her arm out and waved it around with a flourish. 'Well, this it. Not quite a flashy big seafront hotel but we make do. Beggars can't be choosers.'

'The hotel's not big and it's not flashy, and I think this is really nice. It must have been a relief to get out of the Westcliff flat...'

'You didn't have to put up with it as long as we did, you left us to get on with it...' the woman said angrily.

'I'll put the kettle on,' Fred interrupted, trying to break the tension. 'You two sit down and have a natter.'

41

Dot McCabe glared at her husband. 'About what? About why our own daughter can't be bothered to visit her family? About how she thinks we're beneath her now she's got hoity-toity friends? What else?'

'About anything, Dot. You and Gracie could just catch up on all your news now she's here at last. Family is family,' he smiled.

'Gracie doesn't think she is any more.'

'Actually I wanted to talk to both of you to-gether...' Gracie forced herself to stay calm and looked from one to the other. 'Please? It won't take long and then we can have tea.'

As she held her hands out to try and appeal to her mother, Dot reached forward and pointed.

'What's this?'

'It's an engagement ring, that's what I want to talk to you about. I'm getting married. His name is Sean Donnelly.' Gracie smiled and kept her voice calm; she knew she had to somehow get her mother on side.

'Oh congratulations, Gracie, that's good news! Tell us about the lucky young man,' her father said quickly, as if to pre-empt his wife's response.

'When's this happening?' Dot asked.

'We haven't set a date yet, we only got engaged on New Year's Eve. I've known him a long time – we used to work together at the Palace before I went to Thamesview.' Gracie started talking faster and faster in a bid to deflect her mother. 'He's a chef – well, he's an assistant chef but sometimes he gets to be in charge. It's a good job and he earns well, he works strange and long hours but that's the nature of the business for both of us. We both work ha~~

'We're please~~

nice young man a~~

father smiled again.~~

him...'

Fred was doing his be~~

tion getting contentious a~~

to him for it but like King C~~

back the water, he didn't s~~

success; despite her telling them

she could see her mother was just ~~

chance to have another go.

'Does he know about you?' Her mo~~

rupted sharply, unable to hold it in any l~~

'I told you, we've known each other for ~~

time, so he knows me really well. We were frie~~

for years before we got serious...' Gracie deliber~~

ately misinterpreted what she knew her mother

was asking.

'You know what I mean,' Dot snapped. 'Does

he know about the baby?'

'Well, of course he doesn't,' Gracie laughed sar-

castically. 'Why would I tell him that? It was such

a long time ago. It's all done and dusted, old

news, my baby son – despatched and forgotten,

the way you always wanted it.'

'Not for us it's not forgotten. Such a shameful

time for us all, but I'm pleased you realise at last

how shameful it is. You must do or you would

have told him...'

'Yes, okay,' Gracie interrupted to stem the flow

of remonstrations, 'but it's history now, you got

your way and it's over. If I could change it all I

would but I can't, I can't go back in time and not

d.'

get my
y? Oh,
y well

ipsets
don't

saint
ntly.
neet
him
ing

ad.
sit.
re

for you, Gracie, you deserve a
d I hope he deserves you,' her
'Tell us some more about
st to stop the conversa-
d Gracie was grateful
nute trying to hold
and a chance of
all about Sean
rching for her
her inter-
nger.
long
ds

about it.

all got on with our lives since then. You're here and settled, and I'm happy with my life and I don't want anything to spoil it.'

'So you think I'd do that, do you? You really think I'd broadcast something like that to all and sundry? That I'd tell anyone about it?' Gracie was surprised to see her mother looking hurt, as if she was really shocked that her daughter could think something like that.

'I don't know, Mum – you don't like me very much, do you?' Gracie said with sad resignation.

Dot McCabe looked directly at her daughter and stared her down for a few seconds, before turning away without answering. Gracie then looked at her father and sniffed loudly, a gesture full of unspoken meaning.

'I'll make the tea,' her father said as he backed towards the kitchen door.

'Oh no you don't, Freddie, you stay right here! I can't believe our own daughter thinks that way about us. Tell her, tell her she's being cruel and ungrateful...'

Fred McCabe frowned and thought for a few moments before answering. Gracie could see he was stuck in the middle, where he had always hated to be, and was racking his brains for a way to keep the peace.

'Your mother's right, Gracie, that's just nonsense. Why would we say anything out of place to your fiancé? To anyone for that matter? Why would we want it all out in the open now? You bring him round and we'll all be nice as pie and twice as sweet...' he laughed and turned to his wife. 'We'll welcome him and you. We want to meet him if he's going to be our son-in-law.'

Still standing on the far side of the small sitting room, her back right up against the wall and her feet together, Gracie's mother folded her arms tightly and protectively across her chest.

'Providing you're not expecting us to cough up towards the wedding. We've got the twins' wedding to save for, we can't take on any more expense; not that you'd be interested, but we're strapped enough as it is.'

Gracie smiled slightly and shook her head; she was determined to stay calm. She had to somehow get her mother on her side, and if that meant not saying what she was thinking, then that was what she would do.

'Of course not. Me and Sean are doing it ourselves. It's not going to be a big knees-up wedding and reception or anything, just a quiet ceremony at St George's and a small reception at the hotel. Ruby's organising it as a wedding present...'

'She would be, wouldn't she? That Ruby has always been more important to you than your own family.' Dot paused for a second and then suddenly opened her eyes wide and stared at her daughter closely. 'You're not in the family way again, are you?'

Gracie shook her head. 'No, I'm not – and if I was then I wouldn't tell you, not after last time. This time it's all going to be done by the book.'

'Oh stop it, you stupid girl!' her mother snapped. 'Last time you were little more than a child yourself, with no man to marry you. We did what was best for you – which is more than can be said for soldier boy, who disappeared off, never to be seen again...'

'No Mum, you did what was best for *you*,' Gracie said calmly. 'Anything rather than have the neighbours know. That baby was my first-born, he was your grandson, your first grandchild but you gave him away to strangers...'

'It was for the best as we saw it at the time, best for everyone, but especially for you,' her father interrupted. 'You can't blame us for what we did. We thought it was right then and, if I'm honest, I still think it was right, but I think it's also time to stop talking about it. Both of you. It can't be changed, so there's no point in going over it again and again.'

Gracie shrugged and looked into the middle distance. He was right. The same ground had been

46

covered each time she and her mother had been face to face until eventually Gracie had stopped visiting and the rift had widened. But now she needed to know that all would be well when she and Sean went to see them to announce the engagement formally.

'Okay, I'd love to put it behind us,' Gracie said. 'But can you just promise me you won't mention anything in front of Sean when I bring him round? I really want this to work with him – he's a nice young man and I want to be married and have a baby that I can keep, I really do...'

'We won't say anything but, be warned, secrets always come out and then it'll end in tears.' Her father shook his head and waved a finger at Gracie, the way he used to when she was a child. 'Your mother and I won't say a word – today is the last time it will ever be mentioned, but you should think about telling your young man yourself. It's not a good idea to start your married life with secrets,' he said wisely.

'I can't tell him now; I've left it too late. I had a chance and I let it go so now it has to be buried forever. I don't want Sean to know I visited today.'

Fred and Dot McCabe both nodded; her father with a smile on his face and her mother with her usual frown.

'We won't say anything...' Fred said. 'Now I really must make that cuppa. I don't know about you two but I'm parched.'

As she looked from one to the other, Gracie knew instinctively that her secret would be kept safe with her parents, even if it would be mostly for her mother's sake.

For the first time in many years, father, mother and daughter sat down together and had a conversation that didn't revolve around recriminations. The truce was a little uneasy between them but Gracie tried her best. She wanted to make up with them, even if she only managed a superficial relationship as her friend Ruby had done with her own family. But Gracie knew that even if she forgave, she could never really forget what had happened. Sometimes, in the middle of the night, the memory of it was as sharp and clear as if it had only just happened.

FOUR

1946

'Gracie... Why aren't you up? You'll be out on your ear if you're late again...'

'I feel sick and I've got belly-ache, I can't go today...' Gracie McCabe moaned from her bed.

'Oh yes you can,' Dot McCabe shouted from the other side of the door, before flinging it open so hard it crashed against the end of the bed. She turned the dim ceiling light on and went into the bedroom. 'Now you just get out of that bed and get yourself to work. We need the money, you lazy little mare. Get up...'

When Gracie didn't move her mother pulled the bedclothes back in one swift movement. 'What's going on with you girl? Get your backside up now and get going. If you miss the bus you'll have to walk, you're not using my bicycle again.'

'I don't feel well, I feel sick...'

'That's no excuse, get out of that bed right now and get yourself dressed.'

Jennifer and Jeanette, Gracie's fourteen-year-old twin sisters, who had still been asleep in the double bed across the room, sat up quickly and nudged each other. Both were openly amused that it was their sister in Dot McCabe's angry firing line instead of them.

The two girls weren't identical twins; in fact they

were not remotely alike in either appearance or temperament. Despite their mother's best efforts to dress and treat them the same, they were really just two sisters who happened to be the same age, two sisters with nothing in common except for their birth.

Jennifer was quiet, academic and very similar in appearance to Gracie and her mother in both stature and features, whereas Jeanette was shorter, her hair naturally fair and her figure curvy, even at fourteen, with a sprinkling of freckles and a loud laugh. She was also prone to getting into trouble both at school and with the neighbours, something which Jennifer never did.

When they were young they had often bickered but always sided against everyone else, but as they'd grown older their opposing personalities had led them to grow slightly apart and have different friends and hobbies.

As they sat on the bed watching the scene in front of them, Dot McCabe suddenly realised they were there and nodded her head in their direction.

'These two have got to get ready for school. If you're going to be sick then get yourself into the kitchen and get a bowl.'

Gracie threw the rest of her covers off and, with her shoulders hunched and clutching her stomach tightly, she quickly ran from the room, her mother hot on her heels. She knew she wasn't going to be sick as such but she wasn't well enough to go to work. She was tired, she was emotional and she was very scared.

Suddenly she was also fed up with covering up

and pretending. It was time for her secret to come out.

'Stop going on at me all the time!' Gracie screamed with her back to Dot. 'I'm not going to be sick. I'm in the family way, I feel bad because I'm going to have a baby...'

Gracie looked defiantly at her mother and watched the colour drain from the woman's face.

'What did you just say?'

Suddenly aware of the enormity of what she was saying out loud for the first time, Gracie backed away.

'I said, I said...' she stuttered. 'I said, I'm going to have a baby and I can't go to work.'

'No you're not, you can't be,' her mother interrupted. 'Don't say stupid things like that just cos you don't want to go to work, that's wicked...'

'Well I am. I've not had a show for ages and my belly's fat. Look.' With fake bravado Gracie unfolded her arms and patted her eight months pregnant stomach through her thin cotton nightdress, the growing stomach that she'd managed to keep hidden from everyone, both at home and at work.

Dot McCabe's expression was almost serene as she looked first at the ceiling and then at her daughter's swollen belly. She stared quietly for a few moments as she tried to take in the information her oldest child had given her, and then swiftly took two steps forward and slapped her daughter hard around the ear with the flat of her hand.

Then she completely lost control and did it over and over again, with both hands, hitting her as hard as she could.

'You dirty slut, you're dirty … dirty! How could you do that? You disgusting creature!'

Gracie tried to protect her head with her hands but still the blows rained down.

'How could you? Who did it to you? Oh my dear God, the neighbours, the idiots downstairs, they're all going to enjoy this! We'll be a laughing stock. Who knows about this? Who have you told?'

'No one, no one knows. I wanted to tell you before but I was scared,' Gracie cried, her earlier bravery now forgotten.

'And so you should be. What about the father? Is he that nasty squaddie your father saw you with? Is he going to marry you?'

Gracie was sobbing and talking in huge gasps.

'No, he's gone … he said he wanted to marry me but now he's gone and I don't know where and I don't know what to do. As soon as I told him he left me. He disappeared,' Gracie cried, gasping for breath.

Dot's face glowed with anger as she stared at her daughter and the enormity of the situation hit her.

'You stupid, stupid girl! Of course he left you, who wants to marry a girl who's easy?'

The tiny kitchen prevented Dot McCabe from pacing, so instead she turned around on the spot and slapped her own forehead with the palm of her hand.

'No one can find out about this, *no one*. Do you understand me? And I dread to think what your father's going to say when he gets home. Get back into your bedroom now and stay there. Go

52

on, you get back in there; just get in there, get into bed and cover yourself up.' Dot McCabe reached up and took hold of Gracie by her hair, tugging it hard. 'Don't say a word to your sisters; I've got to decide what we're going to do. Go, go, go and stop that snivelling...'

She let go of Gracie's hair, grabbed her by the arm and dragged her to the back bedroom at the end of the long corridor of the upstairs flat.

'You two, get dressed and get off to school,' she told the twins. 'Gracie's sick and I don't want either of you to catch it. Go on. Move. Now.'

'But it's too early...' Jeanette said sulkily. 'Why should we have to go to school now just because Gracie's sick? What's wrong with her?'

'Now!' Dot McCabe snapped with such ferocity that even Jeanette, the normally loud and argumentative sister, didn't answer back. Without another word, both girls started pulling on their clothes. Under the watchful eye of their angry mother they purposefully ignored their sister as she climbed back into her bed and buried herself under the covers.

The double bedroom the three sisters shared was at the back of the property where the family lived. The large, semi-derelict, terraced house in the Westcliff area of Southend-on-Sea was a temporary home to three separate families. The McCabe family had the whole of the first floor, the ground floor housed a noisy family with three uncontrollable young children and the top floor, which was the attic, was home to a young married couple who were related to the landlord. None of the flats were self-contained and, whether they wanted to or not, they all intruded into each other's lives.

Everyone living in the house hated it but it was a basic roof over their heads in the difficult times just after the war. For the McCabe family, it had been somewhere immediate for them to live when their previous home had been declared unsafe after a nearby bomb had shaken the foundations, cracked the front wall from top to bottom and shifted most of the tiles off the roof.

Their floor was relatively spacious but it was also damp, cold, and lacking in most of the basic amenities. They took it in turns to wash at the small kitchen sink and family meals were cooked on a gas stove with three rings and a broken oven, but at least there was a working lavatory which they shared with the couple upstairs. The family on the ground floor were supposed to use the outside lavatory but the children would some-times sneak upstairs to avoid going out into the back yard. The whole situation was unbearably chaotic for everyone in the house but they all tolerated it as they waited for something better.

Gracie pulled the covers right up over her head to block everything out; she was angry with herself for not following her instincts and just running away and hoping for the best.

Because she worked long hours at the Palace Hotel on the seafront she hadn't been home very much for the family to notice her growing belly and at work as a chambermaid she was able to keep it hidden under her roomy overall. But now her secret was out and she was going to have to accept the consequences which she knew would be harsh after seeing her mother's initial reaction.

A sense of impending doom enveloped Gracie as she lay wrapped up tightly in her bed, waiting to see what her mother was going to do. She could feel the baby moving inside her and without thinking, she wrapped her arms around it protectively. She guessed she would have to wait for her father's return from work before she would know her fate but she knew without doubt even her genial and easy-going father wouldn't be able to take her side this time.

Gracie couldn't even begin to imagine what the outcome of it all would be. Engulfed in her own misery, she tried to think of a way to resolve her situation. She thought about running away but she didn't have a clue where to go and she also didn't have the energy so all she could do was wait.

The feigned sickness of earlier became real as hunger gnawed at her stomach but she didn't want to leave the bedroom as she could imagine her mother standing guard outside the door. Gracie didn't resent her mother for the beating she had given her; she understood that she'd pushed her to the limit. To have everyone know that their eldest daughter was unmarried and pregnant, especially with father unknown, would be the ultimate disgrace – both in the neighbourhood and at the church. Gracie knew that she had committed the ultimate sin and for that there would be consequences. She just hoped they wouldn't be as harsh as she was anticipating. She touched her stomach and tried her best not to imagine the baby she knew was inside her, the baby she could no longer pretend didn't exist.

When Gracie heard her mother's footsteps going down the bare boards of the stairs, followed by the sound of the front door opening and closing, she took her chance to go and find something to eat. But as she stepped onto the landing so she saw her mother coming back up the stairs.

'Where do you think you're going?' Dot asked.

'To the kitchen to get something to eat...' but as Gracie answered she saw someone else standing behind her mother.

'No you're not, you've got a visitor.' Dot replied shortly.

'Good day to you, Gracie. Your mother was telling me you have a problem that needs my help...'

Gracie looked at Father Thomas, the parish priest, and her heart sank. In that instant she knew what was going to happen. Her worst nightmare was about to become reality: she was going to be sent to St Angela's.

'Yes, Father...' was all she could say.

'Don't say anything else out here...' her mother looked around furtively as she whispered to both of them. 'Wait until we're somewhere private. There are too many listening ears in this house – I don't want a soul hearing about this, not a soul...'

Gracie's knees were shaking as she turned and headed into the living room at the front of the house, followed closely by her mother and the priest. She felt incredibly ashamed having her very personal and private business discussed in front of Father Thomas but at the same time he was someone she quite liked and respected. Gracie sat down on one of the upright chairs that were crowded around the dining table tucked in the bay window and waited passively for him to outline his plan.

'Now young Gracie, I'm here at your mother's request to seek a resolution to the problem. We're thinking you should be going to St Angela's until this baby is born and then we'll arrange for it to be adopted by a loving married couple who will raise it as their own. You're unwed and just eighteen years of age; it will be for the best. There are many good couples in the parish seeking a baby. It'll be well placed to be having a good future with good married parents.'

Father Thomas' expression was as kindly as it could be under the circumstances and his tone was calm but there was no avoiding the disapproval and disappointment that accompanied his words.

'Thank you,' Gracie shrugged, aware that her fate was sealed.

She'd known of other girls who'd trod the path to St Angela's mother and baby home, a large country house on the other side of Rochford which was run by the strictest of nuns, some of whom were nurses, and used by local churchgoing and non-religious parents alike as both a warning and a threat to their daughters... *If you get yourself into trouble that's where you'll have to go. You'll get carted off to St Angela's, and you know what happens there...*

That day, when the truth had come out and Gracie had been spirited out of the house and driven away under cover of darkness by a silent stranger, had been a pivotal point in her life. She would remember it clearly forever – because it was the day her relationship with her family had been irreparably damaged.

Gracie hated her mother for sending her away so rapidly with no time for any discussion and no say in her own fate and that of her child's; she resented her father for not intervening even though she knew deep down that he had no more say in the matter than she herself did, and it upset her that her sisters didn't understand why she disappeared without a word, never to be a part of the family again.

Gracie had seen a few other girls disappear for a while and then return thinner, sadder and tight-lipped about where they'd been. Everyone guessed they had been to St Angela's but no one ever spoke about it. It was the bogey-man that had to be avoided at all costs.

Father Thomas had been as kindly as he could be with Dot McCabe standing close beside him and had presented the stay at the home as the only solution for her predicament. Gracie would stay there until the baby was born and adopted, and then she could return home to continue her life with her reputation intact, with no one ever knowing that she had fallen by the wayside.

It had all sounded almost reasonable, until the moment she had been led through the doors of the building that looked just like a large country house from the outside.

But inside the home had been another story altogether.

FIVE

Summer 1954

With butterflies that felt the size of blackbirds flapping away inside her stomach, Gracie wandered around the guest lounge at the Thamesview Hotel several times, looking at and touching everything. She ran her fingers along the edge of the marble fireplace, moved a chair a fraction and carefully straightened the new green velvet curtains that framed the sash windows of the room that was going to host her wedding reception. It wasn't a huge space, but it had a beautiful view out across the estuary and was big enough for the limited number of guests they had invited. Ruby had made good her promise to host their wedding breakfast; the ceremony was to take place in the church just up the road in Shoebury and then the informal reception was being held back at the Thamesview Hotel afterwards.

As Gracie looked around and pondered, she found it hard to believe that in just three days' time the wedding she had long anticipated would be happening and that she would soon be Sean's wife. It had only been a few short months since their engagement at the beginning of the year but everything to do with the day was organised down to the last detail, including her beautiful dress that was hanging in wait on the back of the bedroom door.

Gracie tried to calm her pre-wedding nerves by thinking of the occasion rather than the personal aspect of getting married but still she could feel the nerves in her stomach.

After a final look around she closed her eyes and tried to imagine the complex group of invited family and friends in the room together, hopefully laughing, chatting and celebrating her and Sean's marriage.

Gracie McCabe was hoping against hope that she was making the right decision in marrying Sean Donnelly.

She still felt wary about the two families meeting and how they would all interact, but she was less concerned about her own family being at the wedding after their meeting with Sean had gone so well.

Gracie had been so cautious and nervy when they had arrived at the front door, but her father had immediately welcomed Sean, and encouraged her mother to do likewise. And then Gracie had watched in awe as her new fiancé had turned on the charm and her mother had softened in a way she had never seen before; the normally fierce and abrupt woman practically melting in front of her. It had certainly been an eye-opener to see the feminine side of her mother and it made Gracie smile every time she thought about it. Fred McCabe had been his usual amiable self and her sister Jeanette had giggled girlishly and blushed at Sean's humorous flattery. Her other sister Jennifer had stayed unobtrusively in the background looking disinterested but despite that Sean had made every effort to charm her and include her in all the conversations.

'He could charm the birds out of the trees, that one...' Dot McCabe had said under her breath as they were leaving and Gracie thought that was the nearest thing to a compliment her mother could have uttered. For the first time in all those years she allowed herself to think there was a possibility of a truce between them.

Gracie had been so relieved at the successful outcome, and so buoyed by its success, that it had been a bit of a shock when they'd made the journey to Ireland and she had discovered Sean's mother was a completely different kettle of fish to the jolly mammy that he himself had described to her.

The instant they had turned up at the Donnelly family home on the outskirts of Dublin, Gracie had realised that she was in for a rough ride. His mother, father, sisters, their respective husbands and some of the nephews and nieces were all waiting outside in a reception line on either side of the garden path and while Sean had excitedly bounced along and said hello to them all, Gracie had been left behind to face a maternal in-quisition.

Gracie had done her best to be as charming and receptive as Sean had been to her family but when it came to Sean's mother she knew immediately that the woman had taken against her on prin-ciple. The three days spent in Dublin had been a nightmare for Gracie but she'd survived it by telling herself it wouldn't have to happen often as they all lived such a long way away.

His mother Rosaleen, two of his sisters and his cousin Patrick were arriving from Ireland the day before the wedding and would be staying at the Thamesview, along with Babs and George Wheaton, Ruby's foster family from her time in evacuation, and their adopted daughter Maggie, who was going to be a bridesmaid alongside Ruby, her birth mother.

Gracie's parents and twin sisters were going to be at the wedding, as well as Ruby's boyfriend, Johnnie Riordan, and a few friends from the Palace.

Everything was in order.

Mrs Sean Donnelly. Get down off the shelf, Miss Gracie McCabe, you're going to be Mrs Sean Donnelly. You're going to be a blushing bride ... she sang to herself tunelessly as she twirled around in an imaginary waltz across the room and through the doorway, into the reception area. The hotel was eerily empty of ordinary guests, but each room would soon be occupied with the family members and guests who were travelling a distance. Gracie just hoped that everyone would get along for that one day.

As she noted the unusual silence in the building Gracie wondered again at the kindness of her friend Ruby Blakeley, who had forgone four full days of bookings in her hotel to allow room for their wedding guests.

'Ruby...' she called. 'Ruby, where are you? Do you want a cuppa? I'm just going through to the kitchen to make one.'

Ruby put her head out the door on the far side of the hotel reception area and smiled at Gracie.

'I'm still in the office and yes please, I'm gasping in here. I really wish I could conquer this type-writing lark...' Ruby said. 'Actually, shall we go and sit outside, make the most of this very strange peace and quiet? It's almost spooky, it's so quiet. This is the first time since I came here that there hasn't been at least one guest in the building. Even in winter there's usually someone.'

'I know. It's sort of scary...' Gracie ran across the lobby. 'Actually, I've an even better idea. Let's go out for the afternoon. No one's due to turn up until tomorrow evening so we could go and do the things we used to do when we first met, have some fun instead of sitting here all alone, twiddling our thumbs!'

'Oh yes. I vote for ice cream for lunch and chips for tea, but not too much – you have to fit into your dress on Saturday!' Ruby laughed. 'I'll finish off in here and for once we can just go out and lock up. I've had a notice printed for the door to say we're closed until Monday so we can give it a trial run.'

'Great. I'll go and find Henry and let him know he'll be behind locked doors all alone with the telephone!'

Half an hour later the two friends giggled like schoolgirls as they ran down the steps of the hotel and crossed the road to the promenade.

'Where shall we start?' Gracie asked.

'Kursaal, of course,' Ruby said. 'But no more eyeing up the handsome young men who work there, you're going to be a married woman come Saturday...'

'But there's no harm in looking, is there?' Gracie

said mischievously. 'I mean, who can resist a glimpse of muscle on the arms of a fairground boy?'

'I suppose not, as it's a bit of a custom when we go there.' Ruby grinned as they linked arms and strolled in the direction of the town. It was a perfect day for an afternoon off; the sun was shining, the sea was glistening and both young women were happy in each other's company.

They walked slowly all along the promenade until they got to the entrance to the Kursaal amusement park; then Gracie and Ruby ran inside, giggling as they raced each other along the path to the first ride. They then slowly made their way around the park in exactly the same way as they had when they had first met in 1946, just weeks after they had both given birth to their first-born but illegitimate babies.

A couple of hours later they stumbled over to the grass that edged the main area of the Kursaal amusement park and fell down in tandem. They were laughing fit to bust after three consecutive rides on the rumbling rollercoaster which had whipped their skirts, blown their hairstyles to smithereens and left them both with bright red cheeks and white knuckles.

'That was such fun, Rubes,' Gracie spluttered. 'We've had some good times here together, haven't we? I hope this isn't going to be the last time we have fun, what with me getting married and you and Johnny being a real couple all bar the shouting...'

'Of course it's bloomin' well not going to be the last time!' Ruby said. 'I tell you what, we should

64

make a pact. Every year on this date we'll have a day out together where we do stupid things and pretend we're still silly single girls, even if we're not. No husbands, no children, just us two.'

'Oh yes, yes, yes! We'll meet exactly here on the grass...' Gracie looked at her wristwatch. 'At noon, every single year from today, even if we do see each other every day between now and then. Agreed? We'll call it our Silly Day, even when we're sixty and decrepit. God willing, of course.'

'Agreed. God willing,' Ruby said as she held out her hand. Gracie took it and they marked the agreement with an exaggerated handshake. 'Now, what next? Shall we walk the pier and have an ice cream before we go back? Big day coming up on Saturday and as the bride you need all the beauty sleep you can get.' Ruby laughed and pulled a face.

'As my chief bridesmaid, so do you ... especially as we're both getting on a bit now,' Gracie said cheekily.

'Speak for yourself, you're nearly four years older than me!'

'You don't have to remind me; that's why I was so keen to get that ring on my finger before I really was an old maid. I could see myself turning into Leonora before long.'

Savouring the warm summer sunshine, the two women walked slowly along the seafront from the Kursaal to the pier, talking all the way. They stopped at the boating lake and watched for a while but decided against taking a boat out.

'Shall we walk down the pier or get the train?' Ruby asked when they got there.

'How about we walk to the end and then get the train back?'

'Okay, chips on the pier and then we can get an ice cream and sit on the beach, it's such a nice day,' Gracie said. 'This will probably be our last real gossip for ages.'

Despite the fact that Gracie would still be working for Ruby at the Thamesview she would no longer be sharing the flat and her life with her and, despite being her best friend, Ruby would no longer be her nearest and dearest. In a few days' time Sean would take her place, and their lives would take separate paths as a result. Thinking about this, Gracie felt sadness and happiness combined.

'Okay. Now well go and sit on the sand, like we did that first day...' Ruby laughed as they queued at a kiosk to buy their ice creams after they arrived back at the pier station. 'I can tuck my skirt in my knickers and if we wait for the tide to go out we can go paddling in the mud.'

'Oh yes.' Gracie shrieked with laughter. 'Remember that day when I slipped and we had to go back and face the disapproval of Aunt Leonora? I thought she was going to ban me from the hotel forever.'

'She did grumble a lot, I know, but I think that deep down she was envious of us,' Ruby said thoughtfully. 'In her head she would have loved to be out and about being reckless and silly, but she just couldn't do it. It was all there inside her but she just couldn't relax enough to let it out. Sad really...'

'Yeah – I reckon she grumbled because she felt

she had to, but actually she bloody enjoyed all the adventures through us without having to loosen her stiff upper lip!' Gracie smiled.

'I really miss her,' Ruby sighed and looked out at the water. 'She was so good to me. She didn't even know me but she took me in and let me live with her... I know I moaned about her sometimes but I loved her. I think she must have felt likewise or she wouldn't have left me Thamesview.'

'Of course she did, and she left you the hotel because you loved it as much as she did. It was her baby – she gave it to you because she knew you'd take care of it.'

'Oh, that is such a nice thing to say, Gracie Grace...'

The two young women chatted nostalgically as they walked along, ice creams melting over their hands, looking for somewhere where there weren't too many other people, where they could sit and reminisce. Eventually finding a spot which wasn't crowded with day-trippers, they sat on the edge of a narrow strip of pebbly beach that was further away from the Golden Mile of arcades and slot machines.

Tucking their skirts tight under their bare legs, Gracie and Ruby sat down side by side and finished their ice creams in companionable silence, before leaning back and turning their faces to the sun.

After several minutes' silence, there was a crunching on the pebbles behind them.

'Excuse me, you two,' a very correct female voice suddenly said behind them. 'You don't mind if we sit here, do you? It's such a nice spot, away from the noise of all those screaming little kiddywinks further back that way.'

Gracie and Ruby had both been deep in thought, but they sat up quickly and looked round in unison. Two men and a woman were standing behind them, looking ready to settle themselves on the beach near to where they were sitting but politely waiting for a response. One of the men was holding a folded tartan rug over one arm and a cavernous wicker basket on the other and the other man was carrying the jackets they'd obviously taken off because of the sun. There was no doubt they were looking to stay for at least the duration of their picnic.

'Of course not! It's a public beach. And we're leaving in a minute anyway,' Gracie shrugged, without taking too much notice.

She was surprised at the question and also a bit irritated that other people were settling so close on the beach when there was room a little further away. She really wanted to chat with Ruby and enjoy their last outing together before everything changed; she just wanted a fun day with Ruby before her wedding.

'Are you here on a day trip?' the young woman asked as she took the rug from the man, before carefully laying it out just a few feet away from them. Trying to be subtle, Gracie glanced at her.

She was a petite but buxom blonde with a wide smile, classy clothes and a shrill, upper-class voice that carried along the beach. It was obvious she'd dressed for a day at the seaside but without considering the beach.

'No, we live here,' Gracie answered politely. 'We

were just having a sit in the sun before we walk home.'

'How exciting it must be to live at the seaside. We live in the country so we're just here for the day – we drove down from Saffron Walden this morning. Well, Edward drove. It's the first time we've ever been to Southend and we want to see everything; we've already had a good old look around the Kursaal and along by the pier. It's all such fun! Harry and I went on the lake in a boat...' she paused and her hand flew up to her mouth.

'Oh, I'm sorry, you must think we're so rude.' She walked round in front of them and held out her hand to both Ruby and Gracie in turn. 'I'm Louisa, and this is Harry, my darling fiancé...' she said as she pointed to the man on her left, 'and this is Edward, his big brother. Harry and I are engaged, we're getting married next month and Edward will be best man. He came all the way back from Africa especially. How exciting is that?'

'Shhh, darling,' the man introduced as Harry said, as he held his hand up in front of her and smiled affectionately. 'Not everyone wants to know all about our forthcoming nuptials.'

'I'm sorry, Harry, I'm so excited I want the whole world to know!' Louisa joined her hands together as if in prayer and almost bowed as she gazed adoringly at her fiancé.

Gracie felt Ruby's elbow in her ribs and heard her stifled snort but she didn't react.

She wasn't looking at Ruby, Louisa or Harry, nor was she listening to them. Instead Gracie had met the gaze of the man introduced as Edward, and she was completely transfixed.

She could feel herself starting to blush, but still she couldn't look away from the man, who was looking into her eyes with an intensity she couldn't decipher. There was the slightest hint of a smile around the edges of his mouth that inferred intimacy and Gracie was shocked; not only that he could look at her that way, but also that she didn't turn away and break the eye contact. She couldn't – she was hypnotised.

Ruby nudged her again, this time a little harder. 'Gracie? Haven't we got to get back? It's getting late and there's still a lot to do.'

Ruby's words were loaded with meaning, but for once Gracie chose to ignore the 'let's get out of here' signal, although she did force herself to look away from the man and break the connection.

'It's okay, we've got a while, let's stay just a bit longer,' she said, her eyes moving from Ruby back to Edward. 'I'm Gracie by the way and this is my best friend, Ruby...'

'Pleased to meet you, Gracie, and you, Ruby...' the man said as his eyes flickered from one to the other before settling on Gracie.

'Come on now, boys.' Interrupting the conversation, the young woman clapped her hands sharply. 'Let's go and dip a toe in the briney, we didn't come all this way not to at least get our feet wet. Chop, chop, shoes off, trousers rolled up! Let's go and see if it's as nice as it looks...'

Louisa slipped off her shoes and tip-toed barefoot over the stones, down to the edge of the water, where the receding tide was leaving straggling bits of wet seaweed behind on the damp sand. She was wearing yellow tailored knee-length shorts with a tightly fitted matching blouse and had a brightly coloured scarf tied artfully round her neck as a choker. She looked like a film star as she stood with one hand on her hip and the other carefully holding her hair back from her face. There was no denying the fact that she was a beautiful and privileged young woman.

Everyone on the beach turned and watched as she dipped a toe in the chilly water, screamed and then turned and waved madly. Harry was just a few paces behind her, standing on one leg and carefully rolling his trouser legs up to mid-calf, but Edward stayed exactly where he was. Right next to Gracie.

Both brothers were wearing similar beige slacks and white open-necked shirts and both had light brown floppy hairstyles but Edward's hair was gently sun-lightened across the front and he sported a suntan that was deep and noticeably exotic. Next to him, his brother Harry looked pale and mousey.

'Come on, Teddy, and you girls as well, this is such fun even if it is freezing! Why is it so cold when the sun is so warm?' Louisa shouted with a faux shiver as she splashed daintily in the shallows.

Although Edward wasn't moving, Gracie could see Ruby was tempted as always by the water. 'Go on, you go and have a splash with them,' she smiled, 'I'll just sit here and relax for a bit. Go on...'

Ruby put her head on one side and looked

curiously at her friend for a few moments. 'Are you feeling okay? I thought you might fancy a bit of a splash around today. It's such a nice day, and it might be...'

'No, I'm alright,' Gracie interrupted quickly. 'I'm happy to watch for the mo.' I'm comfortable sitting here but I might come down in a bit...'

As Ruby headed towards the water, Edward edged over from the comfort of the rug and sat beside Gracie on the pebble-splattered sand.

'Let me introduce myself properly. I'm Edward Woodfield, but my close friends call me Teddy. As you know, Harry is my brother and Louisa is his fiancée, and we live in rural Essex. Very rural, out in the sticks Essex, heading up to Suffolk. Saffron Walden. You've probably not heard of it!'

'I'm Gracie McCabe, Southend born and bred... Are you and Harry twins? You look very alike. I have twin sisters.'

'Not twins, I'm the elder by one year exactly so I always tell everyone I'm the more important Woodfield brother – although I have to say that Harry is the loudest,' he smiled. 'Do you mind if I call you Grace or do you prefer Gracie?'

'Definitely Gracie, I don't have the grace to be called Grace and I get fed up with all the "there but for the grace of God" jokes, so please don't say it.' She laughed nervously at her often-told joke.

'Not true, I think you're full of grace, but I'll call you Gracie if I have to. You know, this feels so strange, this isn't something I expected when I set out from home this morning...' Edward looked straight into her eyes.

'What's strange? There's nothing strange about sitting on the beach on a nice day, I often do it. Me and Ruby love the beach.' Not completely sure of his meaning, Gracie glanced away, hoping he wouldn't notice her face reddening rapidly under his intimate gaze.

'That isn't what I mean and I think you know that. It's strange, sitting here feeling as if I...'

Gracie didn't say anything but looked at him again, still trying to work out where the conversation was going.

'You know, I persuaded the others to come and sit over here, told them it was the best spot. I've been watching you ever since I saw you on the rollercoaster.' He smiled as he stared at her. 'I made them walk all the way to the pier and back with me; I even dragged them onto the pier ... that took some persuading, I'm telling you! Luckily the picnic basket was still in the car. Phew...'

'You were following us? Why would you do that?' Gracie asked.

'Because you caught my eye when the rollercoaster came around and I could see you laughing. Then, when I saw you and your friend falling about on the grass afterwards having such fun, I knew straight away that you were exactly the girl I wanted to marry.'

SIX

Gracie stared open-mouthed at the man sitting beside her on the beach; the stranger she had met not fifteen minutes before. Unsure how to react she shook her head and started to laugh nervously.

'Oh for God's sake, what a load of old waffle! How daft do you think I am? Flattery won't get you nowhere with me. I'm not that kind of girl.'

'It's not waffle and I never thought anything other than how beautiful you were. That was what I thought when I saw you, though maybe *marry* was a declaration too soon.' Edward pulled a face and paused before looking away in the direction of the sea.

'Harry would say that was typical of me, not thinking before opening my mouth. He says my social skills need honing, but that was what I felt. I still feel it, sitting here beside you.'

He moved a fraction sideways, until he was so close to Gracie their knees were touching. She knew she should move away but she couldn't. As the contact remained, so something made her instinctively place her left hand, along with the engagement ring Sean had given her, out of sight under her thigh.

As she did so a wave of guilt hit her. She should be sending the charming stranger on his way, she should be telling him that she didn't talk to strange men, that she was getting married in just three days' time. She should be saying to him that her wedding was all booked for Saturday, and that she loved her fiancé. She knew she should tell him all of that, and then stand up and walk away.

But she didn't.

Instead Gracie remained there, silent and still, and strangely aware of the scent of his cologne, despite knowing full well that she shouldn't be having feelings like this for anyone, let alone a total stranger.

But despite Edward Woodfield being a stranger, Gracie felt as if she already knew him – because he was exactly how she had always imagined her fantasy man would be. The stranger on the beach was actually the very familiar man of her dreams. He was the right one whom Gracie had always known she would recognise.

Edward was tall and lithe, with long legs and broad shoulders; his features were even, with a charming smile and expressive deep blue eyes that Gracie knew were fixed on her face. But there was a shyness about him that was endearing, and somehow she knew instinctively that he wasn't just a run-of-the-mill Lothario trying to get off with a local girl at the seaside.

She was momentarily dumbstruck. Old flannel she could easily deal with but open sincerity and genuine declarations were something different.

In the background she could hear Ruby calling her from the water's edge but her voice seemed far, far away. Gracie focused on her feet, wiggling her toes in her sandals and shaking a few stray grains of sand from between them. Something strange was happening to her and though she wanted to get up and run away from the obvious danger in front of her, she couldn't.

Even though the touch was so light it was barely there, Edward Woodfield's leg burned into hers, and she was aware of his fresh breath that was far too close to the side of her face. She carried on looking down and didn't meet his gaze, but nonetheless she was completely thrown by both the situation and the palpitations that were getting faster by the moment.

And then he moved an inch away from her. He stretched his legs out in front of him and leaned back with his hands under his head.

'So, what do you do for a living that has you resident at the seaside, you lucky thing?' he asked, gently easing the tension of the moment.

'I've always lived here. I was born here – I'm a Southender who's never lived anywhere else...' she paused. 'But you're not really interested in my life story, are you? It's pretty boring.'

'I am and I'm listening. I want to know all about you and then I'll tell you all about me,' he smiled.

'There's not enough time for all that stuff. Ruby will be back in a minute and then we have to go. I have a lot to do in the next few days...' she paused. Gracie knew she should tell him about her forthcoming marriage, but instead she hesitated just long enough for him to interrupt.

'It's not important; we don't need to know everything about each other immediately.'

As he smiled, so Gracie unintentionally found herself telling him an outline of her life story. It was a sanitised version, but he proved to be a good listener.

76

'And you? What do you do?' Gracie asked, turning it round to him.

'I'm an engineer. I work abroad, mostly in Africa, but I'm back home on leave for Harry's wedding. They're driving me completely bananas with all the planning and organising; it's going to be very formal, which is not my sort of thing, but it's what they want. Or rather, what *Louisa* wants – and usually whatever Louisa wants, so does poor besotted Harry.'

'I thought you looked too healthy and suntanned for England,' Gracie said, carefully avoiding the subject of weddings.

'Hardly healthy,' he chuckled. 'Not that long ago I was burnt to a cinder after a day at the beach and this is the outcome after the top three layers peeled. Luckily I have skin that tans. Gracie, can we meet again? Just the two of us. I can drive down here anytime. I'm in the UK for several more weeks until the wedding. I want to get to know you and for you to know me...'

'I can't do that, I really can't. You see, it's, it's...' Gracie stuttered, unable to get the words out.

'Of course you can,' he interrupted with a smile. 'I'm not going to give up. I want to get to know you, and I want to marry you and whisk you off to Africa with me.'

'Don't talk to me like that,' she snapped. 'You're taking the mickey out of me now. I told you, I'm not some stupid little fairground girl who'll fall for your flannel and flattery and let you have your way, I'm not...'

'I'm not taking the mickey and I've got no other motive. I mean it, I want to get to know

77

you. Please, Gracie? I really mean it and I've never done this sort of thing before. Harry would have a pink fit if he knew I was declaring love at first sight to you. It's just not me.'

He sounded so sincere that Gracie was immediately thrown; she wanted to believe him and to try and understand exactly what was passing between them but she didn't know what to say and before she had time to think of a response Ruby appeared out of nowhere and stood in front of them. She looked from one to the other, glanced down in the direction of Gracie's hidden left hand and shook her head.

'Wow!' she said with meaning.

'Wow what?' Gracie looked up and forced a smile.

'Just, wow,' Ruby said with a knowing shake of her head. 'Shouldn't we be going back home now? You know, things to do and ... well, things to do and guests to prepare for!'

Ruby's subtle reminder brought Gracie straight back to her senses and, shocked at herself, she jumped up and quickly stepped away from where Edward was sitting. He carefully moved back onto the blanket that Louisa had laid out and made a big show of brushing sand off his trousers, then a few moments later Harry and Louisa were back with them.

'Picnic time! I'm famished, let's get the grub set up...' Louisa said loudly, oblivious to the odd atmosphere on the beach.

Gracie and Ruby both watched as Louisa knelt down and started unpacking the cavernous basket, pulling out two plates of sandwiches, a full-size gala pie, a box of biscuits, a selection of fruit and a large home-baked fruit cake. Drinks followed, along with assorted relishes, a cruet set and a full range of crockery, cutlery and glasses which had been strapped into the sides and lid.

'Well, that looks really wonderful. I can't believe you brought all that to the beach...' Ruby said as she and Gracie watched the ceremonial unpacking in fascination.

'Join us,' Edward said. 'There's plenty. Our mother still thinks we need feeding up. I think she emptied the refrigerator straight into the basket rather than divide it up.'

'That's right,' Louisa said. 'Seems she's given us enough here to feed the forty thousand. If you don't join us we'll have to share it with some passing children and those squawking seagulls, I think.'

As she laughed loudly so Harry, her fiancé, joined in appreciatively but Edward merely smiled politely. His eyes, screwed up against the sun, were surreptitiously back on Gracie.

'I'm sorry, as I said it looks wonderful but we can't stay,' Ruby said, taking held of Gracie's elbow and gently squeezing it. 'It was lovely to meet you all but we really do have to get back. Work to do...'

'We do have lots to do but I think we can stay for a bit longer...' Gracie looked pleadingly at her friend. 'That spread looks wonderful.'

Ruby looked at her closely for several seconds. 'Okay, but only if you come for a splash around while the tide's still up. Come and cool off with me.'

As soon as they were out of earshot, Ruby looked at her friend. 'What are you playing at – you and that Edward? I saw the way you were looking at each other. Gracie, you were flirting like you're single!' Ruby hissed.

'I'm not playing at anything. Rubes, he said he wants to marry me. He followed us from the Kursaal, he sat there on purpose...' Gracie said quietly.

Ruby started to laugh but when she saw Gracie's expression she stopped.

'Oh for heaven's sake, that is just stupid. How could he say something like that after five minutes? He must have a screw loose.'

Gracie swished the water around with her feet. 'Maybe both of us have. There's something there; he said he felt it and I know I did. It hit me the moment I saw him. I've never felt anything like this before. He's the right one, I know it. Do you believe in love at first sight?'

'I don't know – but I do know you're marrying Sean this Saturday coming, three days' time.' Ruby paused. 'You *are* going ahead with it, aren't you? I saw you hiding your ring.'

'Of course I am but...' Gracie fiddled with her engagement ring.

'Gracie, don't do this. Let's just go. As soon as we're back at the hotel it'll be as if we never met any of them, as if this never happened.' Ruby grabbed her hand and squeezed it tight. 'I'm telling you, no good can come out of this, let's make our excuses and leave.'

'Let's just stay for an hour or so. That's all, then we'll go home and get ready for the wedding. The hotel is empty and there's not that much to do.

I'll do everything I have to, promise...' Gracie pleaded. 'Please? I just need a bit more time. I'm not going to do anything silly, I just want to get to know him a little bit.'

'You're playing with fire, Gracie and you'll regret it if you take it any further, I'm telling you, but it's your choice. I'm not your mother or Aunt Leonora,' Ruby said.

'I think that the real Aunt Leonora will be up there cheering me on, even if it is through pursed lips. She never found the right one, even fleetingly,' Gracie replied with a smile.

After their few minutes splashing around, Ruby and Gracie walked back up to where Louisa, Edward and Harry were and sat down, just off the picnic rug. Ruby sat next to Louisa and Gracie sat beside her, with Edward at the far end of the semi-circle, in her direct line of vision.

Aware that there were a lot of eyes in the group, Gracie mostly looked at the ground but she didn't have to look up to know that Edward's eyes were on her. She could feel them and the pull scared her.

There was no doubt that Louisa was absolutely in charge of the group; she played host with the picnic and also did most of the talking but Gracie didn't want to join in, her appetite having been replaced by a gnawing combination of nausea and guilt. Her usual common sense had taken flight and she was away in another place ... with the man called Edward, whom she had only just met.

Gracie was in a state of confusion. Her forthcoming wedding to Sean had taken up every moment of her day for months and she had been on countdown ever since they had agreed the date. She desperately wanted to be married and have a family of her own, to leave her past behind. But now that it was about to happen, she had been confronted with Edward Woodfield, who on the surface was her dream man. Suddenly Gracie wasn't sure what she wanted anymore.

'Who wants an ice cream?' Edward asked after they'd all finished.

'I do,' Louisa put her hand up, 'but you chaps go and get them while we clear up.'

'I don't want to go traipsing round looking for ice cream,' Harry said grumpily. 'I seriously need a nap after all that food. There are some empty deckchairs up there; I'm going to get them for us.'

'You get the chairs and I'll go and get the ice creams,' Edward said quickly, 'but Gracie or Ruby will have to come with me as they know where to go, and I don't have enough hands for five cornets...'

Ruby rolled her eyes and looked upwards. 'You go and get the ice creams with him, Gracie. I'll help clear up...' she paused for several seconds, 'but don't get lost, we've got a long shift when we get back.'

Gracie feigned reluctance, but eventually stood up and walked away along the promenade with Edward.

She knew absolutely that she shouldn't be doing it, that she could be opening a door that should, because of Sean, remain firmly shut but she couldn't help herself. She felt as if she had suddenly lost all self-control.

Gracie simply wanted to spend some time with

Edward Woodfield, the man she had instantly recognised as the right one.

The right one at the wrong time.

SEVEN

'Well? How do I look?' Gracie asked nervously, as Ruby stepped back after pulling up the zip on her wedding dress. 'Is it okay? I feel a bit like the fairy on the Christmas tree. I just don't look like me, do I?'

As Gracie spoke she twirled round on the spot in front of the full-length mirror in her bedroom, making her skirt rise and fall. Her freshly lightened hair was curled and carefully pinned up under her shoulder-length veil making her neck look long and graceful, her minimal make-up was carefully applied, and her stiff new satin shoes were on her feet.

As Gracie stared at herself in the mirror she found it hard to believe that she was the bride and that it was actually her wedding day. She had spent so many years seeing a plain kid in the mirror that it was hard to accept that everything had changed for her.

It was the day she had dreamed of, especially after the trauma of being abandoned by the man who was the father of her illegitimate baby, the baby she had been forced to give up.

Archie Cooper had declared his undying love, charmed her, said he wanted to marry her, bedded her and then disappeared without trace, leaving a fearful and disillusioned Gracie to face the consequences alone, with her dreams in tatters.

But that was all in the past, everything was in the past; she now had Sean Donnelly, a nice young man who loved her and wanted to marry her. Her wedding day had finally arrived.

'Oh bloody hell, Gracie Grace! You look lovely – all grown up and sophisticated. You look just like a model bride in *Woman's Own* or even a movie star! You're so beautiful.'

'Beautiful is pushing it, Rubes...' Gracie laughed.

Ruby clutched her hands to her mouth and looked ready to cry as her friend stopped moving and stood with her arms held out, like a ballerina. The wedding dress was mid-calf length with a fitted silk bodice that was darted and shaped to make the most of Gracie's figure; it had a full skirt carefully crafted from silk and lace, with a net underskirt to make it stand out and a neckline that was scooped and edged with white satin, as were the fashionable elbow-length sleeves. Her short white lace gloves were the finishing touch to the bride's ensemble.

All the dresses, Gracie's and both bridesmaids' had been home-made by Babs Wheaton, Ruby's wartime foster mother who was a skilled home dressmaker, as a wedding gift. Gracie was beyond grateful because she could never have afforded something so classy herself.

Ruby's bridesmaid's outfit was the same design as Gracie's but was pale pink satin without the lace or the net underskirts so it hung straight down and fluttered around her calves; Maggie's was almost the same, but hers was full-length and in a design more suited to a child. Each dress had been carefully made with each person in mind and they all complemented each other.

Gracie turned every which way in front of the mirror as she tried hard to recognise herself. No matter how many years had passed, inside she still felt like the plain child with spots and greasy hair who was never really part of anything, either in school or out. The child who was always called names and excluded from playtime games. Now she was looking at a beautiful young woman who didn't look in the least bit like the Gracie McCabe she knew.

'I know I should feel a bit of a hypocrite walking down the aisle in white, what with everything that's gone on but what could I do? Sean's family expect it, the virgin bride and all that.' Gracie frowned as she continued to twist and turn, and study herself from top to toe. 'I wonder why it's still the way? My mother is horrified I'm going to wed in church in white but then she'd have died of shame if I turned up in cream. It's so old-fashioned!' Gracie pulled a silly face.

'It's tradition, I suppose, and the way their generation sees things,' Ruby said.

'I suppose. And talking of tradition, where's my miniature bridesmaid?' Gracie looked around. 'Where's Maggie gone?'

'She's already downstairs with Aunty Babs and your dad. She was jumping around like a flea on a flannel with excitement.' Ruby smiled. 'She looks so pretty and I'm so proud of her. Sometimes when I see her it's hard minding my words. Johnnie says the same; she's our daughter but not a soul except us knows. But she's having the best upbringing with George and Babs so we just have to be grateful and wait until Maggie is old enough to be told the truth. I hope she understands. We were so young, we had no choice.'

'You were brave enough to make the right choice, Rubes, you didn't know Johnnie was going to come back into your life, and Babs and George are fantastic parents to her.'

'It still hurts, though,' Ruby said. 'But enough of that, today is about being happy, it's about you being happy and having a wonderful wedding day.'

She walked over to the open French window and looked out.

'Well, Gracie Grace, this is it. It's just you and me up here now. The guests should all be at the church by now and our cars are already outside, all polished and decked out in ribbons and just waiting for us all. Come and look, and it's such a sunny day...'

As she spoke Ruby went out onto the balcony. Gracie joined her and they both looked down at the cars below.

'Looks like it's time to go to the church then, before I get my dress all mucky – you know what I'm like,' Gracie laughed. 'A bit of rust from the railings would show up a treat on this dress...'

Ruby didn't laugh and she didn't look around, but stayed where she was, looking out towards the horizon.

'You know it's not too late to change your mind, really it's not...' she said cautiously, without looking at her friend. Her expression was serious for the first time that day. 'I know you said you don't want to talk about it again but I have to say this: please, please, please don't do the wrong thing, just because it's suddenly the day. You know what they say: marry in haste, repent at leisure. If Sean's not the one then you're making a mistake.'

'Oh of course it's too bloody late to change my mind, it's far too late! Can you imagine if I jilted Sean at the altar? I'd have to leave the country straight away! The wedding is planned, and the honeymoon and the flat is ready and waiting, how could I back out of all that?' Gracie said, shaking her head slowly. 'And anyway, I don't want to. This is what I want – a husband, a home, a baby – and I know I'll get all that with Sean...'

'It doesn't have to be with him though, does it? I mean, if it's someone else you want, if someone else is the right one then is that fair on Sean?' Ruby persisted.

Gracie shrugged. As far as she was concerned she had made the decision to marry Sean long ago and she was going to stick with it. She had to.

She may have thought Edward Woodfield was the man of her dreams but she was well aware that she didn't actually know him, not in the way she knew Sean. And even without knowing him, Gracie could see that they were from such different backgrounds and class that even if anything were to happen between them, there was no chance his family would ever agree to them marrying.

It just couldn't happen and it wouldn't work, not the way it did with Sean.

'Oh, Ruby,' Gracie sighed. 'I've not made the decision in haste, I've thought of nothing else. But I've known Sean for years, he's a good man and I'm sure I'm doing the right thing for both of us. We're the same kind of people: we're both ordinary and we match. I had a bit of panic the other day, imagining something different but I'm over it now. It was so stupid. I was getting ideas above my station, as my mother would say.'

The two women smiled and waved down to the group of neighbours who were gathering on the pavement outside the hotel, all there to see the bride off. Lots of people that they knew so well, even the small staff from the hotel were out there, waiting.

'Don't go putting yourself down, Gracie. No one is better than you and there's no man too good for you, not even the one whose name you told me not to say!'

Gracie and Ruby moved back from the railings and faced each other.

'Nice of you to say it, Rubes, but that one was definitely way out of my league. A country house and a London flat and living most of the time in Africa? Can you just imagine me out in Africa? None of that is me, is it? I'm just a local girl who's been nowhere and done nothing. I couldn't even keep up with him in a proper conversation.' She smiled and shook her head. 'So, let's go and get on with my wedding day. It's been long enough coming! Everyone thought I was going to be an old maid.'

'Oh Gracie, this is just so final. Are you really sure you're doing the right thing? You can still change your mind...' Ruby said hesitantly.

'I'm sure. It was my very own *Brief Encounter*, like in the film. It was me being daft and getting carried away as usual, but now I'm back where I should be,'Gracie grinned. 'You know what a nutcase I can be. Well, this time I'm being sensible: I'm going to marry Sean.'

'Okay,' Ruby said with a break in her voice. 'I suppose if that's what you really want then it's time to get down those stairs and off to the church.'

They made their way down to the ground floor, where Gracie's father was waiting with Babs and George Wheaton and a very excited young Maggie.

'Can we go now? Pleeease, I want to do what a bridesmaid does...' the child asked, jumping from foot to foot with excitement. At eight years old, she was tall for her age and confident beyond her years.

'Yes, we're going in two minutes. I'm just going to get the flowers and then it's off to the church,' Ruby said, looking wistfully at the little girl. 'You look so beautiful, Maggie. Absolutely beautiful!'

When she came back she handed Gracie her bouquet, gave Maggie her posy and held her own in front of her.

'Right, Miss Impatient, to the cars...' she said.

Gracie watched her friend smile at the child, while at the same time blinking to hold back the tears that were building. She knew it wasn't because of the wedding but because of Maggie, the daughter Ruby could not acknowledge.

The daughter who had been born at the same time as Gracie's own baby, eight years ago.

With her emotions heightened anyway by the stress of her wedding day, it made Gracie tearful to think of her own baby, the beautiful little boy whom she knew nothing about. But she was determined not to let anything spoil the day so she looked at her father, who was standing slightly away from the group, and forced a smile. 'Come on, Dad, let's get to the church. I don't want to be late.'

Her father smiled and patted her hand. 'You look beautiful, my little Gracie, I hope you'll both be as happy as me and your mother, and remember, it's not all going to be easy, marriage is give and take...'

Gracie wanted to say 'you give and she takes,' but she just smiled at him.

The Wheatons and the bridesmaids went ahead to the hotel car which was parked outside, in front of the bridal car. Ruby and Maggie got into the back seat as George Wheaton skilfully moved himself from his wheelchair into the passenger side, leaving his wife to fold the chair and put it in the back, before getting into the driver's seat.

Everyone waved excitedly as they drove off, leaving just Gracie and her father on the steps, waiting for the right moment. Then, with her arm in his, they walked down to the waiting car where Dr Wheaton's new driver stood beside the open door, waiting to help them in. As Gracie gathered up her skirt to avoid it creasing or getting caught in the door so a ripple of applause rang out from the people lining the pavement, making her blush. She paused, glanced around and self-consciously waved back.

Then someone caught her eye.

Over the top of their heads she thought for a moment she had seen *him* standing behind the small group on the nearby corner looking in her direction, but when she looked again, whoever it was had moved.

For a few moments her chest palpitated so much she feared that the fitted bodice on her dress would burst open. *Surely he wouldn't do that? Surely he wouldn't come here?* She asked herself in panic as she looked around again scanning every face, but there was no sign. She wondered fleetingly if Edward Woodfield had come to persuade her to go with him, to jilt Sean at the altar and run away with him to Africa. So many different thoughts flashed through her mind at that moment that she had to shake her head to rid herself of them. She looked all around her once more, just in case, and then climbed into the car to go to the church to marry Sean Donnelly.

Just fifteen minutes later, with the guests all seated and the priest at the altar, Gracie was standing in the cool of the church porch, waiting for the organist to begin playing and give her the cue to start walking. She gripped her father's arm tight and glanced round at Ruby, who winked reassuringly.

'Here we go, time to start walking...' her chief bridesmaid said, as the first notes of 'Here Comes The Bride' echoed throughout the church.

Ruby and Maggie followed as Gracie walked down the aisle on her father's arm. She looked straight ahead and walked confidently but when she got closer and saw Sean standing at the altar with his back to her the enormity of what she was about to do hit her and she was suddenly terrified.

As she looked at the friends and family standing either side of the aisle waiting for her to reach the altar and for the ceremony to begin, it hit her that there really was no going back. This was the moment when her life would change forever. Her chest started pounding again and her feet felt like lead weights in her dainty wedding shoes.

She thought about the signet ring nestling in her jewellery box and felt sick. She had left it too late.

Doubts and uncertainties swelled inside her and she wanted to turn around and run straight out of the church but she didn't, instead she took the last few steps until she reached Sean's side. She turned and handed her bouquet to Ruby, who was one step behind her. As her father stepped back, Sean turned to look at her. He smiled widely and whispered, 'Oh my lord, but you look so beautiful, Gracie...'

Gracie blinked hard and met his gaze. She was there to marry Sean in front of their friends and families and she was sure that was the right thing to do so she forced her doubts away and smiled back. Sean Donnelly knew her and loved her, and that was the most important thing in the world to her at that moment.

Edward Woodfield was a stranger and a nice fantasy man to daydream about in her dotage but Sean Donnelly was the reality, she knew.

EIGHT

After the bridal car had pulled away from the hotel and driven off in the direction of the church, Edward Woodfield stepped out from the shadows of the nearby doorway. With his head down, he walked briskly in the opposite direction to the spot around the corner where he had parked his own car.

He had wanted to see Gracie, to let her know he was there and to see her reaction but when she had glanced in his direction and almost spotted him, he had instinctively jumped out the way and moved out of sight.

Common sense and his innate good manners told him that what he was doing was disrespectful to both her and her fiancé and, despite his feelings, he had no right to disrupt her wedding day. She had told him three days before, after they had kissed behind the ice cream stand, that she was to be married. He had tried to dissuade her then and there but she had been adamant.

When they had said a very formal goodbye on the beach in front of the others Edward had surreptitiously slipped the gold signet ring from his little finger and pressed it into her hand, wrapped in a piece of paper, when the others weren't looking.

'My phone number in Saffron Walden. Think about it Gracie, please. Just think about it and ring me at this number.'

'I already have thought about it. I'm sorry,' she whispered as, with no choice but to take it, she slipped it in the side pocket of her skirt.

They all said formal goodbyes to each other and went their separate ways. He had watched Gracie as she walked away and seen her look back just once. She had glanced over her shoulder and smiled at him, then turned back and walked away with Ruby.

He had watched her go and then sat down with Harry and Louisa, and tried to act as if nothing had happened.

'Nice girls...' Louisa said. 'Both of them. Can you imagine being responsible for a hotel at that age? They must work really hard.'

'I wasn't sure about them,' Harry said. 'The taller one was wearing an engagement ring, I noticed, nothing like as nice as Louisa's so I doubt they've got much money.'

'Heavens darling, you're observant! I didn't notice a ring but I did think she was flirting with Teddy; that was a bit naughty if she's engaged.' Louisa paused and looked at Edward. 'She looked as if she's really taken a shine to you, what do you think?'

Harry laughed and answered instead. 'I thought they were nice enough but somewhat common. Can you imagine staying in a hotel run by those two?'

'It's a hotel for widows and spinsters, you idiot,' Edward snapped. 'And at least they work for a living. You should try it sometime; you've done nothing apart from play at soldiers...'

Harry and Louisa both stared at him, but before they could say anything Edward started piling stuff into the picnic basket.

'It's time we headed back. I've had enough of the seaside.'

'What's got into you, Teddy?' Louisa asked as she studied his face, carefully looking for a clue.

'I just want to get back. It's a long drive...' He took a deep breath and forced a smile. 'Sorry I snapped at you both. Just ignore me, the sea air has worn me out.'

Harry still looked hurt but Louisa simply stared at him knowingly.

'You're right, Teddy darling. It's time to get away from here.'

Earlier that morning on the day of Gracie's wedding and after a long sleepless night, he'd jumped into his car on the spur of the moment and driven at top speed from Saffron Walden in North Essex all the way down to Southend on the coast. Edward hadn't given his action a great deal of thought so he didn't really know what he was intending to do, but something inside was making him want to see what would happen.

Logically he knew there was little chance of Gracie McCabe, the girl he had met and fallen in love with, not going through with her wedding, but he still had the urge to be there and to see for certain. He just hoped it would help him deal with his irrational feelings for the young woman he barely knew.

From the moment he could walk and talk Edward had been the sensible one in the Woodfield-

Barnes family. He was far more mature than his brother, who was almost the same age and, in many ways, he was more mature than either of his parents, who were both unworldly, wealthy eccentrics, wrapped up in their own little bubble of extravagant and luxurious living.

His father was a passable artist who, although he sold the odd piece of work, had an elaborate studio full of unsold canvases and his mother always described herself as an author but she had only ever sat down in front of a typewriter when she was bored and had never even finished a manuscript, let alone had anything published.

Neither of them had made any money out of any of their various ventures over the years, but they had no need to, as they lived very comfortably courtesy of a vast inheritance of estate and income from the Barnes side of the family. They divided their time between their classic country house in Saffron Walden and their art deco apartment in central London, flitting happily between the differing lifestyle of town and country, interspersed with trips to the South of France when they were bored. It was a very privileged lifestyle that they enjoyed to the full.

Edward senior and his wife Elspeth were perfectly suited to each other. They were both dreamers and they lived life with their heads in the clouds, floating happily above the nitty gritty of everyday life. They were a pleasant and popular couple who loved each other and who also loved their two sons, albeit in a rather detached way, keeping them in the periphery of their lives. When they were younger, a series of nannies and boarding schools had provided the majority of Edward and Harry's care and then, when they were grown, the relationship had become more like one between siblings than parents and their offspring.

Their younger son Harry took after his father. He was equally airy with no real aspirations of his own, other than to be married to the seemingly vacuous but very beautiful Louisa, the daughter of a diplomat, who he had met during his enforced spell in the army. Edward sometimes wondered if she was only with Harry because of his potential inheritance, but he never said anything because they were as happy as two children in the playground.

Somehow Edward junior had missed out on the happy-go-lucky family gene and was, to his parents' dismay, eminently sensible and down-to-earth.

Almost from birth Edward had been the serious one in the family, a bit of a loner who was happy in his own company. Growing up he was quiet and hard-working and had always liked nothing better than to shut himself away in the study with a pile of books and some complex problems to solve.

His eventual career path of engineering hadn't surprised anyone, nor had his excellence at university, but his decision to work abroad in a third-world country had shocked them all and no one had expected him to stick it out in Africa.

His parents especially had thought he would be better suited to working and teaching in the closeted surroundings of a university but instead Edward had gone off to work in Nigeria in West

Africa, savouring every moment of his new life on the emerging continent.

He hadn't been sure what to expect when he'd accepted the job but he knew he had to get away from his crazy family if he was ever to have some normality and Africa had seemed far enough away for them not to be able to interfere. Once there and independent he had quickly become absorbed in the way of life. He relished the feeling that he was doing something worthwhile and it excited him like nothing had ever done before. Until a few days before, he had been champing at the bit to finish his unwanted home leave for his brother's wedding and to get back there.

But then by chance he met Gracie McCabe and his usual common sense had evaporated in an instant. He didn't understand his feelings, after all she was a total stranger, but as he'd watched her going round repeatedly on that rollercoaster and then falling on the grass laughing loud and hard, and then followed her as she and Ruby strolled along the prom happily eating ice creams, he had instantly changed from staid and sensible Edward and was acting like an unpredictable lovesick teenager who couldn't concentrate on anything other than his fleeting flirtation with a stranger.

He had had the odd flirtation in the past but suddenly, at age thirty, he was desperately in love for the first time in his life and somehow he'd managed to fall for a girl he didn't even know, a girl who he'd spent just a few hours with, and who had eventually told him she was about to marry someone else.

It was so completely out of character for him

and he couldn't understand how it had happened.

But it had – and he was besotted to the point of obsessed.

Edward followed the wedding car at a safe distance, and when it pulled up outside the church he parked far enough away not to be noticed but close enough to see what was going on. He had hoped so desperately that she wouldn't appear, that she would have cancelled the whole thing en route, or at least delayed it, giving them time to get to know each other.

He had a picture in his mind of her shouting 'stop the car,' he could see her jumping out and running in the opposite direction to the church, but it hadn't happened.

Suddenly she was there and was being helped out of the car by a man he assumed was her father. He watched as Ruby came over to her and straightened her dress and he had a lump in his throat, just seeing her looking so beautiful.

Rather than dampening them, as he had hoped, it intensified his feelings for her.

He watched her make her way up the path to the church on her father's arm, with Ruby and a little girl walking behind them. Instinctively Edward ducked down behind the steering wheel but as he did so he knew it didn't really matter; from her manner and her happy smile he could see she was oblivious to everything except her wedding to another man, an Irishman called Sean whom she had been courting for a long time.

As the small group disappeared inside the dark

porch of the church it finally dawned on him that he really was on a fool's errand. Gracie McCabe was going to marry someone else and there was nothing he could do about it. She wasn't going to spot him in the distance and run into his arms, and he realised how foolish he had been to even think she would on the strength of one short meeting.

He waited where he was until the church doors opened and she reappeared but this time on the arm of her new husband, a chubby dark young man wearing an ill-fitting suit and overly shiny shoes, but looking as delighted as if he had won the pools. Which, in Edward's eyes, he had. In his eyes, Gracie McCabe and her new husband just didn't belong together.

And then everyone was outside and a cloud of rice and confetti flew through the air showering the laughing couple. The photographer was shouting directions and as a family group gathered together for a pose, Edward knew he had lost.

Dejected, he picked up the envelope that was on the passenger seat. It was a letter he'd carefully penned the day after meeting her and had intended to post. He turned it over in his hands a few times and thought long and hard about delivering it by hand to the hotel but then thought better of it.

Gracie McCabe was now someone else's wife. He had no right.

He had watched her go into the church and then watched her come out as a married woman, a happily married woman, judging by her body language. There was nothing for him there so, resisting the urge to stay and watch any more of the ritual of the camera and the confetti, he drove straight back to Saffron Walden.

Normally he would have felt exhilarated as the open-top sports car that he loved swallowed up the miles on a beautiful summer's day. The sun was shining and the wind in his hair was cool and gentle but Edward was unaware of it all. He was in turmoil and he felt really stupid. His actions were so out of character and he felt as if he had had a bit of a brainstorm over the previous few days.

Throughout the drive back he decided to get his head back in order; he thought about the extravagant preparations he was going back to and wondered if he could come up with some excuse to get out of Harry and Louisa's wedding and his best man duties. All he wanted was to be on the aeroplane or mail-boat back to Nigeria as soon as possible. Edward just wanted to get back to his old life and get the now-married Gracie McCabe right out of his system.

It was on the final bend of the narrow country road that his concentration lapsed and he veered off at speed, wrapping the front of his sports car around the trunk of a long-standing oak tree and then tumbling into a ditch. It was a quiet road with little traffic and he was trapped for nearly two hours before he was found and pulled from the wreckage, with devastating injuries.

From the moment Sean had turned, looked her in the eye and smiled at her, Gracie was sure she was doing the right thing and, with her reservations gone, her wedding day went on to pass in a happy blur. The ceremony itself seemed to be over before it had begun and she and Sean exited the church as Mr and Mrs Donnelly, followed by their guests.

Everyone posed patiently for the pernickety photographer who was waiting in the grounds with his camera set up, and an assistant on hand to make sure they did exactly as they were told. While this was going on, the guests grouped into their familiar cliques as inevitably occurred at family gatherings; Sean's family and friends on one side, and Gracie's on the other.

The respective mothers glared across the divide, two equally competitive and assertive women who each wanted to be seen as the senior mother-in-law of the occasion. But although they both pursed their lips with disapproval a few times, neither said anything out of the way.

But all in all, everything about the day was as perfect as Gracie had hoped for. Despite a few showers the sun shone down at all the right moments, everyone turned up and the day went off without even a minor hitch. George Wheaton and Fred McCabe got on like the proverbial house on fire, as did Gracie and Sean's respective sisters.

The twins were accompanied by their fiancés, with Jeanette being in a bit of a huff because she and her twin sister weren't invited to be bridesmaids. Being polar opposite in personality Jennifer, ever the silent observer, didn't seem to mind at all. She stayed in the background all day, quietly watching and absorbing the proceedings rather than actually joining in.

And then it was all over. It was just one day in

their lives but it was a life-changing day for Gracie McCabe, who was no longer sitting on the shelf contemplating spinsterhood. After a few words in church she was Mrs Sean Donnelly, wife and respectable woman.

That night, together for the first time in their new flat near the Palace hotel, Gracie determined she would not give the man called Edward Woodfield another thought. Ever.

As they lay entwined together in the marital bed, she listened to Sean snoring peacefully and forced from her mind all thoughts of Edward, and the twinge of regret she had at not meeting him at another time in her life.

She looked at the ceiling and determined to focus only on Sean, her new husband and the father of her future children.

Bright and early the next morning, Ruby and Johnnie drove them to the station to see them off on the honeymoon Sean's parents had unexpectedly given them.

They were both excited as they headed off for a week in a boarding house in Great Yarmouth, and by the time they came back, happy and relaxed, Gracie was totally focused on her new husband and their future together.

Edward Woodfield, meanwhile, had been forcibly tucked away in the back of her mind as a moment of pre-marital madness, and the signet ring and the piece of paper were in the hands of Ruby, who had been charged with posting the ring back to him as soon as possible.

A new chapter in the life of Gracie McCabe, now Donnelly, was about to begin.

NINE

Six months later

'Guess what, Sean?' Gracie said, pausing for effect. 'I'm expecting. I went to see the doctor this morning and in about six months' time you're going to be a father!'

Gracie smiled at her husband across the dining table, looking forward to his reaction. He'd made no secret of how much he wanted them to start a family just as soon as possible.

'Oh, that's wonderful...' Sean rocked forward in his chair and smiled widely. 'I've been waiting so long for that news. When did you know? Why didn't you tell me earlier?'

'I didn't want to say until the doctor confirmed it, just in case I was wrong, but it looks like we've struck lucky...' Gracie smiled.

'Not lucky at all, Gracie darling; it was just a matter of time. The Donnellys are a fertile family, and this just proves it with another Donnelly baby to add to the collection. Hopefully I'll have a son. We need a boy to carry down the family name.' Sean stood up and went over to hug his wife. 'I can't wait to tell me Mam, she'll be so happy.'

'Well, I was thinking about it this afternoon after I got back from the doctors, and I reckon it will be either a boy or a girl, one or the other. That's worth putting a couple of bob on down the betting shop,' Gracie said seriously.

It was a moment before Sean realised exactly what she'd said.

'You are such a joker, Mrs Donnelly! You fooled me there.' He laughed. 'Wait till I tell me Mam what you just said ... definitely a boy or a girl ... I don't know!'

Gracie smiled but said nothing. One of her biggest reliefs was that Sean's family, especially his mother, lived so far away. He had always talked of them all affectionately but it had only been when they went to Ireland before the wedding to meet them that Gracie had realised how idolised Sean was in his family; in fact, he could do no wrong in their eyes. And Gracie herself was an interloper who could do no right. For some reason his mother seemed to blame her for her precious boy living in England, even though he'd already been there for years before they even got together.

The days she spent with his family were difficult because it seemed that every five minutes someone else popped up to ask Gracie questions about herself and about their relationship. At first she'd thought it was all rather sweet and that they were simply looking out for Sean, the family baby, but as time passed and the questions became more probing she started to wonder if there was something they weren't telling her.

His sisters especially wanted to know every single thing about Gracie herself. When the questioning had first started she'd thought they were really interested in her but by the end of the stay she felt they really wanted to find something out of the ordinary so they could all shrug over the dinner table and say 'we always knew she wasn't right for our baby boy'.

The only time she felt comfortable in the conversation was when Sean's father was around. He was a genial man and she could see he had given up the fight in much the same way as her father always had. Surrounded by women at home, he never got involved in the family arguments, but simply let everything wash over him and disappeared off to his local pub at the first opportunity.

But after they arrived back home Gracie had brushed all her concerns about the family away and got into the swing of arranging the wedding. She decided that so long as there was a distance between herself and Sean's family it wouldn't be a problem, that back in Southend it would just be the two of them in their new life together. But then there had been the visit for the wedding.

The time his mother had spent in Ruby's hotel before and after the big day had been excruciatingly embarrassing and Gracie still cringed when she thought back to it. Because her son was marrying Gracie who was Ruby's friend, she seemed to think it gave her some authority, and she had tried her best to assert herself as the matriarch of the property. To Gracie's horror and Ruby's amusement Sean's mother had constantly aired her complaints about the hotel and everyone in it.

Despite the fact that he had moved away from home so many years before, Sean's doting mother still thought she knew him best. As well as lots of lectures on housekeeping generally, she had given

Gracie a carefully written list of all his likes and dislikes, his food preferences and how best to launder and care for his clothes; she had also criticised the flat that was to be their new home.

It had been at that point that Ruby had taken her friend to one side and made Gracie realise that none of it was personal, that the woman had never got over her precious baby boy leaving home and moving to another country and she would never be happy until he was back home with her.

Now, she could easily imagine how the woman would react to news of the pregnancy and she had frightening visions of her turning up on the doorstop and overseeing the birth and care of her beloved son's firstborn.

But nothing could dampen the mood for Gracie, not even the thought of her mother-in-law. She had looked forward to telling Sean so much because she had known it was what he wanted to hear and that he would be pleased.

Unlike Archie Cooper.

When Gracie had told him the same news all those years ago, he hadn't even stayed until the end of the evening before hot-footing it out of Southend and her life.

It was because this was her second pregnancy that Gracie had known for sure she was expecting but she couldn't admit to that, she had to pretend that it was all new to her; the same as, engulfed in guilt, she had pretended to Sean that it was her first time on their wedding night.

'Let's go out and celebrate,' Sean said now. 'We could go down to the Castle. The lounge bar is nice there, very suitable for a respectable expectant mother.'

'I don't want to celebrate just yet, Sean. Can we wait until the test results come back and confirm it? I know the doctor has said it but I'd like to be completely sure. Just in case.'

'I don't have to wait for test results to tell me what I can see in your eyes. Mam always says you can tell just by looking into a woman's eyes and I can see it in yours, you're alight with happiness.'

As Sean looked at her so happily Gracie felt her guilty fear rise back up to the surface. She felt guilty because she hadn't told her husband her secret and she also felt guilty about the joy she was feeling at her pregnancy.

It was all so bittersweet and she was confused.

With hindsight Gracie knew she should have told him about her previous baby when they became engaged, and taken her chances on his reaction, but she'd left it too late. The moment to tell him had passed and now the secret had to be kept forever. But it was hard.

From the moment Sean had proposed to her, Gracie had been focused on conceiving a baby. She had thought about it constantly to the point of obsession but as her craving had increased, so had her feelings of guilt over her firstborn. She desperately wanted a baby with Sean but she couldn't help thinking that it would be a betrayal of the little boy she had given up, the little boy who was exactly the same age as Maggie.

At the time of his birth she hadn't wanted to give him a name, knowing that whoever adopted him would name him themselves but the nuns had insisted she had to have one to register the birth. So while she was still in the hospital with him she had chosen the name Joseph McCabe on the spur of the moment; after his father, Archie Joseph Cooper, the father he would also never know. The man who had disappeared faster than a frightened rabbit.

Joseph McCabe. Mother: Gracie McCabe, spinster. Father: Unknown.

Gracie had neither a copy of the certificate of birth nor a photograph of her baby. She had nothing other than the picture in her head of him as he was when she kissed him goodbye, just before walking out of the hospital when he was but a week old and leaving him there to be adopted by strangers.

She had gone back to the Palace hotel where she had worked before and managed to persuade the housekeeper to give her a live-in job. It was a basic role and it was hard manual work, but Gracie got on with it without a murmur because it meant she had somewhere to live, and she didn't have to go back to the family home. She got on with her job and her life as if nothing had happened.

In the following years she had successfully blocked the whole traumatic time from her mind and, apart from on relevant dates, it had become something she just didn't think about.

But once she had married Sean it suddenly became all she could think about. While she desperately wanted a baby, the thought of the child she had, in her eyes, abandoned and betrayed played on her mind constantly.

The moment the doctor confirmed that she

was indeed pregnant was one of mixed emotions for Gracie but she tried to brush all feelings of guilt aside and decided to prepare a special meal for Sean that night.

'Have you told Ruby yet?' Sean asked suddenly.

'Of course not, I wouldn't tell anyone before I told you. But if it's okay with you I'll tell her tomorrow when I go to work.'

'Then maybe we could all go out together to celebrate. Maybe Ruby and Johnnie will be next to have one. Once they're wed, of course.' Sean paused. 'When's that going to happen?'

'I think they have to wait a suitable time. Even though Johnnie and Sadie were separated they were still married, and the finger of blame for her doing herself in is still pointing firmly at him and Ruby. And of course he blames himself, which is daft,' Gracie said.

'Understandable,' Sean replied. 'I mean, Johnnie was a married man having an affair; some would say he drove his wife to commit suicide, some would say they are both to blame for the poor woman's passing...' Sean shrugged his shoulders expressively, making Gracie feel defensive towards her friends.

'That's not really fair, Sean. It wasn't like that at all. They weren't having an affair – well, not in the way you make it sound. But anyway the outcome was that she never meant to actually kill herself, it was Sadie being dramatic as always. She thought someone would find her in time. She'd done it before, only this time no one did get there in time...' Gracie said sadly as she thought of the vibrant but damaged young woman Johnnie Riordan had been married to, the mother of his two small children.

'Ah well. They're both still young, and what with Johnnie already having kids, Ruby's going to have her hands full when they all have to live together. The kids will resent Ruby, that's for sure,' Sean said, decisively.

'They're too young for that and they're still living with his sister even though Johnnie spends less time there now he's living down here half the time. But I suppose it'll all come out in the wash eventually, those two were made for each other... Like us, eh?' Gracie smiled affectionately at her husband, trying to change the subject.

'And he's a lucky man,' Sean ignored her comment and continued on his thread. 'I mean, how lucky that his girlfriend could give him a job and somewhere to live. Worth its weight in gold that is. Half the time with his sister looking after them all, and the other in the hotel, carefree and rent-free.'

She recognised the familiar hint of envy in Sean's voice as he spoke about Johnnie and as usual, it bothered her. He mentioned it so often that she knew it niggled away at him that Johnnie had now been given a role in the Thamesview Hotel, even if it was as general dogsbody and occasional chauffeur to the guests alongside Henry.

Because she worked there herself, Gracie knew Johnnie worked really hard whenever he could, for very little pay, just to help Ruby with the running of the hotel. Almost everything he did earn went to his sister for the children. But Sean only saw favouritism and it seemed to rankle with him that Johnnie had sole access to the bedsit in the annexe at the back of the hotel, even though he had declined Ruby's offer for he and Gracie to live there.

Sometimes it rankled with her that Sean also had delusions and expectations over his mother's role in the business. No matter how many times she explained her position, that she was just an employee, they both seemed to be looking for a way to stake a claim on the ownership of Thames-view.

'So it's okay if I tell Ruby tomorrow?' said Gracie, hoping to move the conversation on from how lucky Johnnie was, and back to their baby. 'I'll only tell her if you don't mind. Do you want to tell your mother first?'

'Of course it's okay. We'll tell your parents and I'll write to the family in Ireland first thing in the morning. I'm sure me Mam will want to come and visit us just as soon as she can.'

Gracie forced an enthusiastic smile. 'I'm sure she will.'

'It's a good job that we have two bedrooms, eh? And when the baby's born she can stay as long as she likes to get to know her new grandchild. She helped my sisters out no end when they had theirs. We're lucky I have such a wonderful family, don't you think?' Sean leaned back in his chair, crossed his arms and smiled smugly.

Feeling mildly irritated, but not wanting to comment on his observations, Gracie stood up and started to clear the table. 'I'll just go and get the pudding. I've made your favourite apple crumble especially.'

'Is there custard?' Sean asked with a grin. 'Made the way my mam makes it?' Gracie wasn't quite sure if he was making a joke or not but either way she pretended not to have heard. She silently gathered up the crockery, piled everything onto a tray and took it through to the kitchen. Dumping it all on the draining board she took a deep breath. The last thing she wanted on that important day was to argue with him about either Ruby and the Thamesview or her mother-in-law.

She had spent so long fantasising about the moment she would be able to give her husband the news they both wanted that she was determined nothing was going to spoil it for her.

A baby. She was going to have a baby and this time no one was going to take it away from her.

TEN

The next day Gracie woke up and felt sick. It was an overwhelming feeling of nausea and she wasn't sure whether it was because she was pregnant or because she was suddenly feeling negative about the whole thing, but it took all her energy to drag herself out of bed and get dressed. Usually she jumped up and went off to work full of enthusiasm, but that morning she found it a struggle and for the first time she was late for work at the Thamesview.

It was also compounded because it was more of a journey for her now that she and Sean lived in central Southend. Where previously she had just walked down the stairs to work, now it was either a long walk or a bus ride depending on the weather and the time she had to be there.

'Morning, Rubes... I know I'm late, I missed the bus. I'm really sorry, but if you've got five minutes to spare I'd like a chat in private. Can we go into the office?'

Gracie smiled as Ruby looked sideways at her and smirked. 'Can I make a guess?'

'A guess about what?'

'Well, I don't think you're going to tell me you want to change your day off. That wouldn't turn your face white as a sheet...'

The two women walked side by side to the hotel office on the ground floor that looked out

115

over the seafront promenade. It was a small room that had been created originally from a corner of the lobby but the wide sash window made it light and airy despite the fact that it was filled with shelves of folders, files and papers that went back many years.

It was the only room in the property that hadn't been decorated or at least changed since Leonora Wheaton had died and bequeathed the well-established but rather faded hotel to Ruby Blakeley, the young woman that she had taken under her wing and nurtured as if she were her own. The room was so much a part of the woman that Ruby had grown to love that she had left it exactly as it was, in Leonora's memory.

Gracie moved some papers off the wobbly old dining chairs and they both sat down, Ruby behind the battered old-fashioned desk which took up half of the room, and Gracie on the chair alongside.

'Go on then, tell me...' Ruby said, smiling.

'I'm expecting! Me and Sean are having a baby. It's due in about six months, the doctor reckons.'

'I knew it! Oh, that's such good news. I'm so happy for you, Gracie Grace. I bet Sean's pleased, isn't he?'

'Yes, he is and so am I, but...'

Gracie could barely get the words out before she dissolved into floods of tears.

'Gracie! Whatever's wrong?' Ruby jumped up again and put her arms around her friend. 'I thought this is what you wanted, what you *both* wanted?'

'It is, it *is*,' she sobbed. 'It's everything I ever

116

wanted ever since ... you know ... but somehow it's not how I expected it to be...' Gracie paused and looked around, even though the office door was closed. 'I feel horribly sick and I also feel so horribly guilty, as if I'm betraying the other little one I gave away.'

'Oh, come on, Gracie – you don't really believe that, do you? You've always had such a sensible view about what happened. You know you didn't just give him away, you've always known that; you didn't have any choice, same as I didn't have any choice. The decisions were made and we just had to get on with it...'

'I know it sounds mad,' Gracie gulped in a big breath of air, 'but I had a nightmare last night that I had my baby and they took it away. It was crying and I was running after them but my legs wouldn't work and then it was gone...'

'Oh, Gracie. You never did anything wrong so there's nothing to be punished for, even if that was how it worked. Which it isn't. If you know what I mean.' Ruby smiled reassuringly. 'I'm not saying this right, am I? But you know what I mean...'

Gracie sniffed and wiped her eyes with the back of her hand.

'Deep down I know you're right, but in the middle of the night I can't stop thinking about him. I keep turning it over in my head and I wonder where he is, what he's doing. Even if he's still alive. I mean, I wouldn't even know that, would I? He could be dead, he could be in Australia. I should never have let them do that, take my baby away...'

'Don't think like that!' Ruby interrupted

quickly as she went over to her friend and sat beside her. 'We all make mistakes and that's all there is to it. And we had no choice really, either of us, that's how it was. Now, you stay right there and I'll go and ask Johnnie to make us both a nice strong cup of coffee. If that doesn't make you feel better nothing will. Coffee and fruit cake are coming up shortly to celebrate your good news. I'm really jealous of you, but in the nicest way!'

Gracie Donnelly smiled appreciatively at her friend, who always had the knack of making everything seem okay.

As Ruby pulled the door behind her, her smile faded and she blinked hard as she walked quickly to the kitchen, her head down. She had left the room as quickly as she could because she didn't want to spoil Gracie's moment and she certainly didn't want anyone else to see her looking teary-eyed.

She was naturally delighted for her friend but the conversation about her lost baby had revived the memories of her own ordeal. Like Gracie, she had tried hard to tuck it all away in a separate compartment of her mind and on the whole she succeeded, but every so often something happened and it popped up unexpectedly to torment her. Gracie's pregnancy announcement was one of those times.

It was inevitable and she had been waiting for her friend to announce that she was expecting a baby, but Ruby had still been unprepared to feel as if she'd been punched in the stomach.

The thought of Gracie having another baby had hurt far more than she could ever have thought, not because she didn't want her to but because Ruby wished it was she herself. There was nothing that she would love more than to have another baby with Johnnie Riordan, Maggie's father.

Ruby had been much luckier than Gracie in that she knew where her daughter was, who she was with and how she was getting on; she was also able to see her and have a relationship with her, even it was always as a big sister rather than a mother.

George and Babs Wheaton were her parents, and that's how it was going to have to stay, until the time was right for Maggie to know about her true parentage.

Ruby was eternally grateful to the Wheatons, the couple who had taken her into their home during her evacuation from Walthamstow. She had been a scared ten-year-old away from her home and family for the first time in her life and they'd taken her into their home and cared for her then as if she were their own. They had also cared for her when she discovered she was expecting a baby at the tender age of sixteen and had no one else to turn to.

And it was George Wheaton's sister Leonora who had given Ruby a safe place to stay during her pregnancy at the Thamesview, away from everyone who knew her.

'Leonora, we're so grateful to you for helping us and for helping Ruby. She's got herself into a bit of a fix...'

'I can see that,' Leonora Wheaton said, her stance straight-backed and her expression severe as she looked Ruby up and down. 'And I can see from looking that it's more serious than a "bit of a fix," George. You always did play things down. Anyway we'd better go through to the lounge, you'll never get that clunky old chair up the stairs and we certainly can't carry you.'

Ruby was shocked at Leonora's tone and words aimed at her wheelchair-bound brother but when George and Babs both laughed she realised that it was a form of banter between brother and sister. But she couldn't bring herself to join in because she was mortified to be there. As she followed them into the lounge she felt gauche and stupid and she hated herself for getting in that position, but as everyone was doing their best by her she knew she just had to accept her new situation.

She couldn't go back to the family home in Walthamstow in London which was dominated by her overbearing brothers and if she stayed in Melton with the Wheatons then everyone would know; she had no choice but to stay with Leonora Wheaton in Southend.

Ruby was sixteen and had only met George Wheaton's sister a couple of times, yet now she was going to live with the woman in her hotel. It wasn't where she wanted to be but she accepted it was a good option because she would be able to see out her pregnancy in secret; she wouldn't stand out because she was staying there under the guise of being Leonora's niece: a young, pregnant war widow. Once the baby was born and adopted, then she could go back to her normal life, as if nothing had happened.

After the Wheatons left, Leonora showed Ruby up to her room, which was nowhere near as bad as she had been expecting. She had imagined something basic and solitary but it was actually the comfortable second bedroom in Leonora's private flat on the top floor of the hotel.

'Here you are, Ruby. There are a few rules I expect you to obey while you're here but most of them are just good manners, which I've been told you have. I also expect you to help out in the hotel. It's a small establishment so we all work really hard and you will be required to do the same and earn your keep.' Once again Leonora looked at her belly. 'As long as you're able, of course. I don't want to be accused of taking advantage of you.'

'Yes, Mrs Wheaton,' Ruby said quietly.

'It's not Mrs Wheaton, it's *Miss* Wheaton but that aside, you have to call me Aunt Leonora if you're to be my niece. I hope we can rub along together for the next few months. My brother wants me to take you under my wing, so I shall, but that's not to say I approve of your condition...'

'Thank you, Mrs Wh ... sorry, Aunt Leonora. Thank you for having me and I'll do everything I can to help out. I don't want to be a burden. Aunty Babs and Uncle George have done so much for me.'

Ruby had been determined to just do whatever she had to do to get the whole nightmare over with as soon as possible, but her bottom lip wobbled as she realised that she was going to have to stay where she was right up until she gave birth: there was no going back. She looked down at her feet and sniffed.

'Don't get emotional on me, child. I have enough to deal with already. Can you cook?' Leonora asked suddenly.

'A bit...'

'In that case, go into the kitchen over there and see what you can find for dinner for both of us. I have to go back down and see to my guests.'

That moment had been the start of a relationship between them; they got along together to the extent that a genuine affection developed between the unlikely couple. Leonora had asked few questions of her young houseguest but something had made Ruby confide in her.

Leonora would often sit out on her balcony, watching the liners and fishing boats going back and forth, while Ruby would sit alongside her and talk.

Ruby told Leonora about her family life, about her time in evacuation and also about Johnnie Riordan, the father of her baby. Naturally, Ruby held some facts back; she didn't tell Leonora that he was the local wheeler-dealer in Walthamstow who dabbled in the black market and hung around with local criminals. But she did tell her that she loved Johnnie and that was why she'd left Walthamstow without telling him she was pregnant.

When Ruby had her daughter Maggie, it was agreed that rather than have her adopted by strangers, the childless Wheatons would take her back to their home in Cambridgeshire and bring her up as their own. In the beginning it had been hard for Ruby, but her friendship with Gracie

McCabe helped her through, and when the time came for her to leave Southend Leonora Wheaton offered her a job and asked her to stay.

It was the start of Ruby's new life and she would be forever grateful to the woman who had given her the chance to start anew.

Gracie was standing looking out of the window when Ruby went back into the office. 'I'm such a selfish cow, aren't I?' she turned and smiled. 'I've got everything I ever wanted and still I grumble. Ignore me...'

'Johnnie's bringing the drinks through in a minute.'

'Okay. Quick coffee and then I'll get to work. I'm not ill, I'm expecting a baby so I need to pull myself together and get on with it.'

Ruby looked at her curiously. 'Blimey, that's a quick turnaround...'

'I realised you're right. We didn't give up our babies because we were selfish; we did what was for the best. We're both really lucky with our lives so no more feeling sorry for myself.'

'I know. Despite everything, we've done well for ourselves, haven't we? We're both okay, aren't we?'

'We are. Will you and Johnnie come out with us one evening to celebrate? We could go to a dance in town?'

'Of course we will,' Ruby said with a wide smile, which belied her own inner turmoil.

ELEVEN

Gracie sighed out loud when she heard the doorbell. She really wasn't in the mood to see anyone, least of all someone she wasn't expecting. After the initial euphoria it had turned out to be a difficult pregnancy, and she was making the most of some time at home on her own to put her feet up and rest. She sometimes smiled at the irony of it all; her first pregnancy when she was single and unmarried had been problem-free and yet this time, when she could have relaxed and enjoyed it, it was turning into a nightmare.

The nausea was ongoing and she felt constantly unwell; she was convinced that, despite all the reassurances from everyone, something was going to go wrong with either the birth or the baby. With more than two months still to go she found herself just wishing it was all over.

Gracie crept over to the window and peered round the corner of the net curtains to see who was down at the door but just as she peeked, her sister looked up and saw her.

'Cooeee, Gracie ... only me. Are you going to open this door or what? I'm freezing to death out here!'

As she shouted up to her, the young woman below shielded her eyes with one hand and waved with the other.

Just seeing Jeanette on the doorstep made

Gracie feel nervous. The thought of having to sit and make conversation filled her with dread but there was no way out of it now she'd been seen, so she opened the window and waved back.

'I'll be there in a minute...' she shouted down, annoyed that she'd let herself be seen.

'Well, get a move on then, fatso, or you could throw a key down...' Jeanette laughed.

Although Jeanette and Jennifer were twins by birth they couldn't have been more different in nature. Jeanette had always been the more demanding and troublesome one who, from the moment she was born, had screamed loud and hard if she didn't get her own way. She was the one who made the most noise when she wasn't invited to be a bridesmaid and she was the one who was making all the decisions about the joint wedding that she and her twin Jennifer were planning.

Despite being younger by ten minutes, Jeanette had always been the leader, while her twin was the quiet thinker who no one really ever got to know, the one who, when things went wrong, would withdraw into herself for weeks at a time. It was because of that no one ever really knew what Jennifer was thinking or how she was feeling.

When they were young, the four-year age gap between Gracie and the twins had meant that they were never really close, especially as Gracie had always struggled with her mother's favouritism. From the moment they were born Dot McCabe had focused all her energy on the twins, with Gracie left to fend for herself. Then as the twins grew up and developed their own very different personalities Dot focused everything on Jennifer, the one who caused her the least problems; the one who could seemingly do no wrong.

The three sisters were siblings but had never been friends and Gracie's relationship with them was very superficial and occasional, especially after she had left home.

Although Jennifer had called round a few times to see Gracie after the wedding, Jeanette had only ever been to the flat once, so, because she knew her so well, Gracie quickly surmised that her outgoing sister probably wanted something.

She went downstairs to the shared lobby and as she pulled the door back, her sister bounced past her, taking the stairs two at a time.

'God, it's nippy out there! You took so long I thought I was going to freeze to the doorstep. I've lost my gloves and I need some warmth,' she shouted over her shoulder.

By the time Gracie got into the lounge, Jeanette was already settled in the armchair next to the fire and rubbing her hands in front of the flames.

'Hello Jeannie. Nice to see you too...' Gracie said, but the sarcasm in her voice went straight over her sister's head.

'Thanks, Gracie! I tell you what, I really need a cuppa after the morning I've just had. No sugar for me, though. I'm watching my waistline, it's growing too quickly for my liking, and my bosom. Never mind June busting out all over, so is Jeannie McCabe,' she laughed and Gracie couldn't help but smile.

'Is that because you've chosen your wedding dress?' Gracie asked.

'Actually that's what I want to talk to you

126

about, as soon as you've made me a cuppa. And I could murder a bit of cake as well, if you've got any...' Jeanette smiled coyly and put on the little girl expression that she thought was cute and which men always found endearing, but which had always infuriated the rest of her family.

Gracie sighed but didn't say anything more. Feeling even more nauseous and light-headed than she had before, she went through to the tiny kitchen and made a pot of tea, taking it back on a tray with two cups, a jug of milk and a couple of rich tea biscuits on the side of each saucer.

'That's a bit la-di-dah, what's going on with you? A tea tray? Are you turning into mum?' Jeanette laughed again but Gracie wasn't sure if it was humour or meanness. She always found her sister hard to figure out.

'It's just a tray and you either get your tea on a tray or we squeeze in the kitchen and stand up and drink it. I'm not running back and forth. You can take it or leave it. And no, there isn't any cake.'

'Well, that's bleedin' snappy, even for you. What's up?'

Gracie sat down heavily on the brown utility sofa and with great effort, lifted her swollen feet up on the red leather pouffe that looked like a camel. The flat was fully furnished by the landlord, and although Sean had wanted to put it out of sight in the cupboard Gracie had rather liked the exoticness of it. It made her think of pyramids and sand, and also reminded her of Leonora Wheaton and her dreams of far-flung places.

As Gracie sat back on the sofa she sighed. She felt like a big fat frump alongside her fashionably turned out younger sister. Despite being newly washed her hair was as lank and straight as it had been when she was a child, her skirt was too tight, even with the stretch of elastic holding the fastening together, and the borrowed maternity smock that she was wearing over her jumper was like a billowing tent. She hadn't wanted to spend money on unnecessary maternity clothes and she didn't have the time to make anything so she just made do when she was indoors. But with Jeanette sitting opposite her looking perfect, Gracie felt more like a down-at-heel old tramp than a young woman expecting her first baby.

'In case you haven't noticed I'm expecting and I don't feel well. I hate being like this, a useless fat lump. I just feel horrible all the time, hot and tired...'

'You do look really fat and your legs are enormous, what's going on with them? What are you going to look like when it's due? We'll need to hire a crane to get you out of the chair!' Her sister laughed but Gracie wanted to cry.

'You can be so bloody horrible sometimes, Jeannie...'

'Oh, don't be so touchy, I was only trying to cheer you up. I didn't mean it like that, you know I don't!' Jeanette paused and looked at her sister critically. 'But I mean, you *are* fat, more than you're supposed to be. Are you still working or sitting around all day? That'd make you fat, I suppose, and eating too much...'

Gracie was just a second away from giving her tactless sister a good clip round the ear but she bit back the response she wanted to give. She didn't want an argument that she knew she would lose in her frame of mind.

'Of course I'm still working, we need the money – but not for much longer. And I'm here doing nothing because today's my day off,' Gracie snapped. 'I'm just lucky that I work where I do and that Ruby is so understanding. Most of the time I manage reception and do some office stuff, though if truth be told I sit behind the desk feeling sick and being no use to anyone.'

'I could help out there if you like, you could put your feet up more often then?'

'You've got your own job,' Gracie replied.

'I know but I hate it at that bloody Ecko factory, it's just so boring. The only good thing there is the social club. I'd much rather wander round a hotel looking important like you do. Anyway, I have to change my job...' Jeanette opened her eyes wide and bit her lip. 'Gracie, I've called the wedding off! Mum and Jenny have both gone mad, I'm really in the doghouse with everyone and it's difficult with Mick working at Ecko and being my boss and all...'

'What went wrong? I thought it was all on for a big flash double wedding?' Gracie asked her sister, more out of politeness than actual interest.

'Boring. He became so bloody boring. It was fun being engaged at the start but then I got to know him!' Jeanette laughed loud and hard, and Gracie found herself joining in. 'I did the right thing and gave him the ring back, but now I'm in a fix because he's still my boss and I've dumped him from on high. I was sort of hoping you'd see your way to helping me out.'

129

Gracie shook her head. 'So you're here because you want a job? You didn't just come to see how I am? What a surprise...'

Jeanette laughed and batted her eyelashes. 'I did want to see how you are, really I did, but I also thought I could kill two birds with one stone. Or three birds! A job would be nice, thank you very much, but mostly I really need somewhere to live for a bit. Mum's being such a cow over the wedding and everything. She and Jen are like a pair of old crones together.'

'Well, I don't know where you can go. I hope you weren't thinking about staying at the hotel, that's not allowed...'

'No, I wasn't thinking of the hotel. Gracie, you've got a spare room, can't I stay here? Just for a while. I can pay rent and that'll help you when you have to stop working.'

Gracie looked at her sister and laughed.

'Jeannie, I give you top marks for bare-faced cheek. I never see you and then you turn up bold as brass and want me to give you a job and somewhere to live? You've got more front than Woolworths...'

'I know, but you love me for it,' Jeannie grinned. 'Will you think about it? Please? I'll go nuts if I have to listen to Mum and Jen going on and on about how selfish and horrible I am for mucking up their wedding plans. Never mind my feelings; and then at work I've got Mick looking sadly at me like a stray mongrel staring at a pig's trotter in the butcher's window. Pleeeease?'

Gracie didn't want to smile but she couldn't help herself. Her younger sister had always been able to equally annoy and amuse her, right from the moment the twins had developed very different personalities. It had upset her that she had seen so little of them after the St Angela's episode, her mother had seen to that, but after the fragile peace was brokered by the family going to the wedding she had at least had a little more contact with both her sisters.

'I'll think about it, okay? But it will only be for a little while, until you find somewhere yourself, because we'll need the room once the baby's here. And it would have to be up to Sean as well. We make decisions together.'

Gracie wasn't convinced she could cope with having her buoyant younger sister living there but she didn't feel well enough for a pleading session so it was easier at that moment to take the line of least resistance. And she could also see the benefit of some extra money coming in.

'Where's Sean now?' Jeanette suddenly asked. 'Is he at work?'

'Yes, but he'll be home in an hour, and now you've reminded me I'd better go and start getting the dinner ready. Sean hates it when his dinner isn't on the table,' Gracie answered, hoping Jeanette would take the hint and leave but instead she jumped up.

'I'll do dinner for you. Tell me what it's going to be and I'll do it. You stay there and keep your feet up; it'll help that bloody awful swelling go down.'

Gracie was momentarily lost for words. Whereas Jennifer had always been caring and domesticated, Jeanette never usually did anything of her own volition, even when she was after something. But the thought of not having to drag herself into the kitchen was just too appealing for her to turn the offer down.

'Are you sure? I made the steak and kidney pie yesterday, it's in the larder, but if you can peel the spuds and shell the peas – that'd be a help.'

'Whatever you need doing, I'll do it. You look so rough...' Jeannie pulled a face. 'Sorry, no offence, but you do look dead on your feet. I don't like seeing you looking so worn out, it's not like you.'

With that, Jeanette disappeared into the kitchen, leaving Gracie sitting with her feet up, feeling relieved and just a bit mean. She knew Jeanette was trying to get round her and she was taking advantage of it because she felt so unwell.

It was proving to be a difficult pregnancy, which was a disappointment, because Gracie had been looking forward to being able to do everything properly instead of hiding it all away. She had wanted to savour her pregnancy, talk about it and enjoy the process but instead she had ended up hating every minute. From the early sickness that never went away, through to the grossly swollen ankles and aching back, she could only imagine how bad it would get in the run-up to the birth. She had never anticipated it being such a trial, especially after remembering the ease of the first pregnancy which she'd successfully hidden for nearly the whole duration.

It was also a disappointment to her that Sean, the man who had wanted the baby as much as she had, was acting as if her sickness was an irritant to him. Instead of understanding he was either snappy to the point of rude or else he took no notice of her. She justified it to herself as him being over-tired from working so hard but it hurt her nonetheless. That wasn't how she had envisaged her married life would be.

She could hear Jeanette pottering in the kitchen and although she knew exactly what her motive was, Gracie decided to savour the moment. She leaned her head back and closed her eyes but instead of peace wafting over her there was once again guilt and memories; all she could think about was that the way she was feeling was retribution for giving baby Joseph up.

As Gracie started to doze off, it all came flooding back...

TWELVE

Gracie's welcome to St Angela's mother and baby home had been even more frosty and judgemental than she had dreaded on the almost-silent journey there in Father Thomas's old boneshaker of a car.

Her mother had thrown a few things into a small case, handed it to her at the top of the stairs and then turned away, leaving Gracie to follow Father Thomas out to the car alone. Just before she climbed in she looked up at the window and saw her mother peering around the edge of the lace curtain, but the second Dot McCabe saw her daughter she dropped the curtain, without acknowledging her.

The priest had indicated to her to sit in the back and she had sat bolt upright behind him, clasping her suitcase to her chest throughout the journey, which seemed to take forever. She had actually wanted it to take forever because she didn't ever want to arrive at her destination, but eventually the car slowed right down. Gracie's heart started to pound as they turned off the narrow country lane, pulled into a wide gravelled driveway and stopped in front of an imposing pair of iron gates. They were ornate, tall and wide and were boarded from behind, so no one could see what was on the other side. The high ivy-covered brick wall either side of the gates disappeared off into the distance and was bordered on the inside by tall conifers. Not knowing exactly what was behind the gates made it seem both attractive and frightening at the same time. It could have been either a lovely country house or a ghostly mansion like the ones in the horror films Gracie had seen at the cinema.

'This is St Angela's convent where you'll be staying until after ... well, you'll be staying here until everything is dealt with and you can go back home again,' the priest said, as an elderly man with his head bowed and eyes averted opened one of the gates wide to let the car through, then quickly closed it again. 'You know this is the only option for a young girl like yourself? It's not a punishment, Gracie, it's a solution and I hope you never find yourself doing something so wrong again.'

'No, Father...' Gracie had answered, without really listening.

Driving slowly along the unmade drive that led up to the house, she had been a little reassured by the sight of the grand old building that stood in the centre of what could have been a park. For a moment she was almost relieved; she had been expecting to be confronted by a prison or a workhouse. But although it looked impressive, the silence was eerie, and there wasn't a single person to be seen either in the grounds or at the windows.

Again fighting her urge to run somewhere, anywhere, Gracie had walked up the steps to the double front doors of the main entrance, alongside Father Tom, his hand resting reassuringly on the small of her back. He rang the bell and they waited until a door was opened by a woman in ordinary clothes, who silently waved them into the vast unfurnished lobby, where the tiled floor echoed their every footstep.

The moment the door had banged shut three nuns appeared as if from nowhere, hands clasped and heads bowed in front of the priest. But while he was greeted as a visiting dignitary by the deferential Mother Superior and taken straight to her office, Gracie had been quickly bundled off in the opposite direction with a nun either side of her. Although they walked close to her, neither of them touched her or looked at her. Gracie felt as if she was carrying a communicable disease rather than a baby.

She was marched along in silence by the two women who, in their black and white floor-length habits, seemed to be floating as they swept quickly along the corridor, with a pregnant Gracie trying hard to keep up. When they reached the end of the second corridor one of them said 'Stop' in a voice that made Gracie immediately pause in her tracks. They turned sideways in unison and one of them produced a key from inside her habit, unlocked the door and gently pushed Gracie into a small windowless room that resembled a prison cell. There was a narrow bench running along the wall and a trolley in the corner that was covered over with a cloth.

'Do not speak,' Gracie was told when she tried to ask what was going to happen to her. 'While you are here you do exactly as you're told, and you'll be treated without fear or favour by everyone here. Silence is not a request, it's an order. You only speak when spoken to and follow our orders to the letter.'

She was then given sharply issued instructions on what to do and as the nuns left the room, Gracie heard the click of the key being turned.

As she had been told, she unpacked the limited contents of her small suitcase and laid them out on the bench before undressing down to her underwear and sitting alongside them in her bra, vest and knickers, none of which fitted her anymore. She felt like a child back at school as she sat quietly and waited, aware that compliancy was the best option if she wanted to get through her time there.

It seemed like hours before a different nun arrived, by which time Gracie was shivering uncontrollably and terrified, but this one was more kindly and stated that she had nursing training, before asking a few questions. Some of the questions were intimate but Gracie quickly realised that the young nun was more embarrassed than she was and that made it slightly easier for her. She whipped the cloth off the tray which held a few medical instruments and a clipboard on which she wrote Gracie's name in large letters, before scribbling down some other details that Gracie couldn't read.

After the questions the kindly nun handed her a grey itchy blanket to wrap around herself and then very superficially examined her before making some more notes. Then she read aloud the rules of the convent that applied to everyone, and which were to be obeyed at all times.

After this, she handed Gracie a coverall ankle-length navy blue smock with a high neck and wrist-length sleeves, three pairs of navy blue knickers, two large vests and a pair of ill-fitting lace-up shoes. The final item, which had very nearly made Gracie laugh, was a pair of muddy coloured and well-darned thick lisle stockings, with nothing to hold them up.

'This will be your uniform while you are here. Your own clothes are to be packed away and the case handed over to Sister in charge of your dormitory. You can use your own toothbrush if you have one but everything else is shared.'

'Yes, Sister,' Gracie answered respectfully as she had been instructed. The nun was a young woman who was probably not much older than herself, and Gracie tried not to stare at her, but her natural curiosity made her watch surreptitiously and wonder what would have made her take such a drastic step. The nun's face was expressionless but her voice was gentle as she examined Gracie and gave her the instructions and timetable that went along with life at St Angela's.

When she left, locking the door behind her, Gracie put the clothes on, sat back down on the bench and waited again. She closed her hands into fists and forced her fingernails into her palms, determined not to shed a single tear while she was there.

A different nun again came to take Gracie through the main building, to a part of the house that had been divided into two large dormitories.

'You will be in this dormitory as you are so advanced. I am the nun in charge and if you abide by the rules then your time here will pass far quicker than if you get it into your head to go against me. You have to remember, *your* behaviour brought you here, not us.'

Gracie studied her face as she spoke and decided that she would probably be fair. Firm but fair.

'This is where you will sleep,' she said, pointing to a narrow iron bedstead with a thin mattress and a pillow and two blankets stacked at the end of it. 'You can put your prayer book on the table, if you have one.'

'Yes, Sister,' Gracie said meekly.

There were five beds on each side of the dormitory; two beds were either side of her own and beside each was a hook on the wall and a six-inch wide table with two small drawers underneath. All the tables were bare and all that hung on the hooks was one change of clothes. It was a sparse, cold space which was immaculately clean, tidy and antiseptic. The dormitory that was to be her home for the duration housed ten young women, all in similar stages of pregnancy, and who had mostly been banished by their families in an attempt to hide the shame that an illegitimate birth would bring. There was another dormitory on the opposite side of the building but for some reason that nobody knew, the two groups weren't allowed to mix.

Whispered conversation in Gracie's dormitory told an assortment of stories of girls who had either been led astray or raped but the single word that applied to them all was 'shame'; either their own, or that of their parents.

The nuns and the devout auxiliaries at St

Angela's weren't cruel as such but they were harsh and unforgiving of the circumstances in which the girls in their care found themselves, so the day was spent in a mixture of housework, cooking and prayer, with a designated rest hour in the afternoon to 'keep their strength up for the ordeal of childbirth'.

There was little opportunity to make friends as there was a constant changeover of the women of all ages who were there and who mostly remained until six weeks after the birth.

Like many of them there, Gracie accepted her situation because she knew that her mother wasn't prepared to have her at home or send her away to distant relatives, as was sometimes the case in large families. She had no choices.

But Gracie had been lucky in that when Father Thomas had taken her to St Angela's, she was already eight months pregnant, so she had spent just a few weeks in the home before being sent to the maternity hospital because of complications which had resulted in a long and hard labour.

Some of the young women spent as long as three months at the home before the birth and up to six weeks after under the care of the nuns, working and praying, hidden away from the world as if they were criminals. Everything possible was dealt with inside the dark and depressing building and on the rare occasions they were allowed outside unaccompanied, the furthest they could go was the ivy-clad brick wall that enclosed the property, shielding it from outside eyes. If they needed to venture further for whatever reason they were accompanied by a nun and had to walk in silence, with their hands clasped and their eyes downcast.

When Gracie's time finally came she had baulked at going to hospital, especially after hearing how other girls had been treated there, but there had been no choice. At St Angela's there was no choice in anything. It was like being in prison and being punished for the sin of having sex and falling pregnant outside marriage. Being coerced and deceived was no excuse in the eyes of the nuns and visiting priests.

A couple of girls who came in at around the same time as Gracie had been defiant and tried to fight the system but as she watched their misery after punishment Gracie knew it was a useless fight. The parents and the nuns would win in the end, they always did.

But as luck would have it, having to go to the maternity hospital turned out to be the best thing that could have happened to Gracie, because it was there that she had met and become close friends with Ruby Blakeley, who was in a similar situation: young, pregnant and unmarried, and mother to a baby that would be given up.

It had been a lucky meeting because Ruby's billeting family from her time in evacuation had been regular visitors and had witnessed how the nurses were so hard on Gracie because of her being from St Angela's. George Wheaton was a doctor and had intervened forcefully on her behalf, making her hospital stay a little better.

But they had no power over the nuns at the home where she was supposed to go on discharge for another six weeks, which would be spent caring for, feeding and bonding with the baby that would then be taken from her and given to someone else anyway.

Knowing she had no choice but to give her baby up, Gracie was determined not to go back to the home and have to suffer any further indignity. When her last day in the hospital had come around, she'd calmly done everything she was asked, signed everything she had to sign and then, when no one was watching, had slipped out, leaving her baby there for his inevitable adoption.

She walked out of the hospital, wearing the clothes she had been wearing when she first went to St Angela's, and walked all the way back to the family home in Westcliff.

Her mother was mortified that she had been disobedient to the nuns and had told her so, in no uncertain terms, so Gracie had turned around and walked out again.

THIRTEEN

When Gracie woke up she was so disorientated it took her a few moments to get herself together, but when she heard clattering coming from the kitchen she remembered. Jeanette.

She closed her eyes again and thought about what her sister had proposed.

The thought of Jeanette staying with them and being around every single day was daunting, but because she felt constantly tired and under the weather Gracie also liked the idea of having someone else in the flat to help out, giving her the chance to rest at home. If Jeanette was in the spare room for a couple of months and paying her way then she could do just that and there would be the added advantage of it being a deterrent to the mother-in-law. She decided she would put it to Sean and see what he thought.

Jeanette had completely prepared the dinner while she was asleep on the sofa, so Gracie had little choice but to invite her to stay and join them.

'Well, that was tasty...' Sean said as he put down his knife and fork and looked from one to the other. The three of them had spent the meal chatting and Gracie found she had enjoyed having her sister there. She was a third person to keep the conversation moving when Sean was off in one of his trances, his favourite way of avoiding interacting with his wife.

'Gracie prepared it but I cooked it...' Jeanette said with a grin. 'She wanted to put her feet up as it was her day off and she was feeling a bit poorly so I offered to help. I'm quite domesticated sometimes.'

'Gracie's always wanting to be putting her feet up nowadays,' Sean replied, as if his wife wasn't there. 'I never knew anyone make so much fuss over being in the family way. It's not an illness for pity's sake, it's perfectly natural.'

'Don't be like that,' Jeanette said lightly. 'She's doing her best, it must be hard to do everything when you're expecting and you've got fat ankles.'

'That's nonsense and I've never heard any excuse like it,' Sean said, his irritation at his wife undisguised. 'What about the women who have four, five, six children, one after the other? Gracie has an easy job at Thamesview doing whatever she wants and no other children at home. How can that be doing her best?'

Gracie wanted to respond but she was once again feeling light-headed and detached and simply couldn't be bothered. She'd heard it all before from Sean, who was turning out to be intolerant in a way she could never have imagined. The genial young man who said he loved her had morphed into a snappy bad-tempered grump in the course of a few short months, and it bewildered her.

'Some of us are more fragile than others,' Jeanette said with a casual shrug.

'You can say that again,' Sean said sullenly, without looking at either Gracie or her sister.

'I was talking to Gracie before you came in,'

Jeanette said brightly, 'and, now that my engagement is officially off, and Mum and Jen are cheesed off with me, how about I become your lodger? I could help Gracie with the housework and cooking, that'd make it easier for you, and I can pay rent to help out when she gives up work, help towards your rent and all that.'

Gracie peered up through her eyelashes and could see from his expression and his silence that Sean was considering it.

Once they were married and living together it had surprised Gracie how dependent and demanding her new husband actually was. He wanted everything doing for him, as per the list his mother had given Gracie just before the wedding. Everything had to be just right, the way his mother had always done it, and probably her mother before that.

It had never occurred to Gracie that someone who had lived away from home for so long would be so set in his views on how a wife should be, but that was just how Sean had turned out to be.

For the first few months of their marriage Gracie had loved playing house in their new home and looking after her new husband, but once she was pregnant she had anticipated a little consideration from him, especially in the bedroom. However, Sean was focused on his own needs only.

All his kindly little ways, the compliments and the generosity of spirit that had attracted her to him seemed to have faded away after she became his wife. As she had grown larger, so he had become more distant and deprecating by the day.

'So, what do you think then, Gracie? Should we

let Jeannie come and stay here with us until the baby comes?' His voice snapped her back from her thoughts.

'If you think so; maybe it might help. I have to stop working very soon, it's not fair on Ruby having to carry me, so the money will help towards the rent...' Gracie smiled at him and touched the back of his hand. 'It won't be long now, and then well have our baby and everything can get back to normal. I'm really sorry I've been so useless over the past few months.'

Sean smiled back in acknowledgement but it was fleeting and without affection. Then he swiftly looked across at Jeanette, who was looking expectantly from one to the other.

'Okay, you can have the spare room but only until the baby comes and then my mother will be coming to stay,' Sean said forcefully. 'And of course you have to pay rent and help Gracie out around the flat. No rent, and I'll be chucking you out myself right away.'

'Oh, thank you both so much.' Jeanette jumped up from her chair, laughed and clapped her hands theatrically. 'I'll move in tomorrow! I'll go back tonight and tell Mum and Dad. Jen'll be pleased to get me out of home and get the bedroom to herself! And of course she'll love having Mum to herself as well. Those two deserve each other. Bitches, both of them!'

'One more thing...' Sean said quickly. 'We don't want you around us all the time. You'll just be the lodger.'

'You won't know I'm here, Sean.' Jeannie winked.

Gracie smiled and pushed to the back of her mind the niggling feeling she had that it could all end in tears and another family feud, instead concentrating on how much the extra rent would help. She told herself it would only be for a couple of months, and if it helped her keep Sean happy in the meantime, then it would be worth it.

'Have you seen Jennifer lately?' Jeanette asked them both as she cleared the table. 'She is so furious with me but I don't see why, she'll have the wedding all to herself now. She and Mum can plot away to their hearts' content.'

'I've not seen her for a while,' Gracie replied. 'And probably won't now you're here. She'll take a few weeks to calm down and then she'll be back to normal. Quiet.'

'You mean boring...'

The two sisters laughed together. It was just a gentle bit of amusement, with no malice intended, but Sean looked annoyed as he pushed his chair back and stood up. 'If you two are going to chatter on then I'm going to the pub. It's like being in the room with a pair of budgerigars in a cage.' Then he looked at Jeanette. 'But it was a grand dinner, Jeannie – you should be training Gracie...'

As the door closed behind him Gracie and Jeanette looked at each other, open-mouthed.

'What's wrong with him?' Jeannie asked. 'Does his mood always turn on a sixpence?'

'It's my fault,' Gracie said. 'I seem to do everything cack-handed lately.'

'Give over... It's not your fault you're off-colour

and that little strop was uncalled for. He was digging and digging away at you tonight, it's not right.'

'He's just overworked...' Gracie said, but as she defended Sean and his behaviour she couldn't help thinking about Ruby's ex-boyfriend Tony, the abusive and controlling man her friend had so nearly married before Johnnie had come back into her life. Gracie had disliked him from the word go but Ruby had been too blind to see him as he was and had tried hard to convince Gracie that he was just a bit misunderstood. It had taken a major fight, in which Ruby was really hurt, to make her see sense.

She really hoped she wasn't being as blind as Ruby had been but there was something very wrong with the way Sean was behaving, and she had no idea what it was. All Gracie knew was that something had changed.

FOURTEEN

Gracie and Ruby were sitting opposite each other, with a pot of tea on the table between them and a cream cake each. To avoid Ruby getting caught up in hotel business, the two young women had agreed to meet up in town away from the hotel and all its distractions, and they had both arrived at the same time at the agreed spot outside Keddies, the big department store in Southend High Street.

After some slow-paced window shopping around the store, they had gone up to the restaurant so Gracie could take her weight off her already aching feet. Feeling frumpy and self-conscious alongside her friend, she pulled her coat tightly around her hard-to-hide bump and settled down into her chair as low as she could to try and hide. But she was still painfully aware of how dishevelled she looked compared to her friend.

Ruby was tall and shapely with dark auburn curls, an air of self-confidence and the ability to look classy under any circumstances, which had come about as a result of her happy years in evacuation with George and Babs Wheaton, the village GP and his wife.

Gracie loved her friend dearly but she sometimes felt a tinge of natural envy that Ruby had been given the opportunity to break free from her dysfunctional family in London and make

149

something of herself.

It had only been a couple of weeks since Gracie had had to give up working at the Thamesview on doctor's orders, but already she was starting to feel bored and excluded from her old life. She hadn't anticipated how much she would miss her job, until about the third day of being at home, when she realised she had no one to talk to.

Feeling so worn down by the pregnancy she had thought she wanted more relaxation time but instead she had ended up feeling like a lonely spare part in her own home. Jeanette was at work during the day and often out in the evenings, and Sean was working a lot of extra hours at the Palace to make up the shortfall in their income so instead of enjoying having more time to herself, Gracie found herself sitting around feeling bloated, tired and depressed. She understood why Sean wasn't as attentive as he had been when she was slim, full of vitality and ready to party at the drop of a hat.

'So go on, tell me about life as a lady of leisure,' Ruby asked.

'Ooh, you sound like Jeanette, she said that to me,' Gracie said. 'It's okay, I do get a bit bored but, believe it or not, it's helped having Jeannie there. She's not around too much but when she is, she makes me laugh. If you thought I was mad, you should see her when she gets going. She doesn't stop. She's so different from Jennifer. It's hard to believe they're twins.'

'Did she get another job?' Ruby asked.

'No, she's still at the Ecko. She hates the job but loves the social club so she decided to brave it out with Mick. I almost admire her cheek. I think she's got someone else in tow already; she rushes about a lot and is a bit secretive.' Gracie laughed as she reached for the teapot and poured a cup of tea for each of them.

'I'm pleased it's working out with Jeanette there but I still find it hard to believe. She's a bit of a handful, that one, isn't she? She looks and acts a bit dim but deep down, I reckon she's sharp as a tack.'

'Oh, I'm not under any illusions about her but she has helped me out. Jen pops in occasionally and makes the right noises, but she's got her wedding on her mind so she always seems distracted. But at least she and Jeannie seem to have made up, which is nice. That double wedding arrangement that my mother came up with was doomed from the start...'

'Blood's usually thicker than water, though not in my case, of course.' Ruby rolled her eyes and pretended to shiver as she thought about her own dysfunctional family. 'So, tell me how you got on with the midwife yesterday. Not all that long to go now; just a few more weeks and you'll have your baby. I'm so jealous, I want one as well!'

'Oh Rubes, I hope you don't mind but I don't want to talk about the midwife or babies. I'm fed up with baby talk already and it isn't even here yet. I want to talk about ordinary things! Tell me all the gossip; tell me what's going on with you and Johnnie!'

As long as they'd known each other Gracie had never kept secrets from Ruby but she didn't want to get into a position where she had to fib about the state of her still-new marriage, so she tried to

151

steer the conversation away before it got there.

'Okay, no babies just this once, but next time you tell me. I'm looking forward to being God-mother proper!'

'Okay, next time, but back to you and Johnnie now...' Gracie laughed and relaxed. She was never as happy as when she and Ruby were together. They knew each other so well and conversation was never the hard work it had become with Sean of late.

'It's all going along nicely, touch wood,' Ruby reached down and tapped the table leg three times. 'Johnnie's back at the hotel right now looking after things for me. I was scared he'd find it boring or that he'd hate having me in charge but he does whatever I ask. He's even doing some of your work so I haven't had to take anyone on. He's a fine old jack of all trades; he can do bed-making and book-keeping, almost at the same time.'

'No more dodgy dealings?' Gracie smiled.

'No more dodgy dealings,' Ruby said as she pulled a face. 'I hope he stays away from that stuff, but then, it's in his blood. He loves a bit of ducking and diving so we'll see. I don't mind a bit of it so long as he stays legal. There's a line he knows he can't cross anymore and he's promised that the really dodgy stuff is all in the past.'

'Any nearer to wedding bells and babies for you? I was hoping our babies would be able to be play-mates...'

Ruby's face dropped. 'I don't know when it can happen. It's still all such a nightmare. The poor bloke has got everyone on at him over Sadie and the kids. Even his sister Betty isn't being as understanding as I would have expected. He's definitely the villain of the piece, with me not far behind.' Ruby looked sad and shrugged. 'Now she's not here she's suddenly Saint Sadie. They're acting like he murdered her or something. It's all wrong.'

'But surely they all know she was unstable and she was the one who ran off with the crazy Greek waiter, who had trouble written all over him?' Gracie said sharply, feeling defensive of her friend.

'I know, but when someone dies like that they always look for someone to blame. They don't want to accept that I had nothing to do with his marriage going to the wall. We hadn't seen other for five sodding years, I mean you know what happened...'

'I know exactly what happened and so does Johnnie's sis, but everyone loves a scandal and that's what Sadie was so good at. Alive or dead...' Gracie shook her head. 'It's so tragic but not unexpected. Sadie always was as mad as a hatter and one step away from doing something crazy for attention. But it'll die down eventually, I'm sure. Anyway, how's Maggie? I haven't seen her since the wedding...'

'I saw her at Christmas and for her birthday as always. Uncle George has been a bit poorly since he had that fall from his wheelchair so they haven't been anywhere. I must go up to see them. Do you want to come as well? Have a day out?'

'I'd love to – but is it a good idea with me so far gone?'

'Oh, you've still got several weeks to go, it should be fine,' Ruby said reassuringly.

'Hmm. Can I think about it? I just feel so

bloody awful all the time, I'd hate to spoil your day. But I hope they come and see the baby when it's finally here ... which can't be soon enough, the way I'm feeling. And Sean is really fed up with me. Tells me I'm imagining it all...'

'Sean's being an idiot and I'll tell him when I see him!'

Gracie smiled at her friend. Despite being married to Sean and expecting his baby she still thought of Ruby as the biggest constant in her life. They were friends and confidantes and each could rely on the other absolutely but Gracie still couldn't bring herself to be completely honest about how things were between her and Sean. She simply hoped all would be well after the baby was born.

The two friends sat together and talked for well over an hour before Ruby had to get back to the hotel, leaving Gracie to reluctantly head off in the other direction to get the shopping, before catching the bus back home. She loved their flat and had made it as homely as she could on their limited budget but since Jeanette had moved in it had seemed less like their own home.

As she walked along the pavement and could see the front gate getting closer she felt herself involuntarily going slower and slower. She was unhappy and detached, as if she was far away. Her head was floating as if it was filled with cotton wool and her legs burned despite the chill in the air. When she eventually got there she stopped and leant on the front wall to catch her breath, not wanting to actually go back into the flat she was starting to dislike. But then her baby kicked hard and she felt ungrateful. She reminded herself that she had everything she had wished for: a husband, a home of her own and soon she would have her longed-for baby. She shook her head to clear it and as she put her key in the door, she rubbed her belly. 'Here we are, baby, this is where you're going to live – you, me and your dadda,' she said, dreamily talking to her baby as if it was actually there already. 'Now, Mamma's going to go upstairs and have a warm cup of milk and a rest before Dadda and Aunty Jeannie get home from work. Milk is good for both of us the midwife said...'

Jeanette was going to be at work all day and she had no idea when Sean would be home, so Gracie hoped she'd have enough time for a nap to try and assuage the feelings of misery that were plaguing her. She felt so guilty about being a bad wife she wanted to make sure she was wide awake for Sean that evening.

Then, as she trudged up the stairs, she heard whispering coming from the front room and she was instantly furious again. Jeanette had been told that no boyfriends were allowed into their home. Gracie flung the door open, ready to confront her, only to be surprised to see Sean there with Jennifer, her other sister.

They were sitting opposite each other, he on the sofa, she on the chair, but there was something about the way they were laughing together, something intimate, that made her think they were laughing at her. She wondered if they'd heard her talking to the baby.

'What's going on? I thought you were at work today, Sean. I wasn't expecting anyone to be in...'

she said, keeping her tone as even as she could.

'What do you mean, what's going on? My shift changed, I'm working twelve hours tomorrow instead...' Sean frowned and shook his head, looking angry that Gracie was questioning him.

'Jen! I didn't know you were coming to visit...' Gracie continued, looking from one to the other curiously. Something wasn't right but she couldn't figure out what it was. 'What are you doing here?'

'I just called round on the off-chance. The office is closed today because they're doing some painting. You don't mind, do you? I thought Jeannie would be here...' Gracie's sister looked around as if she was expecting Jeanette to appear as well. 'I'll go if you want me to; I don't want to be getting in anybody's way...' Jennifer's tone was apologetic as she looked at her sister.

'No, no, it's alright. I was shocked to see you, that's all. As I said, I didn't expect anyone to be here, not Sean, not Jeanette and certainly not you,' Gracie said, trying to soften her voice.

'Coming back early for a lie-down again, were you?' Sean asked with just enough of a hint of disapproval in his voice to make her feel awkward, especially as he was right. 'Good job you're not a farmer's wife or a mother of six, like my mam was. She didn't have to take to her bed every five minutes, I'm sure...'

'Oh stop it,' Gracie replied defensively. 'I walked back from town and my feet are killing me so I came home to change my shoes before I go to the shops. I got the vegetables at the market on the way home but we need some groceries, and I've just got my last pay-packet from Ruby. She gave me a nice bonus.'

The silence in the room was deafening, until eventually Jennifer stood up. She smiled as she straightened her skirt with her hands and then picked up her coat from the chair. 'I'd better go. Tell Jeannie I was here...'

After she'd gone Sean jumped up from his seat and rounded on his wife with a ferocity she'd never have thought him capable of. 'What was all that about? Why did you talk to me like that in front of your sister? Honest to God, I don't have to answer to you and you've no right to make me look small that way...'

His expression was angry and his stance almost aggressive as he stood in front of his wife and railed at her.

'I was just surprised, that's all, and don't shout at me.' She felt the tears well up. 'I'm sorry, this is all just too much for me. I feel so ill... I'm sorry, I didn't mean to upset you!'

It was at that moment that Gracie hated the person she had become and she understood why Sean was fed up with her. He worked long and hard every day at his job and then came home to a miserable fat wife who moaned constantly about feeling poorly and tired.

She sniffed away her tears, walked over and slipped her arm around his waist.

'I am sorry, Sean. I'm unreasonable and I know it. I'll try and do better, I promise. You were up early this morning to go to work; you go and have a sleep and I'll bring you a cuppa later. Go on, you deserve it.'

He looked up at her and for the first time in

months smiled as if he meant it.

'I think I'll do that. You could come and join me, you know. Just because you're expecting a baby shouldn't mean we can't ... you know ... it's allowed. I checked with Mam. Come on...'

He winked and Gracie smiled back at him, but her heart sank. It was the last thing she wanted, but she knew she had no choice if she was to keep Sean in a good mood.

FIFTEEN

'We can't do this anymore, it's wrong and Gracie's not stupid. She'll guess if she finds us together. She's only gone to the shops. You have to leave, please...'

Sean Donnelly tried to pull away from the young woman next to him on the sofa, who had her hip pressed tightly against his and an arm curved possessively around his neck. Her skirt had nicked up and she was showing both stocking tops and suspenders as she pulled him closer in towards her; when he tried to move away she kissed his face and nuzzled his neck while running her other hand seductively up and down his inner thigh.

'But I love you, and you love me, I know you do. Let her find out, then you can leave her. Leave Gracie and we can be together. We could go to Ireland, we could go anywhere, we don't have to stay here in crummy Southend. And just think, if we were together we could do this all the time without you having to be scared about *her* catching us.'

Her voice was low and sexual and her words directed straight into his ear as she let her hand hover lightly over the fly buttons on his trousers.

'I don't love you, I don't. I love my wife, I've told you so, over and over.'

Sean Donnelly said the words he knew he was supposed to say but he could feel his heart beating faster in a mixture of desire and panic as he tried half-heartedly to push her hand away.

'I'm a married man with a baby due soon and this should never have happened, never, never. You have to leave and don't come back. Please? Don't keep doing this to me, I can't stand it.'

He was in turmoil trying to think of a way to get Jennifer McCabe, his sister-in-law, out of the flat before Gracie got home and discovered them together, but she was showing no sign of going anywhere.

And deep down Sean didn't want her to. He just wanted her to drag him off to the bedroom again.

'But you do love me, you know you do! It's silly, you already said Gracie doesn't care about you anymore and anyway...' Jennifer's face was up close to his as she smiled slyly. 'How do you know the baby is yours? We all know what Gracie's like. She's always been the same, out having fun, sleeping around. You know that really, don't you?'

He frowned as she stared into his eyes. His desire faded as his guilty anger rose; he knew he was betraying his wife and he didn't like being reminded of it.

'Well of course it's mine, don't you dare to suggest such a thing about my wife,' Sean snapped. 'Now please, you have to leave...'

'But I don't want to, my darling.'

For Sean it was the defining moment, when he realised that he was backed into a corner that was all of his own making; it also dawned on him that Jennifer actually wanted Gracie to catch them together. She wanted her to find out what had been going on.

'You have to; we can't be caught like this.

Please?' He begged as his panic levels rose.

'But that's daft. I'm your sister-in-law and I can be here sitting alongside you. That's not wrong, even if this is...' She smiled slyly and very slowly started to undo his buttons, and Sean could feel himself weakening once more.

'Not here, Jen, please not here...' he sighed half-heartedly. There was something about her that he couldn't resist, despite knowing full well that he should.

When he thought about it when he wasn't with her, Sean was fascinated that someone so seemingly ordinary and demure on the outside as Jennifer could be such an able seductress behind closed doors.

What had started as a mild flirtation with Gracie's sister had quickly taken a turn for something more serious the moment he had let himself be physically seduced by her. It had become an affair and now she wanted more from him; she was demanding more from him, and he was only just starting to realise the enormity of what he'd done.

He had had sex with his own sister-in-law.

Sean Donnelly loved his wife, he always had. He had taken a shine to her the first time he crossed paths with her at the Palace where they both worked and had slowly but surely fallen for her. But he loved the Gracie he had married, not the Gracie she had become. He was in love with the fun-loving effervescent young woman who was always game for a laugh and a good night out, but since she had been expecting she had become someone completely different and he was no longer sure of where he stood or how he felt about her anymore. All he knew was that he couldn't resist Jennifer.

Sean had been brought up to believe he was number one; his mother had done everything for him and idolised him unconditionally, as had his older sisters. They all still did, and he could do no wrong in their eyes. Hence, he had expected that he would be the centre of his wife's universe. But since Gracie had been expecting, the unborn baby was taking precedence and Sean hated being in second place.

Gracie was constantly tired and distracted and he felt side-lined; it was as if everything was too much trouble for her, in the kitchen and in the bedroom. She just didn't want to do anything anymore, other than sit around and grumble and he didn't like it; in fact he didn't like *her* anymore.

She was his wife and from his experience Sean thought that wasn't how wives behaved, expectant or not.

And then one afternoon a few weeks before, when Gracie was out visiting the midwife and he was at home on his own and full of self-pity, Jennifer had turned up on the doorstep to visit her sisters. He'd had no choice but to invite her in but then, to his surprise, he had discovered that she was actually good company.

She listened to him intently, laughed at his jokes, massaged his ego and sympathised over Gracie's personality change and her obsession with her baby, and empathised with him over Jeanette's untidiness and her loud voice.

Sean was starting to get to know Jeanette be-

162

cause she was living with them, but he had never had anything to do with Jennifer, who had always been the quiet, unremarkable one in the background who nobody really noticed, because her pretty, bouncy twin invariably hogged the limelight and overshadowed her.

That first visit, Jennifer had left before either of her sisters got home and Sean had found himself not mentioning her visit to either one of them. He didn't know why he hadn't told his wife or her sister about what was then an innocent visit, but something had stopped him and afterwards, he found he couldn't stop thinking about her.

And then she had visited once again when only Sean was home, and then again, and then one day the inevitable had happened. Jennifer McCabe had flattered and cajoled her sister's husband into bed. The marital bed.

Sean had been mortified afterwards, but knowing that Jennifer was soon to be married he had tried to convince himself that it was a one-off caused by Gracie's frigidity; he had tried to convince himself that he would be able to forget about his momentary aberration but she kept returning and he had found himself further and further sucked in. Soon he was meeting her elsewhere when he was supposed to be at work. He even put his job at risk by sneaking her into vacant rooms at the hotel.

In a few short weeks it had gone from a mild flirtation to a full-blown affair.

'But I love you, Sean, you know I do, and I want to be with you. Forever.'

'I've told you, Jen, nothing can happen between

us again, it can't,' he pleaded. 'It was a mistake. I'm a married man and you're her sister, my sister-in-law – it's just not right. Oh my dear lord, this is Gracie's home, whatever were we thinking? And what would your fiancé say?'

Sean pushed her away. He was close to tears as he tried to make her realise the enormity of what they'd done but Jennifer merely smiled seductively and stroked his face.

'Don't be so dramatic, my sweet. None of that matters. We're meant to be together, we both know that and I'm going to call my engagement off to-night. We don't have to meet here, you know that – there are lots of places we could go... We could get a room at the Palace again, you wangled it before...' she paused. 'But if you tell the truth then we won't have to sneak around, will we?'

Sean Donnelly's head was telling him to force her to leave, to physically throw her out and be prepared to deny everything if Gracie found out, but there was something hypnotic about her. Each time he tried to get away from her she reeled him back in like a fish on a line, playing with him until he gave in.

Jennifer McCabe, the quiet girl whom he had never bothered to get to know, had turned out to be absolutely irresistible in the bedroom and he was addicted to her.

Sean now realised she was also very dangerous.

'No, Jen. Really. Maybe if we'd met before Gracie and I wed it would have been different but this is adultery and it's wrong. I'm ashamed; my mother would kill me and Gracie would never do it to me...'

'Well, you don't know she won't, and she might have already...' Jennifer paused and looked directly at Sean. 'There's a big family secret you don't know, a secret I know I'm not supposed to know but I do – and if you're good, I'll tell you as well...' Her teasing tone was the one she used in her bedroom talk and he could feel himself getting excited.

'No, stop it. You're making trouble, now you have to go,' he pleaded.

'No, no, no, listen. I have to tell you, let me tell you...'

Jennifer's dark brown eyes were wide open and wild with excitement. 'A few years ago, when Jeannie and I were still at school...'

The sound of the front door opening and closing nearly gave Sean a heart attack. He jumped away and opened the front room door, just in time to come face to face with Jeanette. He took a deep breath and smiled as he tugged at his dishevelled clothing.

'Jeannie! Your sister is here to see you, she's in there. If Gracie gets back, tell her I'm off up to the newsagent for some fags – I've run out.'

'You can have one of mine,' Jeanette smiled and rummaged in her handbag.

'No! I've got to go...' Sean ran down the stairs and out of the front door as if he was being chased.

As Jeanette watched Sean hot-footing it down the stairs, breathing deeply, with his face bright scarlet, she knew that something had happened. Her first guess was that her sister had probably been doing what she was good at, causing friction.

'Well, twinnie, what have you been doing to scare the hell out of the brother-in-law? He just ran like I've not seen anyone run since the bloody Blitz!'

Jennifer said nothing but her sly secretive smile told her sister all she needed to know.

Jeanette knew her twin better than anyone, they had spent all their lives together, and at that moment she knew she'd been doing something she shouldn't – and that it most likely involved flirting heavily with Sean Donnelly.

From when they were tiny children Jennifer McCabe had been held up as the perfect example of a daughter while Jeanette was derided as the uncontrollable one. But Jeanette had an insight into her sister that no one else had; as they were twins, she could read her like a book. She had always loved her but most of the time she didn't like her. Jennifer was devious and calculating, which made her an expert in getting away with everything. It also meant that whenever Jeanette tried to say anything, no one took any notice of her.

'Are you causing trouble for Gracie now? I can't believe you sometimes – you have to stir the pot, whether it's friends or family. Why can't you leave her be? She's got more than enough on her plate without you adding your bleedin' two-pennorth...'

Again, Jennifer smirked. 'And you always have to take Gracie's side against me, your beloved twin. But not to worry, I'm off home now. Do you know, it's great without you there. We all get along like a house on fire and Mum is so much happier with just me!'

'Oh bugger off, you smug cow!' Jeanette interrupted her angrily. 'I know you're up to something and if I find out you're causing trouble for Gracie, I'll make you suffer for it, I promise.'

'I could always ask Sean if I could come and live here as well. I could share with you, couldn't I? Twins in a bed, like we used to be, eh?'

'I'd sooner share with Ghenghis Khan. He's safer than you, you nutcase. I swear you've got a bleedin' screw loose...'

Jennifer laughed long and hard as she strutted out onto the landing. With a flourish she snatched up her coat and handbag from the hallstand at the top of the stairs.

'Me? But you're not allowed to be horrid to me, sister Jeannie. I'll tell Mum that you're both ganging up on me. Who do you think she'll believe?'

Jennifer sauntered off down the stairs with a backward wave, leaving Jeanette steaming mad. She knew with certainty that her sister was playing games with Sean and she hoped that he wasn't playing back – but from his behaviour towards his wife lately she guessed that he was.

'What did Jen want today?' Jeanette asked Sean as they were having dinner.

'She wanted to see you; she asked if she could wait. I knew you wouldn't be long...'

Sean looked down at his plate and concentrated on cutting into his lamb chop but there was a slight redness rising up his usually pale face.

'Well, that's a bit bleedin' strange because I wasn't supposed to be here. I said that this morning. It's just chance that I came home early...'

'Yes, you did say you wouldn't be home. You told us both,' Gracie said. 'Maybe Sean wasn't listening? Or else he forgot, he forgot when I was going to see Ruby as well.'

'Oh for the love of God, what's going on with you two?'

Sean pushed his chair back so fiercely it crashed backwards onto the floor, and at the same time tipped the table away from himself sending the crockery flying, nearly hitting Gracie on her pregnant bump. It was her speediness in crossing her arms protectively that saved her from it.

'Oi, be careful, you could have hurt her and the baby! Bloody hell, Sean, that was so dangerous ... and unnecessary...' Jeanette snapped as she stood up and started pushing everything back into place. Gracie meanwhile was still sitting in her chair, looking stunned.

'Oh give it a rest, the pair of you! Everything is always my fault,' he shouted furiously. 'Your sister comes round here, *your* sister, not mine and I'm supposed to remember who's going where and doing what? I don't fucking care what you two are doing or not doing. I'm sick of it, I'm sick to death of this whole fucking marriage thing!'

'It was just a joke, of course we don't expect you to remember what everyone's doing. It was a joke,' Gracie said quickly trying to ease the atmosphere. She looked at her sister. 'Sean's been working hard lately, he's tired.'

'Too right I'm tired, sick and tired of all this nonsense going on here. I'm off out to get some peace. I'll be back when I'm back...'

With much crashing and banging, Sean stormed out, leaving both young women shocked.

After the main front door slammed shut, making the window frames rattle, Gracie looked at her sister.

'What was all that about? It came from nowhere.'

'You said it yourself,' Jeanette murmured with a shrug, 'he's just over-tired and being bad-tempered. It's what men seem to do! Miserable idiots, the lot of them. Mick was starting to get like that, which is why he had to go...'

Gracie forced a laugh but she couldn't hide her distress at seeing her husband lose control as he just had. She hugged her bump protectively.

'It wasn't like him to do that, I don't understand...'

'Saint Jennifer can have that effect on people. Five minutes with her would make the Pope himself feel like shooting someone.'

'Oh, that's not fair! Jen's not that bad,' Gracie said. 'It was probably something I said. I seem to upset him all the time lately, can't do right for doing wrong.'

Jeanette put her arm round her sister and hugged her in an unusual display of sisterly affection.

'It's him, darling, not you. He's being unreasonable but maybe he is just tired and bad-tempered. Even Dad used to get like that sometimes, remember? Now you stay there, and I'll clear up. Then we can just sit and listen to the wireless in peace, or dance. We could put some records on and have a dance...'

Gracie sat down heavily. 'Not a good idea but

thanks Jeannie, I'm glad you're here. It's all a bit strange, isn't it?'

'Pardon? Oh go on, say that again, just once more,' Jeanette rubbed the back of her hand across her brow feigning shock. 'Oh my good God, did you really just say that?'

Both sisters laughed but it was uncomfortable laughter because they both knew there was something very wrong about Sean's completely irrational eruption over something so minor.

Gracie was noticeably bewildered but Jeanette was inwardly seething; she knew that it had something to do with her twin sister being there earlier and she could guess what had gone on. Jennifer had played games with her sister's boyfriends in the past but Jeannie hadn't expected this, not with Gracie and Sean being married and expecting a baby.

She hoped she was wrong because that would be too sinister, even for Jennifer.

SIXTEEN

'Come with me, Sean,' Jennifer McCabe begged, 'please come and talk to Mum and Dad. They'll tell you it's all true. I want you to know what she's like and if they tell you, you'll have to believe them...'

'We have to stop this. I've told you, can't be doing this anymore. Please Jennifer, please go away. I don't know what I was doing messing around with you.'

'But when you know that what I'm saying is true you'll be able to leave her with a clear conscience. Please?'

Because his guilty conscience was driving him to distraction Sean had tried his best to distance himself from her but she wasn't having any of it. Jennifer was nothing if not determined and he was increasingly weak when it came to her. After he had lost his temper so dramatically when Gracie had so nearly caught him out Sean was quite rightly jumpy whenever Jennifer was around but she was having none of it. He was also well aware of Jeanette's watchful eye on him whenever she was around. As the weeks went on he became increasingly guilty but he couldn't seem to do anything about it.

Sean Donnelly was losing control of the situation.

'No, Jennifer, I can't do it. I don't want to do it

– I have a baby to think of. If it wasn't for the baby...'

'But we *can* be together, it's possible,' she continued, her words tumbling out. 'If you'll just listen to me about Gracie, no one will blame you for leaving her when they know why you had to.'

'Now stop this. I'm not leaving Gracie and that's a fact. I'm not. She's having our baby in a few weeks, can you imagine the scandal? I'd lose everything, my family would disown me...'

'But you'd have me...'

Jennifer had been hanging around outside the Palace hotel, waiting for Sean to finish work and although he tried to disentangle himself from her, she kept grabbing his arm and pulling him, trying to get him to stop and talk to her, to listen to her telling him about his wife.

'Just come with me,' Jennifer pleaded. 'Let me prove it to you. Let Mum tell you. Your precious Gracie had a baby years ago. She had to go to St Angela's and it was adopted, she's been lying to you all these years...'

Sean stopped in his tracks.

'St Angela's? What do you mean, St Angela's? I thought that was...' he paused mid-sentence. 'Isn't that where the wayward girls go?'

'It *is*! I heard Mum and Dad talking about it. Before you and Gracie got married, she went to see them, to tell them not to say anything to you. Seems it was some squaddie she picked up on the seafront and she ended up with a bastard bun in the oven.' Jennifer dropped her chin and fluttered her eyes, feigning sadness. 'Sean, I'm sorry, I didn't want to tell you like this but I love you. I couldn't let the lie continue...'

Sean was confused. He didn't want to believe a word Jennifer was saying because he knew she was trying to get him away from Gracie, but there was something about her insistence that unsettled him, especially as he remembered that Gracie hadn't wanted him to meet her family in the first place. He tried to think but couldn't, because Jennifer was going on and on at him.

'You're lying...'

'And she's been seeing him since you've been married, someone else told me,' Jennifer continued, the spiteful lies pouring out of her mouth. 'That Ruby, her friend from the hotel where she works, knows all about it. You ask her – she even let them use a room there. I mean, when you think about it, it probably isn't your baby she's carrying, it's his...'

'Stop it now! I don't want you saying things like that about my wife – who's also your own sister, for pity's sake. Look at me, Jennifer, I don't believe you.'

Sean spoke so quietly he was almost whispering, scared someone would see or hear them, because they were still too close to the Palace for comfort. Standing on the pavement nearby he was all too aware Gracie still had friends at the hotel from when she worked there herself. Perversely he thought that while he could explain Jennifer away at the flat, there was no excuse for them to be arguing in public. He could easily imagine the questions if someone overheard the conversation.

Dropping her hands down to her sides Jennifer shrugged and turned away. 'Okay. If you don't care that she's making a fool out of you then that's your business but come and talk to Mum. She'll tell you what she's like. You're a good man, Sean – you deserve to hear the truth.'

Sean looked straight into her eyes. 'If that's what you thought and if it's true, why wait until now to tell me?'

'I wasn't in love with you before.'

Despite the fear of being seen or heard, Sean was suddenly relieved the confrontation was in public, because in private, when they were alone together, he simply couldn't resist Jennifer McCabe. She did things to him that he'd never experienced before and she drove him crazy with lust.

He had tried to put an end to it but he wanted to be with her every second of every day in a way he had never wanted with Gracie. Every waking moment he found himself thinking of her and re-living their time together; he was completely besotted with his own sister-in-law, but every so often an element of doubt about her crept into his mind. He found it hard to accept that someone who seemed so demure in public could behave like an experienced whore in private but when he had asked Jennifer about her experience, the experience she had used to so successfully seduce him, she had simply laughed.

'*Don't all girls do this with the man they love? And you're the man I truly love so I do things with you I've never done with anyone else. It's instinctive and it's just you, Sean. I promise. Just you.*'

He hadn't been completely convinced about her sincerity or her truthfulness but he was wearing the blinkers of lust combined so nothing else truly

174

mattered. He was besotted. Even at that moment, standing in the middle of Southend High Street, he wanted to snatch her up and drag her off to bed. For a split second he thought about going back to the hotel with her but he resisted.

'I have to go,' Sean said quickly. 'Gracie's expecting me and I don't want to see you again. You're lying about her. I know you're lying.'

This time Jennifer let him go. As he cycled away, she smiled after him, her eyes bright with manic pleasure, knowing full well he would be back.

And even if he didn't come back then she would just go and find him and reel him in. She walked round to the bus-stop plotting and planning her next move because she knew that Sean wasn't convinced. Yet.

But she had no doubt he would be, after the coup de grâce she was intending to deliver the very next day.

Jennifer McCabe was brimming with excitement the following day when she and her mother got off the bus at the top of the High Street. As they started to walk down the street, she began her speech.

'Mum, I've been thinking,' Jennifer said, as casually as she could. 'I want you to tell Sean about Gracie and that baby. The one she had at St Angela's. You should tell him, you know, it's your moral duty...'

Dot McCabe stopped in her tracks and turned to look at her daughter walking alongside her. Her expression was neutral but her hands were tightly clenched around the wicker handle of her shopping basket. Jennifer had a very slight smile playing on the edge of her mouth; she looked as if she really wanted to grin widely but was fighting it.

'I don't know what you're talking about.' Dot shook her head, feigning puzzlement. 'Now let's get the shopping. I need to be back in time to cook your father's meal, I have to get to the fishmonger and back while it's still fresh. I've got no time for your flights of fancy, Jennifer McCabe.'

'Come on, Mum,' Jennifer laughed happily, 'don't pretend you don't know what I'm talking about. I just want you to tell Sean the truth about Gracie and her baby, the one she had adopted.'

'I don't understand...' Dot said as she started walking forward, gathering pace as she went. 'This is madness. Your madness alone,' she said almost to herself.

'Oh Mum, I know all about it so you don't need to pretend. Sean needs to know the truth about our Gracie; he should have been told, she should have told him – but she obviously hasn't and he doesn't believe me.'

'Well of course he doesn't believe you, you stupid girl, and why have you been talking nonsense to your sister's husband?' Dot asked incredulously as she carried on walking at a pace that had Jennifer struggling to keep up with her. By the time they reached the railway bridge both of them were breathing quite heavily.

It was an unseasonably chilly day and although it was dry, there was a slight frost on the ground and the pavements were quite slippery. Dot McCabe was wearing her astrakhan coat, stout boots with a zip up the front and a felt hat, whereas Jennifer was shivering and slipping around in her more fashionable court shoes. Her straight black skirt and tight-fitting brown jumper did nothing to keep the chill breeze off her body, but knowing where she was going, she was dressed up to impress Sean Donnelly rather than to keep out the cold.

'I don't know what you're talking about. I thought you were helping me with the shopping, you didn't mention anything like this on the bus...'

'If I had told you, you wouldn't have come, would you?' Jennifer smiled and grabbed her mother's arm. 'Sean should be leaving work soon. He's on a split shift, and were going to meet him. He always comes this way, up the High Street to York Road on his bicycle, then right turn. He's a creature of habit.'

Her mother pulled away. 'How do you know about your brother-in-law's shifts and habits? I don't know what's got into you, Jennifer McCabe, but you're acting like you're away with the fairies again. I just don't know where your madness comes from, it's not from my side of the family...'

'Of course I'm not mad, I just think it's dishonest not to tell him.' Jennifer shook her head and looked at her mother with a condescending expression on her face. 'I know what went on and you have to tell Sean. He should know about the other baby. You have to tell him the truth, tell him what happened...' Jennifer's tone was as urgent as her eyes and smile were wide.

'This has nothing to do with you, why are you interfering? Gracie's expecting a baby, she's fragile. Why in heaven's name would you want to upset everyone with this nonsense?'

'Oh look!' Jennifer looked ahead and waved. 'Here he is now...'

As Sean cycled up the High Street Jennifer jumped out in front of him.

'Sean! Cooeee, Sean! Mum's got something to tell you...'

Scared, he tried his best to ignore both Jennifer and his mother-in-law and started to cycle on past but she reached out and grabbed the handlebars, nearly pulling his bicycle out from underneath him.

'Sean, come and talk to my mother, she'll tell you all about this.'

As Jennifer held onto his bike and laughed, his mother-in-law was moving from foot to foot on the pavement and looking nervously at Sean, who was still in the road on the other side of the High Street. The cars were driving up and down in between them but that didn't stop Jennifer trying to pull him over to where her mother was standing.

Sean and Dot had never got on but they'd never fallen out with each other either; their meetings were too few and far between to warrant anything even remotely resembling a relationship, but he had always tried to be respectful and polite on the occasions they did cross paths. Likewise she had never said anything wrong to him but she'd never said anything nice either.

'I don't want to be part of this nonsense, Jennifer McCabe,' she told her daughter angrily. 'If Sean has anything he wants to know then he should ask his wife, it's got nothing to do with the rest of us...'

'You see, Sean? She's not denying it. Gracie is a slut. Your wife had someone else's baby and never told you, and she's been doing it since. She has...'

Dot McCabe took a few steps across the road till she was face to face with her daughter and then she slapped her hard across the face.

'I'm ashamed of you, Jennifer, and disappointed.' She stepped back and then turned her attention to Sean. 'And as for you, Sean Donnelly, I don't know what's going on between you two but you should be ashamed of yourself. If you want to know anything, you should ask your wife, not her sister. Shameful, shameful, and Gracie being in the family way an' all...'

Sean carefully propped his bicycle upright with the pedal on the pavement and looked at Jennifer.

'Why did you do that?' he asked her. 'And in public... People are looking, anyone could see and hear you.'

'Because you wouldn't come with me to see Mum,' she smiled. 'Sean, you had to know and now you do. Now we can be together...'

Without saying another word, Sean pushed her backwards so hard she went flying across the icy pavement, just righting herself before she fell against a shop window. She was still stumbling around when Sean jumped on his bike and sped off in the direction of home.

Her mother walked back over to her.

'Oh Jennifer, I don't understand. I thought you'd grown out of all that jealous stuff and nonsense,' Dot told her sadly. 'Why did you have to make trouble like that? We promised Gracie we wouldn't ever mention it again and now you've gone and told him just to upset her.' She looked at her daughter. 'How did you know? No one knew...'

'Walls have ears!' Jennifer smirked.

'You were eavesdropping...'

'Of course I was, but it doesn't matter. He needed to know and Gracie should have told him. It's only right.'

Jennifer looked at her mother, her eyes wide with mad excitement. 'And she didn't tell him so I did. I never promised anything, did I? And now Sean can free himself of her.'

'And then what, Jennifer?'

'You'll see soon enough. Now, what were you saying about the fishmonger?'

'I'm going home, Jennifer. Wait till I tell your father what you've done. Wait till your fiancé finds out...'

'I broke off the engagement last night,' Jennifer grinned. 'And it was you who always taught me to tell the truth and shame the devil. That's all I did...'

'That doesn't mean you have to act like the devil.'

As Dot McCabe turned on her heel and walked off, Jennifer walked down the High Street to Pier Hill and settled down on a bench overlooking the Pier to think about what had just happened. She could easily imagine the explosion that was about to occur in her sister's home and she fully intended to be around to savour the fallout.

She was besotted to the point of obsession with Sean Donnelly and she was determined to have him – regardless of what anyone else thought.

Including Sean himself.

SEVENTEEN

Following her altercation with Sean in front of Jeanette, Gracie had given herself a good talking to and tried her best to pretend that everything was fine. She just wanted it all to be as it was before, when she and Sean were first married and they were happy.

Gracie had done her best to disguise her swollen ankles with thick stockings and had dressed as smartly as she could considering her size and lack of suitable clothes; she also made sure her hair was brushed and that she had at least a dash of lipstick and powder on to hide her pallid complexion. She was determined not to mention feeling tired or unwell ever again. If the dates were right she only had another couple of months to go and she just had to get through that time as best she could. Once they had the baby she was sure everything would be fine again. She'd be fit and well, and back to her normal self.

As part of her promise to herself Gracie was in the kitchen preparing a nice meal for them both, knowing that she and Sean would be eating alone as Jeanette was going to be out dancing in town with her latest boyfriend. She had started the preparations well in advance and moved from foot to foot as she stood at the cooker, trying to keep the circulation going in her legs to stop them aching. She paused and leaned back against the blue Formica drop-leaf table that they had bought together from a local furniture store.

'We can do the kitchen yellow and blue,' she'd said as they carried it up the stairs not long after they'd moved in. 'This is the first thing that's really ours and not the landlord's. It's so exciting, I love it.'

Sean had laughed long with her. 'How can you say you love a piece of furniture, it's only a table?'

'But it's *our* table and it's brand new. New, new, *new*! It's a symbol.'

Gracie had clapped her hands and jumped up and down on the spot for a moment, and then flung her arms around her husband's neck. 'Our very own kitchenette table, bought with our own money.'

He had laughed as he pulled her in close and kissed her hard. 'I love you, Gracie.'

'And I love you, Sean.'

But that was before she was pregnant.

Before Sean had changed.

She heard the front door open.

'Gracie? Where are you, Gracie?' Sean came running heavily up the stairs, bellowing at the top of his voice as he went.

'In here...' she shouted back from the kitchen, pleased that he was talking to her. 'What's the matter? You sound upset.'

'Of course I'm upset...' he shouted as he stomped along the hallway towards her.

'What's happened?' As Gracie spoke, she felt the same fluttering in her chest that she used to feel when she was in trouble at home or school. She knew something was wrong. The tone of his voice told her far more than the words. She had known the previous night that something was troubling him because rather than sniping at her the way he'd been doing for the past few weeks, he had ignored her. He completely ignored her, it was as if she wasn't there. Jeanette was out and by nine o'clock Sean was tucked up in bed facing the wall. Something was wrong but she didn't have a clue what it was.

She turned round from the cooker and smiled as he appeared in the doorway, and for a few disconcerting moments he simply stood there with his head on one side, looking at her.

Staring as if he'd never seen her before, as if she was a complete stranger.

'Has something happened at work?' Gracie asked nervously.

'No, nothing has happened at work – but it did on the way home. I've just seen your mother in the High Street with Jennifer. They had some really interesting news for me, really very interesting...' he paused and continued staring.

'What's that?' Gracie asked. 'Has she set a date for the wedding?'

'No, nothing like that. Gracie ... did you have a baby before? With someone else? *Did* you? Did you?' His voice rose with each word as he blurted it all out. 'Tell me it's not true, Gracie. Tell me?'

As she looked at him and felt the anger that was so obviously brewing inside him, Gracie's heart started beating so fast she thought she was going to collapse and she wondered how she could play for time while she decided what to say.

'What do you mean?'

183

'The question is easy...' Sean stared at her, his eyes so dark and furious she was suddenly not just nervous but scared also; she had never seen him look at her like that before. 'Did you or did you not have a baby with someone else? Did you go to St Angela's? Yes or no, tell me now...' his hands were down by his side but his fists clenched and un-clenched in time with his rapid breathing.

'Sean, it's difficult, let me explain...' Gracie wan-ted to reach out to him but her instincts made her back right away until she was up against the Formica table, their table, tucked in the corner of the room. She pressed herself into it thinking that she really wanted to slip over the top and out of the window; she wanted to run as far away as pos-sible. She didn't want to be there and she didn't want to have this conversation.

'I can see from your face that it's true so no, there's no way you can explain this away. You've lied to me all this time. Why? *Why?*'

As he spoke she could see his anger slipping away, only to be replaced by an expression she hadn't seen before: a combination of disbelief and utter despair. For one awful moment she thought he might burst into tears.

'Please Sean, I didn't lie, I just didn't say any-thing,' Gracie pleaded, 'and it was a long time ago, before I even met you. I'm so sorry, I was just too ashamed to tell you about it. I thought you wouldn't want to marry me.'

'And so I wouldn't have. But I'll be guessing Ruby knows all about it, and Johnnie? The man who pretended he was my friend? I can't believe that you didn't tell me; that you let me think you were a virgin, that bold as brass you walked down the aisle of a Catholic church dressed in white.' He moved closer to her. 'How could you do that to me and my family? You're a hypocrite, Gracie, a bloody hypocrite, and you're not who I thought you were.'

'I'm so sorry,' she said as the tears welled up. 'But I am who you thought I was, I'm still me, so why does it really matter now? We're married, we're happy, we're having a baby together. Please, Sean, I made a mistake. I wanted to tell you but the time was never right...'

'All that's gone, it's gone. And how do I know this baby is mine? You've been seen with other men, God Almighty. Mam was right; you aren't good enough for me.'

He raised his hand as if to slap her, but changed his mind as she flinched. 'No. I've never hit a woman in my life. You're not worth it, Gracie McCabe. Our marriage is over.'

Gracie stood still, her arms wrapped around her baby, sobbing to the point of hysteria. 'Sean please, let me explain, please...'

'Pack your bags and leave. This marriage is over.'

'What about the baby?' Gracie was so distraught she could barely get the words out.

'But it's likely not my baby, is it?' said Sean. 'It's his. It was just another lie from you. I know you're still seeing him, the squaddie – you've been seen with him, at the hotel. Now get out or I'll throw you out myself...'

'But I haven't seen him since the day I told him I was expecting and that was in nineteen bloody forty-five...'

'No. Not true. Your sister told me you'd been seen with him, that Ruby let you use a room at the hotel like it was a whorehouse. All of you, so fucking deceitful...'

Gracie tried to understand exactly what he was saying but all the words were blurring and she was so confused she got entirely the wrong end of the stick.

'Jeanette told you that? But she doesn't know anything about that time, she was just a kid. No one knows except Mum and Dad...'

'No, it wasn't Jeanette it was...'

At that moment Jeanette appeared. 'Talking about me again?' she laughed, but stopped abruptly once she sensed the mood in the room.

'What's going on? Are you two fighting about me? What am I supposed to have done this time?'

As Sean turned to her it gave Gracie the chance to get out of the confines of the kitchen and into the sitting room, with Sean and Jeanette close behind.

'Did you know your sister had an illegitimate baby that was adopted? *Did* you? Did you live under my roof and not tell me that?'

With eyes wide open in shock, Jeanette looked from one to the other.

'Whatever are you talking about? Gracie? What's going on here?'

'Oh yes, you pretend you don't know. Everyone knows except for me, it seems,' Sean said quickly. 'But it was Jennifer who told me. Everyone else thought it right to keep it a secret from me, to not tell me that my wife was a liar and a slut.'

Sean's poisonous emphasis on the last word

made both sisters flinch but as he said it every-thing fell into place for Gracie and Jeanette at the same moment. It was as if someone had thrown a jigsaw puzzle up into the air and suddenly, all the pieces had landed together in exactly the right place.

It explained Jennifer being in the flat more often than ever with her sly smiles and strange comments, but it also explained Sean's seemingly irrational behaviour, his unexplained absences and his unusual reactions to everyday things.

'Ah Jennifer, the saintly sister...' Jeanette laughed without humour. 'I should have guessed Jennifer's filthy hands would be all over this.' She looked at Sean. 'She's done this before, you know. She's gone after boyfriends of mine – she does it for fun. I swear she has some sort of mental problem...'

Gracie took deep breaths as, aware of the move-ments of her baby inside her, she determined to stop crying and calm herself down. 'Why are you listening to Jennifer?' she asked. 'Why her over me?'

'Because she really cares about me – and it seems to me that at this moment she's the only person who does.'

Gracie's mouth dropped open as she tried to take in the fact that Jeanette had been right all along about the deviousness of their sister and no one had seen it. She also knew by looking at his face that she had no argument that would change how Sean thought of her. She took a few more breaths and then pushed past him.

'Are you two having an affair?' Gracie asked, but he didn't answer. He simply looked down and shrugged his shoulders very slightly.

'Okay, you win, or rather bloody Jennifer wins; I'm leaving. Are you stopping?' Gracie asked her sister.

'If you're going, I'm not letting you go on your own and anyway, why would I stay here?' Jeanette glared at Sean as she spoke. 'I bet Jen'll be gloating on the doorstep before we get to the corner; she'll be all over this idiot like a measles rash in no time.'

Gracie gathered up a few necessities as Sean watched over her. She didn't say another word and she didn't look at him. At the top of the stairs she thought he might help her with her case but he simply stood back with his arms crossed to let her pass, leaving Jeanette, who was already carrying her own bag, to snatch it out of her hands.

'You're stupid and gullible, Sean – do you know that? Jennifer hates to see anyone happy. She's always been like it; she's jealous, she's spiteful and if you think she's doing this for any other reason then you should be living in the bloody lunatic asylum, not here...'

'Maybe, but it wasn't Jennifer who had a baby and didn't tell her husband, was it now? You can't blame her, Gracie did this to herself.'

'It's not too late, Sean. Can't you two sit down and talk about it? Please?'

'No. It's too late, what's done is done. She's a liar. I can never trust Gracie again, not ever, so there's no point.'

Jeanette glared at him but said nothing else, simply ushered her heavily pregnant sister downstairs and out of the front door.

'She should have told me...' Sean shouted at the top of his voice as Jeanette slammed the front door.

'This is all well and good but where are we going to go?' Jeanette asked as they stood side by side on the pavement outside. 'We could go to Mum and Dad's and explain...'

Gracie managed a laugh. 'And you think Mum would chuck Jennifer out so that we could stay there? Never in a million years! She'll say I deserve this, she might even be pleased I've got my come-uppance. No, we'll go to Thamesview. Ruby would never see us out on the street.'

'I'd forgotten about her. Okay, we'll walk to the rank at the station and get a taxi. You can't go on a bus like that, you look terrible.'

Gracie could feel her whole body throbbing. Her legs were leaden and the baby inside her was kicking madly as if in protest at the disturbance. If Jeanette hadn't been there it would have been easy for her to just lay down on the pavement then and there and go to sleep.

'I'm so stupid. Sean's right about that, I really am one stupid fat cow. I should just go throw myself off the end of the pier and be done with it. I've lost everything...'

'Don't talk like that, you've got a baby to think about,' Jeanette said as she linked an arm through her sister's. 'We'll go and talk to Ruby and then we'll plot the best way to slowly and painfully kill our sodding bitch of a sister.'

As Gracie walked away from her home with just a few basic things packed into a small suitcase, the rent money in her purse and Jeanette's arm in hers helping her along, so Jennifer, who had been standing in the shadows further along the road, went and knocked on the door.

She made Sean tea, gave him sympathy, hugged him close and then took him to bed.

Sadly, Sean Donnelly simply couldn't resist her. He'd never known anyone as seductive or addictive as his sister-in-law. He was madly and blindly in love, even though he knew deep down that she was devious and nasty, and had most likely exaggerated the truth about Gracie's past.

But at that moment Sean wanted to believe it was all true. He wanted to think that his wife had betrayed him, and now she was gone and he could be with Jennifer with a clear conscience because it was all Gracie's fault.

But even as he bedded Jennifer once again he couldn't get Gracie and his baby out of his mind and she knew it.

'Let's run away together...' Jennifer said as they lay side by side in Sean and Gracie's marital bed.

'I can't do that – I have a job, there's a baby...'

'You can get another job, so can I, and the baby isn't yours anyway, I already told you that. Why don't you listen to me? I'm always right, you should listen!'

There was a brittle edge to her voice that unsettled Sean. When he didn't answer she continued.

'I looked in the *Evening News*, there's a hotel in Brighton that's looking for staff. We could both work there. It'll be fun and we won't have to see Gracie or any of them ever again.'

'I can't do that ... the baby...'

'Oh yes you can, Sean. Now listen to me, we're leaving tomorrow and going to Brighton.'

As Jennifer spoke, she slipped slowly out of the bed and walked across the room. With a flourish she turned on the ceiling light then twirled gracefully back towards him as if she was a revue dancer. As she reached the bed she pulled the covers back, leaned over him and carefully put her hands on his shoulders. She stared into his eyes for a few moments, before very slowly lifting one leg in the air and swinging it over his naked body. She was completely naked and framed under the beam of light from the ceiling.

'Is that okay? We'll leave tomorrow?' she asked as she sat upright on him, put her hands behind her neck and slowly gyrated her hips down onto him.

'Yes...' he groaned. 'Tomorrow...'

'Good!'

EIGHTEEN

'I don't care what you say, I'm going to have to telephone the midwife, Gracie. This isn't right, you're white as a sheet and shivering...'

'I'll be alright in a minute, it's just cramp.'

'It's not just cramp, though – I can see that by looking at you, and you're burning up,' Ruby said as she leaned over the sofa and touched her friend's forehead. 'Oh I'm so bloody, bloody angry! This is all Sean's fault. Johnnie is fit to kill him – he was all for going round there straight away and dealing with him. He still wants to, it's unbelievable...'

'That's silly, it wasn't all Sean's fault. It was my sister; she stirred it until he didn't know whether he was coming or going. And it's my fault.'

'How is it yours? He turfed you out, he wouldn't listen...'

'He was made to look stupid and he reacted. I should have told him; you said I should, Mum and Dad said I should, but I didn't say a word and now he thinks I lied about everything.' Gracie grabbed hard at her stomach and gasped. 'Oh God this is agony! I feel like I'm going to explode...'

'I'll have to ring the midwife.'

Gracie and Ruby were in the flat at the top of the Thamesview. Gracie was curled up on the sofa and Ruby started pacing back and forth, a worried frown on her face and her arms folded tightly across her chest.

'Okay okay, you go down and ring the midwife. Hopefully it'll stop you wearing a hole in the lino...' Gracie tried to smile but it was hard; she was in so much pain she could barely think, let alone smile.

She knew that Ruby was right, that something was definitely amiss, but she didn't want it confirmed. She could feel her baby moving and kicking, and as long as that was still happening she didn't want to push her luck. Feeling the baby was the one thing that'd comforted her in her misery.

Gracie was aware she was in labour but she was hoping against hope that it would stop because it was about a month too soon and the thought of possibly losing another baby, albeit under different circumstances, was just too unbearable.

When she and Jeanette had turned up at the hotel three weeks previously after the big row with Sean, Ruby hadn't asked for explanations or reasons, but had taken one look at Gracie and bundled them both inside. Leaving Johnnie to deal with everything downstairs, Ruby had quickly made up the bed in Gracie's old room, gathered up enough bedding from the linen cupboard for Jeanette to take the sofa and then gone into full mother-hen mode, while at the same time cussing Sean Donnelly to kingdom come.

Gracie had been silently grateful for her friend's care and support; she had curled up in a ball in her bed with the curtains tightly closed for two days and had then wandered round the flat in a daze for several more days, until Ruby had eventually taken her to task.

'Gracie, I love you and I'll happily look after you, you know that, but only you can look after your baby and you're doing it no good by not eating or sleeping, or getting any fresh air. Now get your coat, we're going for a walk and then you're going have some soup, whether you want to or not. Come on, think of the baby...' Ruby smiled persuasively.

'I don't want to go out; I don't want to see anyone.'

'Too bad. Get your cardi and shoes ... now! We'll just be two women taking a stroll and we'll walk in the other direction, towards Shoebury, so there's no chance of seeing any of your old chums from the Palace. We've got bags of time. Johnnie is in charge and doing very nicely.'

After some grumbling, Gracie had given in, and the two of them had walked and talked as they used to but neither of them mentioned Sean specifically.

Ruby did most of the talking, chatting away about all the minutiae surrounding the running of the hotel, the buying of the property next door and giving updates on the Wheatons and Maggie. Gracie knew she was trying hard to lift her spirits and distract her, and she did her best to respond but it was hard to smile when her life, with everything she had ever wanted, had fallen apart so dramatically. And it had all been her own fault.

From being in the place she had always wanted to be, with a husband, a home and a baby on the way, Gracie was suddenly back where she started. A pregnant young woman on her own.

But after the walk she'd picked herself up as best she could and tried to make herself useful in the hotel, to earn her board and keep her sanity.

Breathing hard after running back up the stairs, Ruby went over to the sofa and checked Gracie again.

'The midwife is out on a call so you need to go to hospital. We've both had babies and we both know this isn't right. I'm taking you to hospital, like it or lump it...'

'I don't want to go to hospital, Rubes. I can't face going there again, not after last time, and anyway it's not due for ages, it's too soon for it to be born. I just want to stay here and hang on until it passes...' Gracie sobbed, the words tumbling out as she tried to ignore the griping pains that were building inside her.

As she spoke, she wrapped her hands around her stomach protectively. The pain was intense and she felt as if she was going to be sick but tried to keep calm, hoping that if she could keep it under control that the pains would go away. But instead, they intensified.

'No more arguments,' Ruby said firmly a few minutes later. 'I'm taking you to hospital now. The car's out the back but I don't want you traipsing through the kitchen and garden, so we'll go down to the lobby and then I'll get Johnnie to bring it round.'

'I don't want to go to hospital...' Gracie cried. 'I told you, it's too soon.'

'I know you don't want to but you have to, you have to think about the baby, not yourself.' Ruby's voice was calm and soothing as she tried to re-assure her. 'I'll be with you all the way. Up you get and I'll help you down the stairs.' She paused for a moment. 'Would you sooner I called an ambulance to take you? Would that make you feel better?'

'Nooo, no ambulance...'

They slowly made their way down to the ground floor, and then Ruby and Johnnie put Gracie into the back seat and drove as fast as they could to the hospital.

As the car whipped along the roads Gracie was back in 1946, the year she had given birth to her baby Joe.

'Stop making such a fuss, you stupid child! This is pain of your own making...' the nurse had told her as she was struggling with her labour. 'You girls from St Angela's are all the same when you come here, lots of fuss and nonsense and shouting...'

Gracie had been in heavy labour for nearly twenty-four hours when she was rushed to the hospital by ambulance. Terrified by the stories she had heard of the way St Angela's girls were treated at the hospital, she had pleaded with them not to send her but it had been in vain. The ambulance was called and Gracie had been bundled in alone and taken to the maternity hospital in a uniform nightdress and dressing gown, wearing black plimsolls. As she was admitted, she was more mortified by the way her appearance shrieked St Angela's than she was of the pain and once there, it had turned out to be everything she expected and more.

Eventually her baby had been born; he was a big baby and she had the stitches to prove it, but he was also healthy and loud with a big appetite. Most of all, he was the most beautiful baby she had ever seen and the thought of having to give him away haunted her every moment.

She had visits from the Adoption Society and the hospital Almoner, even Father Tom made a fleeting visit during his rounds of visiting the sick, but no one else. Neither her mother nor her father came to see her because she was officially a St Angela's girl and the shame that went with that was usually too much for parents to bear.

Then a few days into her stay, a tall, elegantly dressed woman came and sat down beside her bed. 'Hello, my dear. My name is Mrs Wheaton. I'm visiting young Ruby over there...' she pointed across to where there was another young woman sitting upright in her bed with a man beside her in a wheelchair. 'I know you've not met but Ruby told me the nurses have been particularly hard on you?'

Gracie smiled politely. 'It's okay. I'll be going soon, I'm being taken back just as soon as...' she paused. 'I can put up with it.'

'Well, I'm disgusted by what she's told me. I don't have any authority but my husband over there is a doctor and he's going to make sure nothing else happens. Now, is there anything you need?'

'I'm fine, thank you.' Gracie had murmured. 'I'm from St Angela's and I'm not allowed to have anything...'

The woman laughed, a gentle tinkling laugh that engulfed Gracie in kindness. It was the first time anyone had said a kind word to her since the day she'd been sent away.

'Oh well now, we'll soon see about that. I'll be back

in a minute; you'll have the same as everyone else...'

Gracie had wanted to cry, but instead she looked at the girl called Ruby again and smiled. That was the start of their friendship.

'You have to push harder if we're going to get this baby out... Come on, Gracie, push! There's no time for this shilly-shallying around.' The midwife's voice was becoming more intense with each command. 'Push this baby out, PUSH or you'll have to have a caesarean section. You don't want that, do you?'

Gracie shook her head to clear the déjà vu. Through a haze of gas and air she vaguely realised that there were more nurses around the foot of the delivery bed than there had been before, including the ward sister. There was an atmosphere of carefully restrained urgency in the delivery room, but the pain was so unbearable she hadn't got the energy to think too hard about it. As she lay there sweating and shivering, her feet immobilised in the stirrups attached to the bed, her dignity long gone, Gracie wondered if she was going to die. It even passed through her mind that she would actually choose to if it'd mean an end to the never-ending agony that refused to let up. She knew something was wrong because it hadn't been anything like that when she'd given birth to baby Joe.

She couldn't even remember how long she'd been there, how long it had been since Ruby had driven like a mad woman out to the hospital in Rochford where she'd been taken straight to the maternity ward.

She remembered the pain escalating while she

was in the car and Ruby screaming, 'Hang on Gracie, hang on! You can't have it in the car...' but although the pain had continued to worsen during the rest of that day and night the baby still hadn't arrived.

They were already into the next day when the labour finally moved on and Gracie managed to do as she was told; she pushed and pushed so long and hard she felt quite demented but then she felt the baby slip out and the relief was so overwhelming she started to cry hysterically.

But almost as quickly she calmed down and began to think straight she realised there was silence in the delivery room. No baby crying, no words spoken. Just silence.

'What's happening? Is the baby okay?' Gracie asked, her slow, drawn-out words still slurred by the gas and air.

'I'm sorry, my dear, your baby is stillborn. He must have died in the womb...' As the word was finally said it echoed round her head.

Stillborn.

He.

Her precious baby, a boy, was dead. She didn't have one. Her longed-for baby hadn't even taken a breath. Gracie looked around at the sympathetic faces but she couldn't say anything. She was so shocked, she hadn't any words.

But as she was trying to fight her cotton-wool brain to absorb the information, the physical pain which had subsided started again, with the waves building inside her until it was so unbearable she started screaming. Suddenly the furious activity in the room started all over again.

'Call the doctor,' she heard the Sister say urgently. 'There's another one in here. Call the doctor right away, this one's all wrong. I can see a foot, the baby's the wrong way up and it's coming out that way. Tell him it's an emergency...'

By the time the next baby was painfully delivered with forceps Gracie was slipping into unconsciousness and haemorrhaging. She was unaware of being taken away from the maternity ward to the main part of the hospital and she was also unaware of the major operation that had saved her life – but it was an operation that also meant she would never have another baby.

It was nearly three days before Gracie recovered enough to fully understand that she had given birth to twins, a boy who had died in the womb some weeks before and a tiny girl who was alive but small and fragile, and being cared for in an incubator.

When she was finally told the full gravity of her experience Gracie had accepted it all calmly. She had expected to be punished for giving up her first-born and she had been.

There would be no more babies. Ever. The price for Joe had been paid.

'Have you told Sean?' Gracie asked Ruby when she visited with Jeanette. 'He should know...'

'We tried to find him because the hospital wanted to speak to him to get permission for your operation but we couldn't. He's left the Palace and the flat. No one knows where he is.'

'Is he with Jennifer?'

'I don't know,' Ruby turned sideways to Jeanette and looked at her. 'Do you know? Have you heard anything?'

'Not a dicky bird and neither have Mum and Dad.' She looked at her sister. 'If its any consolation they're mortified at what she did to you and they blame her for Fay being born too early; Mum is going mad with anger and shame. She can't believe that the good girl out of the three of us has turned out to be the devil incarnate.'

'I just wondered if Sean knew I'd given birth...' Gracie's voice faded as she turned away and looked down the ward. 'I remember being here last time but I was in that bed over there, tucked safely away in the corner in case I infected anyone with my immorality. It's so strange to think back on that time and everything that's happened since. It seems so long ago in one way but as if it was only yesterday in another...'

Ruby leaned over and gently squeezed her arm, to remind her not to say anything more in front of Jeanette. Ruby's own place in the story had to remain a secret; not because of shame but because of her daughter Maggie, who had no idea that she wasn't the natural daughter of Babs and George Wheaton. It was a secret they were all honour bound to keep until the day came when she would have to be told.

Gracie looked round and it was a few seconds before she realised what Ruby meant.

'Sorry, I'm rambling, none of it matters now and at least this time I'm a respectable married woman – even if the husband has buggered off with the sister to God knows where and isn't interested. So long as I'm called Mrs and have a ring on my finger I can be treated as a human

201

being. Yippee, I'm not a fallen woman anymore!'

As Gracie laughed humourlessly so her eyes filled with tears. Ruby and Jeanette both leaned forward and touched her reassuringly but neither said anything.

The three of them sat in silence until the nurse came in and rang the handbell to let the visitors know it was time to leave.

'Do you want me to keep on trying to find Sean?' Ruby asked cautiously. 'I know Johnnie could find him but I told him to hold off until I'd spoken to you.'

'I don't know. He should know but he had his chance... Oh I don't know, maybe I have to just get on with it, get used to it; accept it's just me and the baby.'

'And me...' Ruby said quickly. 'I'll always be here, and so will Jeanette and your Mum and Dad, eh Jeannie?'

'We'll all help you, Gracie, really we will.' Jeanette took her sister's hand and squeezed it. 'You're not on your own like last time.'

Gracie forced a watery smile. Jeanette's affectionate gesture meant so much to her at that moment.

'Thanks. Who'd have thought it, eh? Gracie McCabe fucks it up again.'

'Shhh,' Jeanette grinned. 'I thought you liked them thinking you were respectable?'

'So, I wonder where we go from here?' Jeanette asked Ruby as they walked out of the building. They wandered over to the nearby wall together and perched on the edge of it. Ruby pulled a pack of cigarettes out of her handbag and offered one to Jeanette.

The two young women were chalk and cheese visually. Ruby was tall and slender, with dark red hair hanging carelessly around her shoulders and casually dressed in slacks and blouse, while Jeanette was short and round, with a head of bleached platinum-blonde curls, scarlet lipstick and high heels.

'I like your dress,' Ruby said with a smile. 'You're looking very glamorous for a hospital visit...'

'You never know who you might meet. Think of all the handsome young doctors that must be wandering around these corridors. It'd be a shame to miss an opportunity like this; someone well-heeled and a bit brainy would make a nice change from the hard-up morons I usually meet!'

Ruby laughed. 'Maybe you should become a nurse, you could take your pick then...'

Jeanette looked at her. 'I never thought of that. Do you know, you might have given me an idea there. I hate my job; maybe it's time for a radical change, time to be more responsible. You don't think I'm too old, do you?'

'Not a chance and it sounds interesting! Meanwhile, what do we do about Gracie? I don't want her to think I'm organising her life for her but we have to set something in place.'

'Yes, but what?'

'Let me think about it while you go back in and ask for a leaflet about nursing.'

'Shall I ask if there's one on how to snare a doctor?' Jeanette laughed.

'You could try but I doubt there'll be any left...'

NINETEEN

'Oh just look at her, she's a little baby doll...'
Ruby said as she and Gracie stood side by side
looking through the glass that separated the
nursery from the corridor. 'And she looks like
you already, though she's got Sean's hair. Just
look at it, a real mop for such a tiny scrap...What
have the doctors said? She looks like she's come
on a treat.'

'She has,' Gracie said. 'She should be able to go
home soon, another week maybe. She's done
really well but they think she'll probably always
be fragile, and maybe even a bit slow at doing
things.'

Gracie shook her head and gently touched the
glass, moving her fingers back and forth as if she
was waving to her daughter. Every time she
looked at Fay she felt the same helplessness sweep
over her.

'They just don't know what the future holds for
her; she was stuck for so long. I mean, none of us
knew she was even there, but at least she's alive.
Unlike her poor little brother. You know, I still
can't believe it. How could I have been walking
around with a dead baby inside me and not
known?'

'It must be so hard for you. Even I feel muddled
by it all,' Ruby told her. 'It's so strange, I'm so
happy for this little one who's survived everything

and is here with you but so heartbroken for the other one you lost. And for you, having to have that operation.'

Gracie turned to look at Ruby.

'I'm never going to have another baby, Ruby. This is it for me. One adopted away, one dead and the other still struggling. What did I do to deserve this? It's not fair. I'm not bad, not like some...'

'You're not bad at all, you're just unlucky and you're right, it's not fair.'

'Was it my fault? I was sure something would go wrong, something inside was telling me but no one listened. Not the doctor, not the midwife, they thought I was a nervous new mother and Sean thought I was just being an idle cow. Perhaps I was. Maybe that's what caused it, me not doing the right things. Oh, I don't know...'

Gracie's voice quivered as she spoke. She was determined not to cry any more but every time she touched or even just looked at her baby she had an instant image in her head of the other one and she started all over again.

It had been the day after the birth and the operation when the full impact of what had happened had really hit her. With her emotions all over the place, Gracie had no idea how to separate out the joy and the grief overwhelming her. They were so entwined she couldn't imagine how she would ever accept that there should have been two children. There was the joy of having a baby girl, tempered with worries over her health and the shock that she should have been a twin, that she had actually been carrying two babies. Gracie had tried listening to the nurses on the maternity ward, who told her that as she thought she was only having one baby, the loss of the twin she didn't know she was expecting wasn't so bad, but it didn't work. She still grieved for the baby boy that had been stillborn. Added into the mix was the emptiness that she felt at the news that she would never be able to have another child. It had been so much for her to absorb that she had switched off.

But now the time had come when Gracie knew she must come to terms with it all if she was to be able to look after the baby that she still had, the one she had yearned for, for so long.

'It wasn't your fault, you know it wasn't,' Ruby said quietly as they both looked back at the baby in the crib. 'No one realised that you were carrying twins, and the little boy died several weeks ago, according to the doctors.'

Gracie sighed but didn't respond.

'It's no wonder you felt so ill, though,' Ruby continued, 'but considering what happened you're so lucky to have this little one. She'll be okay and we'll all look after her. Aunty Babs can't wait to get her hands on her and Maggie wants to meet her.'

'I know I'm lucky; I do know that – I just don't feel it at the minute...'

'Have you thought of a name for the other one? He was born and he was Fay's brother, you may want to tell her about him one day?'

'I've decided to call him Phillip. Phillip and Fay, they're the boy and girl names Sean and I chose for either eventuality, not knowing we were going to have one of each...' Gracie's voice

206

wobbled as she said the names out loud.

'Once you're feeling better we'll go up to the church and have a mass said for him. The mass card will be something to remember him by.'

'Oh hell, Ruby! I'm so scared of taking her home and looking after her; I can't even imagine being alone with her...' Gracie started to cry again. 'How could this happen? Why me? All I ever wanted was a husband, a baby, a home and now it's all gone up the Suwannee. Whoosh! Gone on the back of my stupid lie.'

'It's not your fault your sister turned out to be such a cow and who'd have thought Sean would be another stupid weak bastard? Honestly, if I had a gun I'd shoot him right now, right between the legs.' As Ruby said it she took imaginary aim and fired. 'POW, POW! Now that might make him realise what a disgrace he is.'

Gracie managed a weak smile. They had been such good friends for so long she couldn't imagine what it would be like at that moment without Ruby supporting her.

'I might have a solution to some of it, you know...' Ruby continued. 'I've been talking with Uncle George, you know he does all the finances, and you know we're buying the ramshackle house next door? I mean, it was going for a song, so it would have been daft not to. We're going to have it as part of the hotel eventually, but in the meantime we're doing it up and Johnnie and I plan to live in the basement flat there when the furore over Sadie has died down. It's going to be a real classy gaff for us!'

'That sounds like a good plan...' Gracie said.

She tried her best to look pleased but she couldn't help feeling a little tinge of envy at Ruby sailing high while she herself was at rock bottom.

'Yes, but that means you and Fay could have the Thamesview flat all to yourselves. Permanently. Or maybe even the basement there, if we have a rearrange. Jeanette is welcome to share with you but she'll have to pay some rent and you can work in the hotel, like you've always done...'

Gracie thought for a moment before responding.

'But I'll have a baby and anyway, I'm not your responsibility, I have to stand on my own two feet. Though having my old job back would be a help. Maybe Mum could look after Fay...'

'We'll manage all that. We've managed all the other rubbish life has chucked at us, haven't we? Meanwhile we'll all have to cram into the flat together for a bit longer and try not to drive each other nuts, or you can go and convalesce with Babs and George in Melton. They've offered...'

Again, Gracie forced a smile.

'That's nice of them but...'

'You don't have to make up your mind now, think about it,' Ruby said, in a kindly tone.

'I don't think Jeanette will want to stay at the hotel. She's done far more for me than I would ever have expected from her but she'd never survive stuck with me and a baby,' Gracie told her friend. 'She's a party girl at heart; she wants to be out and about with a different man on her arm every night of the week...'

Ruby laughed. 'Did you know that this party girl is applying to train as a nurse? Oh yes, she's full of surprises, is your sister. Well, they both are – but Jeanette in a good way!'

'A nurse?' Gracie laughed for the first time in so many weeks. 'Well, I never did! I wonder what Mum and Dad would say about that?'

'Why don't you ask us?' the voice behind her said, making her physically jump. Gracie spun round to see both her parents standing behind her. Her father was smiling but her mother was looking down at her feet.

'What are you doing here?' she said to them, then quickly followed it up with, 'I'm sorry, I didn't mean it like that. Of course I know why you're here.'

For the first time, Gracie found herself feeling sorry for her mother. Dot McCabe stood beside her husband but her head was bowed. Gracie thought she looked as if she had aged ten years since discovering that the daughter she had favoured over the other two had been the one who had done the worst thing imaginable: broken up a marriage, her own pregnant sister's marriage, and then gone off with her sister's husband.

'Look,' Gracie said, pointing at the window. 'Second from the left, that's Fay, your grand-daughter. I'm hoping I'll be able to take her home soon.'

Her parents stepped forward in unison and stared through the window at the baby, and as they did, Gracie noticed that her father put his arm around his wife's shoulder. She couldn't remember the last time she had seen anything remotely affectionate between them.

'She is so tiny ... is she going to be alright?' her

father asked.

'I hope so, but it's still early days. She was distressed when she was born – hardly surprising as she spent weeks beside her dead brother...'

Dot McCabe made a strange sound, and Gracie was shocked to see tears rolling down her cheeks.

'Don't do that,' Gracie said. 'I wasn't trying to upset you, I wasn't. It's just a fact.'

'I've got to get back to the hotel now so I'll leave you to it,' Ruby said tactfully. 'I'll see you tomorrow evening...'

'You don't have to go...' Gracie said.

'Yes, I do.' Ruby looked at Fred and Dot McCabe. 'Nice to see you again. You should come to the hotel sometime; we'd love to see you.'

'We might just do that,' Fred McCabe smiled. 'We've got a lot to thank you for, Ruby. Without you, I dread to think what might have happened to Gracie and the baby.'

With a quick wave Ruby disappeared out of sight, leaving Gracie and her parents standing around awkwardly.

'She said *we*, are you going back there?' Dot McCabe asked.

'I think so. At least I'll be able to have the baby at work with me, I have to earn a living...'

Her mother still looked at the floor. 'You and the baby could come home to us. We've got plenty of room.'

Gracie smiled but didn't answer. She was actually lost for words.

Gracie had agreed with Ruby that Johnnie would go round and tell her parents about the baby. Initially she'd baulked at the idea but Ruby had been persuasive, telling her that they should know and that Johnnie Riordan was the most neutral person to do it.

They hadn't been to visit while Fay was in the special unit and Gracie was recovering from her surgery but they had kept in touch with Ruby by telephone. Fred McCabe would walk to the phone box most days and ring the hotel to ask for an update, and Ruby would pass on any messages.

'Have you seen Jennifer?' Gracie suddenly asked. 'I was just wondering if Sean knew he had a daughter. Are they still together?'

'We've not seen hide nor hair of either of them since the night Jennifer flew in, packed a small bag and went straight out almost immediately. She didn't mention Sean and we didn't know at that point – it was Jeannie who told us exactly what she'd done. I'm so sorry...' Fred started to say but his wife quickly interrupted him.

'No.' Dot put a hand on her husband's arm and looked at her daughter. 'Gracie, *I'm* sorry. It was all my fault. I didn't know Jennifer was in the house when I was talking to your father after you'd been to visit, when you asked us not to tell Sean. I didn't know she was listening or what she'd do, but it was my fault.'

Dot looked again at the baby. 'I always knew Jennifer had a streak of madness in her but this is wrong. So wrong...'

Gracie didn't know what to say. She looked closely and saw tears in her mother's eyes for the first time. Gracie had never seen her mother cry before.

'Oh, it wasn't your fault, it was mine. I know that now,' Gracie said. 'I should have been honest with him and then Jennifer wouldn't have been able to do what she did. My fault. But I'll still smash her face in when I see her – selfish jealous bitch, messing with people's lives for the fun of it.'

'Gracie!' Fred McCabe said sharply, but with a slight grin.

Gracie forced a smile. 'Sorry but it's true. Thanks for coming anyway.'

'We've had our differences, we all have. Let's hope we can have an end to it,' Fred McCabe said gently. 'Things like this make other things seem unimportant.'

Dot folded her arms defensively and for a moment Gracie thought she was going back on the attack but she didn't, she simply sighed and slumped down into herself. Gracie saw how old and haggard her mother looked and she felt another surge of pity for her.

'An end to it would be nice,' Gracie said. 'It would be nice if we could be more of a family again, just don't expect me to forgive and forget about Jennifer.'

'I don't think any of us will be able to forgive Jennifer for what she did,' Dot said sadly looking at the baby on the other side of the glass, 'but maybe this little mite will be the one to heal some of the wounds.'

TWENTY

Gracie and Ruby were rushing around the hotel, changing beds, dusting and vacuuming the rooms and landings and scrubbing the bathrooms. They were trying to get everything done because there was about to be an influx of short-notice guests.

Ruby had taken her uncle's advice and advertised the hotel in a new women's magazine, and straight away a group of young war widows had contacted them and booked all the rooms and three meals a day. It was a fantastic coup for Ruby and the hotel but it meant a lot of extra work for everyone because the women were holidaying for a week.

Jeanette had been helping out and was upstairs in the flat babysitting for baby Fay and Johnnie Riordan was doing all the shifting and lifting and things that involved a bit of muscle.

'We really have to impress this group and then they might recommend us. We need the business so badly after the lull we've just had,' Ruby said as they made yet another bed.

'It was a brilliant idea to advertise, we'd got into the habit of relying on the old guests but they're slowly dying off!' Ruby pulled a face. 'Thoughtless of them, eh?'

'You are so bad...' Gracie laughed.

'Well, it's true. We need to get some younger guests in. Did I tell you about the new idea we're turning over?'

'No, go on...'

At that moment, Mrs Madison the cook came huffing and puffing up the stairs to the first floor where Gracie and Ruby were piling up the linen from the bed changes. The woman was well over sixty, overweight and struggling desperately with painful arthritis and swollen joints, but she was reliable and Ruby knew she needed the wages, so the workings of the kitchen were organised to make it easy for her.

'There's someone downstairs for you. A visitor ... in the lobby,' she said, leaning hard on the door handle as she tried to catch her breath.

'Oh hell! I'm not expecting anyone, Mrs M. Can you deal with it? We're running round like a couple of blue-arsed flies up here to get ready in time for the group,' Ruby said, as she dragged a linen bag along the landing for Johnnie to collect and take downstairs.

'Not for you, dear, for Gracie. He wants to see Gracie...' she puffed the words out.

Gracie frowned. 'I'm not expecting anyone either.'

'I'm sorry, dear, but it's your so-called husband. He wants to speak to you urgently, he said. Not my place to tell him to sling his hook – unless you tell me to, that is?' the woman said with a nod of her head in the direction of the stairs.

'Sean? Downstairs?' Gracie's jaw dropped as she absorbed exactly what Mrs Madison was saying.

'That's what I said. Shall I send him packing? Just say the word, dearie. I'll happily boot him up the arse for you, little toe-rag that he is...'

'No, it's okay,' Gracie said quietly. 'Tell him I'll be down shortly. Thank you, Mrs Madison.'

As Mrs Madison left the room so Gracie stared at her friend.

'Well, that's a bit of a bolt. Bugger it, Rubes, what am I going to do? I don't want a scene anywhere but especially not here.'

'It's up to you. I think all of us would happily send him packing. Maybe he wants to see Fay? Maybe Jennifer's been in touch with your Mum and Dad and she's told him?'

'Well, he's not seeing her, not just like that after not a peep from him for all this time,' Gracie said sharply, 'and anyway, he said he wasn't the father, so why would he want to?'

'You don't have to tell me!' exclaimed Ruby. 'If you want, I'll send Johnnie to get shot of him, but if you want to see him then I'll go up and tell Jeanette to stay put with Fay. Can't have your baby sister ripping his head off his shoulders in the lobby, can we?' Ruby grinned as she gave Gracie a reassuring hug.

'I don't know if he knows what happened. No one's heard from Jennifer so maybe he doesn't know. I'll just have to see how it goes...' Gracie said nervously.

'Well, if you want me, just shout. I'll be straight down once I've got the gun...'

Gracie went down the stairs slowly, each step making her more nervous, but when she was nearly at the bottom she sped up and tried to look calm and business-like.

So much had happened in the year since they had got married and especially since the day that

215

Sean had thrown her out of the flat. Gracie had got herself back together with the help of both Ruby and Jeanette, and her prime focus now was Fay, her precious daughter who she loved more than she could ever have imagined. It was Fay who made up for everything that had gone before in her life. Everything.

Her daughter was still tiny and needed extra care to avoid catching any chills and fevers or childhood illnesses but with three mothers around to help protect and care for her, she was thriving and happy. Gracie wasn't going to let anyone jeopardise that – especially not Sean, the father who had denied her even before she was born.

As she neared the bottom of the stairs she looked over the banister at Sean Donnelly, the man who she had thought would be part of her future forever. She watched him for a few moments until he looked up.

'Well, well. The wanderer returns...' she said calmly, but coldly.

Sean Donnelly looked up at his wife and grinned sheepishly.

'Hello, Gracie! You look nice, you've had your hair cut short, it suits you...'

Gracie immediately felt her blood starting to boil as she recognised his trait of turning on the charm. She hated that he seemed to think she was stupid enough to fall for it.

'I don't want to hear rubbish like that from you, Sean. What do you want?'

'I want to talk with you, can we go somewhere private? This isn't the right place, in here with others around.'

Gracie stopped on the bottom step, one hand gripping the polished round on the banister post and the other on her hip. She felt better having a conversation when she was standing taller than him.

'I haven't got anything to say to you. You told me what you thought of me the day you threw me out.'

'I was wrong the way I behaved, and I'm sorry. Please Gracie, can we talk?'

Gracie thought for a moment. She wanted to turn her back and walk away but at the same time she wondered what he had to say.

'Wrong? You think you were wrong, do you? Well, fancy that, lover-boy!' Her emphasis on the last two words was pure sarcasm but it seemed to pass him by.

'Please?'

'I'm working and we're busy. We can go into the office but you have to make it quick, I have a living to earn.'

Gracie kept her expression as neutral as she could as she spoke. She couldn't believe that he could stand in front of her with his shoulders drooping and a hang-dog expression on his face and expect her to make small talk as if nothing had happened.

'How have you been?' he said to her back as she led him along to the office. 'You look very thin...'

'Unlike the fat lump of lard you chucked out, eh? No, don't answer that, I've got no time for niceties. Just tell me what you want and then leave. I've not got time for you.'

Sean sat down on one of the old dining chairs

that had been demoted to the office and beckoned for her to do likewise, but instead she went around the desk and perched on the window ledge, with her arms folded tightly around her.

'I'm okay here...'

'I won't beat about the bush, Gracie. I'm so sorry, I was a fool. You lied to me and it upset me but I can forgive you if you forgive me. I was an idiot...'

'*I* lied to *you*?' She stared at him before continuing. 'Okay I did, but about something in the past, before I even knew you. In the present you were sleeping with my sister behind my back, and in our bed...'

'I shouldn't have, I know, but you pushed me into it...' He shrugged his shoulders and frowned, as if he didn't quite understand why she was upset with him.

'I made you sleep with my sister? Tit for tat?' she interrupted him sharply. 'Come off it, you think I believe that? You'd started with her before you knew anything about my past, my secret; she was the one who told you. She's a spiteful bitch and you're stupid. Neither of you know what loyalty is.'

Sean looked down at the floor. 'You're still my wife, it's our anniversary...' he mumbled.

'No, I'm not your wife, and our anniversary is something I want to forget about. Well, legally I'm your wife but that's all. You chucked all that away when you buggered off with my sister!' Gracie's self-control was slipping and her voice was getting louder. 'Traitors, the pair of you, wrecking it for everyone! My mother's not been out of the house,

218

she's so distraught. We could have had everything together...'

As she'd walked slowly down the stairs to see Sean, Gracie had promised herself she'd stay calm and not cry but it was hard. She wanted to scream and shout and beat him around the head with her fists, especially as she was aware of baby Fay upstairs. Her beautiful fragile daughter who, if life hadn't been so cruel, would be sturdy and strong and still have her brother alongside her in her cot. Instead, he was in a tiny coffin in the local cemetery.

All she had of her son was the smallest few threads of hair that one of the midwives had given her, tucked inside a small cellophane envelope and marked 'Baby Donnelly'.

As she blinked she wondered how much Sean knew, whether Jennifer had been in touch with her mother and father since he got back.

'I see you've given birth...' he asked.

'Oh, top marks for bloody good observation, Sean! You've remembered that, have you? That I was expecting your baby?' she clapped her hands slowly. 'Of course I've given birth, I'd have thought even you could work that out...'

'Was it a boy or a girl? Can I see it?'

'So you don't know? You haven't seen anyone?'

'I only got back to Southend yesterday. So? Boy or girl?'

Gracie thought for a moment before answering. She knew she would hate herself for sinking to his level but she knew what her response would be. As she looked at him and took in his guilt-free smile she hated him more than she had ever hated anyone, and she wanted him to suffer at least some of the pain she had.

'Yes, I had a boy. He was stillborn – he'd died in the womb, which was why I felt so ill...' she paused. 'Not that you cared.'

She knew she was wrong to mislead him and she also knew he was bound to find out but she wanted to hurt him. Really hurt him. 'Not that that's relevant, of course, as you were sure he wasn't yours anyway.'

Sean Donnelly's expression was one of genuine shock and for a moment she thought he might even cry.

'I never said that. Gracie, I'm so sorry, I can't believe this...'

'You did say that! You listened to Jennifer's poison and believed what you wanted to believe to justify putting your sexual wants above your unborn child, to justify sleeping with your own goddamned sister-in-law!'

At that point she could feel all the grief of the past few weeks simmering away just waiting to erupt, but then as she looked into his eyes she saw his face crumple. For a moment she felt guilty, but only for a moment; then she remembered exactly what he'd done to her. She decided she would tell him about Fay but first she wanted him to feel the same pain that she had.

'Now, I have to get back to work... Is there anything else?'

'I'm sorry, Gracie. I really am.' Sean stood up and walked towards her. 'I don't understand what happened to me; I had a mental blackout or something. The past few weeks have been hell and I was scared to come back but I want my life back to how it was before she came along. I'm sorry.'

'Evil is as evil does...' As Sean neared her she moved away from the ledge and stood upright.

'Gracie, I don't understand how all this happened, but surely we're both as bad as each other?'

'No, we're not, so don't try and tar me with the same brush. Now do me a turn; get out of this hotel and out of my life and never come back.'

He looked stunned and stared for a few moments before answering.

'No, I won't. I'm going to be around and I'll keep coming back until you forgive me. I love you, Gracie, I always have. We're right together – Jennifer isn't important.'

He leaned over to kiss her on the cheek and Gracie felt herself softening. At that moment she nearly gave in. He was her husband and the father to Fay, the little girl he was entitled to get to know and vice versa.

'Please Gracie? I'm so, so sorry I did what I did. You have to take me back. I'll forgive you if you forgive me...'

'Is it all over with you and Jennifer then?'

Sean's eyes darted from his feet to Gracie's face and back to his feet again before he smiled and held his hands out to her.

'Look, you have to help me here. Me mam's going to be spitting feathers. She's coming over next month with Yolande. I want everything to be back to normal for when she gets here, else she'll kill me for sure. And you as well...'

As Gracie looked at his expression, the reason for his apology fell into place. He didn't want his mother knowing exactly what he'd done. Gracie felt her resolve strengthen once again as she moved past him and walked over to the door.

'So this is because you want to appease your mother? It's not because of our marriage? Our baby?'

'Be reasonable, Gracie.' He put his palms together as if in prayer, a pleading gesture that made her feel quite ill. 'Please? We all make mistakes. You let me think you were a virgin, you never even told me that you'd had an illegitimate baby. For God's sake, are you surprised I went off the rails? Come on, darling...'

'But you seduced my sister, that's not the same as going out and getting drunk.'

'It was the other way round, I promise you it was. It was Jen who came after me and my mistake was that I fell for it...'

Sean's easy use of her sister's name told Gracie all she needed to know.

'Oh, that's enough. Goodbye, Sean,' she said as calmly as she could before she turned to leave the office.

'I'll be back...'

'Don't, we've got nothing to say to each other. Just get out.'

'Do our marriage vows not mean anything? It was a year ago, our first anniversary, how can you ignore that?'

'GET OUT...' she shouted at him.

Gracie pulled the door open for him and then stood stock-still as he went through it. She watched as he walked through the lobby and then turned and ran out of the building without another word.

As Sean left, Ruby came down the stairs.

'How did it go with him?' she asked.

'I can't talk about it, I'm so bloody furious. He's little boy sadness and blackmail, but one thing I do know is that I have to keep a close eye on Fay, because once he knows about her, he'll sure as hell be back.'

'You need to have a nice strong brandy, but I suppose a cuppa will have to do while we're working.'

'I'd better go up and tell Jeanette what's going on,' Gracie said, but then she stopped and shook her head as the full impact of what she'd just done hit her. 'My mother was right all along. I *am* a nasty piece of work.'

'Oh Gracie Grace, you know that's not true! Come through to the kitchen, we'll have a tea break and you can tell me what happened.'

'I can't talk about it, I have to think. I've just done something that makes me as bad as him. Or worse.'

Gracie's voice was filled with panic and as she looked at Ruby, she felt physically sick. She had denied her baby's very existence to the child's own father. The same as he had denied his daughter before she was born.

'I'll have to go after him...'

Gracie ran out of the hotel as fast as she could and looked both ways, but there was no sign of Sean Donnelly and she had no idea where he was staying.

At that moment she hated herself more than she hated him.

TWENTY-ONE

Ruby Blakeley was wearing unflattering dungarees and a headscarf knotted on top of her head in an attempt to keep the dust at bay as she mucked in to help with the refurbishment of the house next door to the Thamesview.

'I feel like a Land Girl,' she said to Johnnie. 'They used to work in and around Melton during the war and I thought they looked so unkempt, and yet here I am, looking like something the cat's dragged in...' She stood in front of him in an exaggerated ballet pose, arms high and one leg gracefully pointing to the side.

He reached out and touched the tip of her nose.

'You look gorgeous in whatever you wear, but I'm not too sure about the dusty face powder. It's a bit pale for you and it's turned your lips white...'

'Sheeesh... And have you looked in a mirror lately? You look as if you've suddenly aged fifty years, your hair is covered in dust and paint. But as Babs used to say, you can't make an omelette without breaking a few eggs. Or nails...' she held her hands out in front of her. 'Look, every single one of them is done in.'

'Tea break time, I think. You sit on this 'ere comfy orange box and I'll nip next door and fix us something,' Johnnie said.

'No, I'll go – you finish that last bit of wall

before Babs and George arrive. I really want them to be impressed with our efforts, both in here and next door. Anyway, I need to check they're doing what they should be doing in the kitchen. That new daily doesn't do much if I'm not waving the whip.' Ruby flicked an imaginary whip.

'Oh, they'll be impressed alright, we've all worked like navvies and it's coming on a treat in here! It'll soon be habitable downstairs, and the rest will come in time. Probably another year before the whole building is fit for what you want it for!' Johnnie replied.

'*We*,' emphasised Ruby. 'Fit for what *we* want it for...'

'No way is there a *we* in this business! I don't want to be labelled a gold-digger. I've already overheard talk about me being after your inheritance, especially from Sean. I think he thought he should have been part of the business.'

'Well, we both know that's not true so whoever's saying that can go and take a long walk down a short pier because they don't matter – especially when it's someone like Sean Donnelly saying it!' Ruby shook her head angrily. It infuriated her that people who knew nothing about her relationship with Johnnie Riordan, the love of her life from the moment she met him on her return to London from her evacuation, felt that they could pass judgement.

'Go and make the tea, woman – I've got men's work to do...' Johnnie laughed and pointed to the doorway that was missing a door, as Ruby curtsied. 'Yes, master...'

Ruby had been able to buy the vacant property

next to the hotel at a bargain basement price because it had fallen into such disrepair it wasn't habitable. The reclusive old lady who had lived and died there had no family that anyone knew of and had refused all offers of help from her neighbours in her final years. In fact, as best they knew, no one had even been allowed over the threshold since before the war.

In its day the house had been an expansive family home but when the owner's husband and two sons had all been killed in the First World War she had never recovered and had gradually closed up all the rooms as they were, spending her final years living in just one room at the back of the house. It had taken a long time to settle her affairs but finally the house had been put up for sale and, as Ruby and the Wheatons had already done their sums, they were ready to jump right in and buy it at a bargain price.

It had been a challenge to clear it out and do the very essential repairs but now it was starting to look like a home again. The body of the well-built house was still firmly standing so Johnnie had happily taken it on as his project, which was to convert it into an annexe to the main hotel.

Times had moved on and although there was still a market for a ladies-only establishment, there was a bigger market for family holidays in Southend, so the idea was for the annexe to become a basic bed and breakfast establishment for families, with a self-contained flat in the basement.

It was an ambitious project and it was taking up all of Ruby and the Wheatons' inheritance from

Leonora Wheaton, but it was a good investment. They were making progress and Ruby and Johnnie had welcomed the challenge.

'Here you are...' Ruby said as she arrived back from next door with a tray in her hands. 'Not quite Leonora style, but the best you're going to get, Master.'

Johnnie took it from her and they both perched on the newly sanded window seat that looked out over the shambles of a garden that was being used as a dumping ground for all the débris from the house.

'Thank God the labourers are back tomorrow.' Ruby sighed heavily. 'I have to get back to the hotel. Gracie's doing her best but it's hard with Fay. We may have to take on someone else soon.'

'She does well, considering. It's hard enough for me with two boys living with Sis in Walthamstow – I can't imagine working with a young baby in tow. I feel sorry for her, but you have to think about the hotel...'

'How are the boys doing?' Ruby asked. 'It seems forever since we've been able to sit down and talk properly. We're either flogging ourselves working or falling into bed dead beat.'

'I know, but there's an end in sight. Hopefully once this place is finished and the furore over poor Sadie has died down then we should be able to settle down, all of us. We can get married and have another child...'

Ruby laughed. 'That's a bit of a leap, Johnnie. But one day, maybe one day.'

'Definitely one day soon.' Johnnie leaned forward and kissed her. 'I love you, Ruby Blakeley.

Always have, always will...'

'Me too!' she smiled.

Ruby was happy with her life. She loved Johnnie, she loved the Thamesview and she wanted to have the opportunity to love Johnnie's two young sons as if they were her own; the only sadness was their own daughter Maggie, who had no idea of her true parentage. Maggie Wheaton looked on Ruby as her older sister and Johnnie as a sort of uncle.

In the beginning it had been hard for Ruby to even see Maggie as part of another family but gradually she had adjusted and she really did sometimes forget that she had given birth to her, that she was her natural mother.

Ruby and Johnnie had both had a hard time of it but they were starting to come out the other side of the trauma that had surrounded Johnnie's ill-fated marriage to Sadie, his volatile and unpredictable young wife. No one knew for certain but it seemed that in a fit of pique, she had made a dramatic suicide bid that had succeeded because the person she was expecting to arrive and save her, her errant boyfriend of the moment, had stood her up.

Sadie was found the following day in her best dress and high heels, wearing full make-up, lying on the floor with her head inside the gas oven. It had been traumatic for everyone but especially for Johnnie, who had two sons with her, two very young boys who had lost their mother because of a moment of madness.

Ruby Blakeley and Johnnie Riordan had a long history together going back to when she first returned to her family after her wartime evacuation to Cambridgeshire in 1945. It had been a brief relationship but it culminated in Ruby becoming pregnant on the one occasion they had got carried away. In fear of her older brothers' reaction she had run away back to Cambridgeshire and the Wheatons before being taken to Southend, where no one knew her to have the baby. Maggie. The newborn had been adopted by Babs and George but it had been five years before Johnnie and Ruby met up again and he discovered they had had a child together. In the intervening years he'd married Sadie and had two children with her.

'Will Betty let the boys come and live with us now, do you think?' Ruby asked.

'They're my sons, she can't stop them but I'd like it to be with her blessing. Betty, Tony and their kids are the only family the boys and I have got now Mum has passed on... Apart from you and Maggie but they don't ... can't know that.' Johnnie paused and smiled at Ruby. 'It's a bloody shame that she disapproves of you and me being together, especially as it's because of Sadie. You and I did nothing wrong, it was Sadie who was unfaithful but she became a saint when she died and we can't change that,' he said sadly.

Ruby took his hand and smiled sympathetically. 'She'll come round soon enough. She loves you and time heals, I know that more than anyone! Meanwhile we'd better get this up and running as quick as we can then!'

Ruby jumped up, touched her toes a couple of times then flexed her arm muscles, exaggerating the movement. 'Let's get building!'

Johnnie grabbed her with both arms and hugged her tight.

'Okay. Back to work here for me and back to the kitchen next door for you. You're right and one day...'

'One day...' Ruby smiled and then she hesitated.

'Before I go, though, there's something I want to ask you about, but to do it I have to break a confidence...'

'This is to do with Gracie and Sean, isn't it?' Johnnie guessed.

'Sort of, but more Gracie. Promise me you won't say anything? I shouldn't be saying this but I don't know what to do...'

'Try me,' he said reassuringly.

For the first time, Ruby told Johnnie about the day she and Gracie had met Edward, Harry and Louisa at the beach, and about Gracie's reaction to Edward.

'The day she married Sean she gave me the ring and card he had given her and told me to send it back. But I didn't...'

'Uh-oh.' Johnnie pulled a face.

'I just didn't know how to do it, what to say. Oh, I don't know, but I just didn't.'

'And...?'

'And then after the wedding a letter came in the post. It was addressed to me and there was a short note and a sealed envelope for Gracie.' Ruby pulled a guilty face.

'And I bet you didn't tell her about that either? Oh, Ruby, I can see where this is going...'

'You're right, I didn't tell her, and now I'm wondering if I should have.' Ruby looked at Johnnie. 'I don't know what the hell to do. She deserves something nice to happen but would bringing up the name of the one she called "the right one" be the right thing?'

'But if this was all that time ago then he might be married. At the very least he'll be back in Africa, like you said.'

'So?'

'So what?'

'I'm asking your advice here, Mr Riordan. Help me! Should I tell her about it? Should I give her the letter after all this time?'

'I suppose it depends on why.'

'In what way?'

'Why do you think you should give it to her now when you didn't back then?'

'I don't know...' Ruby said thoughtfully. 'I just thought he might make her happy?'

'And if it all goes pear-shaped then she'll be taking another kicking.'

'Oh bugger it, Johnnie, you're too logical for me! I'll have to think a bit more...'

'Sorry, love. Just think about what you'd want if it was you.'

Ruby smiled and said a silent thank you for having him.

'I'll think about it, but now I really do have to get back.'

Johnnie Riordan kissed her on the cheek and watched her leave, but instead of getting on with the renovation he sat down again and thought about Sadie and his two sons.

When he married the unstable and volatile Sadie he knew he wasn't in love with her, but Ruby had disappeared from his life and he was persuaded into it by Sadie's surrogate father Bill Morgan, a local villain with a fearsome reputation who was also Johnnie's employer and landlord.

Despite knowing that Johnnie had caught Sadie in bed with someone else, she had told a good tale to her father who had taken her side. Johnnie had lost everything in one fell swoop. He had taken his two young sons, Martin and Paul, and moved back in with his sister.

Her suicide was a low point in his life and he knew he would always feel guilty about it because of his sons. Just the thought of them growing up without their mother made him feel sad for them but he also felt angry with himself for not anticipating that Sadie would self-destruct so dramatically.

He stood up and went back into the hotel.

Suddenly he had the urge to go and see his sons.

TWENTY-TWO

'Gracie, once I've washed my hair and changed, can we talk? There's something that's been bothering me for a while...'

Gracie was busy with the Brasso, polishing the handles and finger plates on the doors that led off the lobby but she stopped in her tracks.

'That sounds a bit frightening. You're not going to sack me, are you? I know it's hard with Fay and everything but I don't how I'd manage without this job, especially as I live here as well. Oh God, you want the flat for you and Johnnie, don't you?'

Gracie stared at Ruby, her eyes wide, her expression fearful.

'Oh stop it,' Ruby said fiercely. 'As if I would. I couldn't manage without you – or Fay! No, there's something I have to tell you that might make you a bit peed off with me ... but I want you to remember that if I did the wrong thing, then I did it with the best of intentions, I promise.'

'Now you're really scaring me,' Gracie exclaimed. 'You have to tell me right now, even if you do look like a walking bag of flour!'

The hotel was quiet at that time of day so the lobby was empty, apart from Henry who was sitting behind the desk reading his newspaper, being a presence just in case anyone needed anything.

Henry was a tiny, wiry man with a handlebar moustache and a thatch of pure white hair, which he kept under control with vast quantities of Brylcreem. A widower and a pensioner who was well into his seventies, he loved his job and spent far more time at Thamesview than he was paid for. Although he was slowing down with age he was reliable and popular and could still turn his hand to most things. But most of all he was quietly spoken and his manners were impeccable, so he went down well with the lady guests.

'Are you alright for a bit longer, Henry?' Ruby asked him.

He looked over the top of his glasses. 'Aye.'

'Can you tell us if Fay wakes? She's in her carrycot in the office, she's only just gone off...' Gracie said.

'Aye,' he said as he looked down again.

Ruby and Gracie exchanged glances and smiles. It was a standing joke that Henry never wasted a word.

'Shall we go into the garden? I shouldn't be around people, I look such a mess...' Ruby said.

They took the shortcut through the kitchen and, as there were no guests out there, went over and sat on the wooden garden bench. Gracie could feel the now-familiar anxiety building in her chest as she waited for Ruby to say what she had to say.

'Okay... Can I start by mentioning the name Edward Woodfield?' Ruby said cautiously, watching for a reaction from Gracie. 'I know you said don't mention his name again and I haven't up to now, but I've been thinking about this...'

'You don't think he's anything to do with this

234

mess, do you? I didn't do anything with him. I left him that day and never saw or heard from him again. It was a bit of stupidity but it wasn't the same as what Sean did to me...' Gracie said defensively.

'No, no, I never thought that at all, but look, Gracie, there's something I didn't tell you. A few weeks after you'd got married a letter arrived here; I think it must have got lost in the post because of how it was worded. But anyway, it was addressed to me but there was another one for you. It was from Edward. I didn't give it to you because you'd already asked me to send his ring back so I knew you wouldn't want it. But now...'

'Now what? Why are you telling me? Have you still got it?' Gracie fired the questions, not really knowing why she wanted to know.

'I've got the letters and the address card *and* the ring. Everything is together in an envelope in the back of the safe. I didn't know what to do with it and I didn't want anyone else finding it, but now I think I should give it to you to decide what you want to do.'

Gracie looked at her friend but didn't say anything. Her emotions were in turmoil as she thought about the man she had met so fleetingly, but who had made such a big impression on her. She leaned back and closed her eyes to the sun.

Although she had occasionally thought about him, Gracie had tried her best to put Edward Woodfield away in her memory and she had mostly succeeded. It had been a harmless interlude with a handsome stranger who had momentarily turned her head. It was simply a swan-song before she married Sean and there was nothing more to it.

Gracie had known then that Sean wasn't the right one, that their relationship wasn't like the crazy love affairs of the cinema screens, but she had loved him and she had genuinely thought they would be right together in a comfortable married way. But it hadn't been enough, she realised with hindsight, because she wasn't in love with him and, as it turned out, Sean was never in love with her either. They had both settled for the ease of second best.

The moment Ruby mentioned Edward's name Gracie was back on the beach that sunny summer's day, and as his name returned to her consciousness she realised she could see him as clearly as if he was standing right in front of her. It was as if she had been given permission to think about him again.

Gracie Donnelly had blocked Edward Woodfield from her mind for so long but suddenly, she was back there with him.

'You know, maybe Sean was right about me, even if he didn't really know it,' she said, shaking herself back to the present. 'Maybe I *was* the one at fault; I did do him wrong, didn't I? I should never have married him – not when I could feel like that about someone else?'

'It could have worked without your sister.'

'I think if it hadn't been her it would have been someone else. I suppose I might have done what so many women do and turned a blind eye to it but the rot set in when I didn't tell him the truth in the first place. You told me that, didn't you?'

'Now you make me sound like a know-it-all,' Ruby smiled.

Gracie sat forward again. 'You all told me I should have told him about my first baby and I ignored you. I thought I knew best and I never thought anything like this could happen. It must have been hell for him to find out that way...'

'Sorry, Gracie Grace, but he was already at it with your sister by then, that's how he found out! He's put the blame on you to protect himself.' Ruby paused. 'But back to Edward...'

Gracie stood up. 'I'll be back in a minute, I must check on Fay.'

'Henry would have called you.' Ruby called after her, but Gracie didn't answer, just turned away and walked quickly to the office. She put her head round the door to check on Fay, who was sleeping in her carrycot. Again she gazed in wonder at her tiny daughter, the baby she had dreamt about having for so long. Gracie loved her with an intensity that she could never have imagined before she was born but her love for Fay was tinged with sadness at the loss of her baby son.

Ruby walked up behind and looked over her shoulder at Fay as well.

'You did what you thought was the right thing for both of you, and it would have stayed right if your sister hadn't decided to screw up everyone's life.'

'But it all comes back to me really, doesn't it? If I'd told Sean right in the very beginning I wouldn't be in this mess. If he hadn't married me it wouldn't have been the end of the world. I was just so bloody determined not to be the old maid...'

'Well, it's done now and as Leonora used to say, *You have to work with what you have, not what you want.* You might not have everything else at the moment, but you do have Fay.'

Ruby enunciated the words carefully, using the clipped tone that Leonora Wheaton had used when she was passing on her tips for life. 'But back to what I was saying. I still have the letters, if you want to have a look. I put them away at the time because I knew you wouldn't want them, but now...'

'But now what? Now I'm on my own with a baby? Can you imagine Mr Country Estate, works in Africa, Woodfield being interested now?' Gracie laughed. 'I feel like Leonora must have done as she watched her ships sail out of sight; I think that ship has long sailed. And anyway, I didn't even know him. He could be a mass murderer for all we know!'

'Give me a minute...' Ruby said.

Gracie watched as Ruby went over to the far wall, moved a rather dull painting of an Edwardian lady and opened the safe where she kept all her personal papers. She pulled out an envelope. 'Here, take it and do what you want with it, but I knew I had to tell you.'

Gracie picked it up and stuffed it in her pocket. 'You do know I'm not angry with you, don't you?' she said, turning to Ruby. 'I'm angry with myself. I've got it all wrong once again but as you said, at least this time I've got my baby and for that I wouldn't change a thing.'

'I know.' Ruby smiled. 'I tell you what, you go upstairs for a break, I'll keep an eye on Fay. I've got a mountain of paperwork to do...'

As she spoke, Johnnie knocked on the door. 'Am I interrupting?'

'No, I was just leaving.' Gracie smiled.

She went up to the flat, kicked her shoes off and curled her legs up on the sofa.

Then she took the letters Ruby had given her out of her pocket.

She read the one addressed to Ruby first and then looked at the envelope addressed to her, knowing that once she let the genie out the bottle there would be no putting it back.

As Gracie looked at it, she felt a surge of guilt over Sean. Even though she had been faithful, she had betrayed him in so many ways. She hadn't been honest about her past and she had married him knowing that she had feelings for someone else that she hadn't explored.

TWENTY-THREE

Saffron Walden

Edward Woodfield looked up from his newspaper and smiled at his sister-in-law, who had just joined him at the table.

'Good morning, Louisa. Nice day, isn't it?'

'I hope it stays like this. I need to do some sun-bathing – I'm looking so pasty and wan. We should all be down in the South of France with Ma and Pa.'

'If you can persuade Harry, then good for you – he's not really a sun person...'

'Then we have to educate him. Could you pass the toast, please?'

Edward smiled at her and passed the toast rack with a flourish.

'Now you're captive, I have a question for you. I was wondering about it last night. Do you know what happened to my car after the accident?'

'Ooooh, that's a random question out of the blue, the car...'

'I know. I've only really just thought about it, it's been a strange old year! Did Pa send it to the scrap yard? I loved that car, not to mention my favourite tweed jacket that was on the back seat!'

'I don't know. I think the car was dragged up here by one of Pa's tractors and dumped in the old stables, but I don't know if it's still there. Your

240

things were bundled up into a case and, I think, put into your room but there was a lot of blood so the jolly old jacket may have had its day.'

'I'll have to go and take a look. Do you think the car was past redemption?'

'I didn't see it but it was really smashed up from what I heard. You rammed it to smithereens! That poor old tree will take yonks to recover, but it's still there as far as I know. I bet Hooper will be able to tell you all about it, he knows everything. Do you want me to ask him?'

'No, it's really not important, I was just ruminating over things, remembering the last time I drove the poor old dear.'

They were sitting out on the patio of the house in Saffron Walden. Edward and Harry's parents were both away in France and Harry had already finished his breakfast and gone off to check the tennis court, ready for a game with his wife.

'I guessed you'd been thinking about the accident,' Louisa said sympathetically. 'You were really shouting out in your sleep last night as if you were reliving it. We heard you as we went to bed. Do you remember what you were dreaming about?'

'No. How would I? I was asleep.' Edward's tone was sharp but he smiled nonetheless.

Over time he'd learnt to accept Louisa and her forthright approach to everything. She was never subtle but she was never phoney either and she had been a good friend and support to him since the accident. Edward appreciated it, but every so often, when she was in full flow, he just wanted to run away and hide from her directness. He had always found it difficult to discuss anything personal.

'Well, I know that, you old silly, but sometimes we remember our dreams and nightmares the next day,' she smiled patiently. 'But you sounded so distraught. I listened outside your door in case you were in trouble but you calmed down again. Harry said you're bound to still have nightmares after everything you went through...'

Edward shook his head. 'Harry understands, does he? I doubt it...'

'Don't be so mean about your brother!' Louisa wagged an index finger at him. 'Harry was worried sick about you after the accident, as were we all. You nearly died. Now get back to your newspaper and don't be such an old misery-guts. The sooner you get yourself back to the wilds of Africa, the better!' She slapped his hand playfully, making Edward laugh.

'You've become such a tormenting little sister. I really don't know how Harry puts up with you.'

'Because he loves me of course, and he also loves you, so don't you forget it!'

After the car accident it had been ten days before Edward Woodfield had come out of the coma, and then many months of rehabilitation to recover physically from the injuries. The metal plate in his head and the pins in his leg still caused him discomfort, but the agonising pains he had suffered in the aftermath of surgery had finally gone.

However the scar that ran across his face was a much more permanent reminder of the accident that nearly cost him his life, because every time he looked in the mirror it was the first thing he saw, even though he'd grown a full beard and moustache to cover most of it. He wasn't sure how he'd cope with so much facial hair when he went back to the climate of Africa but in the meantime he felt happier with his face covered.

As well as disguising his facial scars he had adjusted his way of walking to accommodate his slight limp and the scars on his legs and chest from both the accident and the surgery were hidden out of sight when he was dressed. One of the worst things for him during his recovery had been the kindly words and patronising head patting from all and sundry. They meant well but Edward found his dependency excruciatingly embarrassing.

During his time convalescing he had sat around a lot and put on weight. His face had filled out and his belt had been let out a couple of notches but he didn't mind too much about that, he knew once he was active again and back in the equatorial heat he would soon get back to normal.

He was aware how fortunate he was that his family had ensured he had the best private medical and nursing care, because without it he may well have lost a leg, if not his life. He was grateful he was alive and functioning, but a year on and he was going crazy in the family home; hence declaring himself fit and well, and ready to go back to West Africa.

The sprawling country house in Saffron Walden was not only home to his parents but also to Harry and Louisa. The shape of the building meant it naturally divided into three sections and the family made the most of that, with the parents having the accommodation at one end, Harry and Louisa at the other, and Edward in the smaller mid-section.

When everyone was in residence they would eat together as a family and socialise in the drawing room and the gardens, but apart from that they all respected each other's space even though there were no formal boundaries.

There was also a cottage in the grounds, where Mrs Hooper the housekeeper and her husband lived. The middle-aged couple had worked for the Woodfields since before the war and between them did everything to keep the whole property, inside and out, in good working order.

Edward's parents and brother were horrified at the thought of him going back to Africa but he was determined to return and get on with his life as soon as possible. He loved his job but it was also the easy, outdoor lifestyle which he missed. He often thought affectionately about the large colonial house he had shared with two other engineers, Paulo who was Italian and Olivier, a Frenchman. They were all single men of a similar age who worked for the same company and they got on well together as housemates, despite being different nationalities. It was a good life but one he could lose if he wasn't cleared fit to return at his company medical examination.

The company had contacted him the previous week to ask after his health and to tell him that his job was still open and so was his accommodation, but not for long. His temporary stand-in was due to return to England and if Edward wasn't fully fit then the posting would have to be filled by someone else.

He had to get back soon if he wanted to keep his job but he also wanted to do so. 'Joking aside, Louisa, I'm ready to go. This has been a long hard road for everyone and it's time we all got back to some sort of normality,' Edward said.

'Oh, Teddy darling, I'll hate to see you go back to Africa but I know you want to. How will you get on if you need any healthcare while you're there? Is the company okay about your accident?'

'They are so short of qualified people wanting to work there they're actually trying to get me back as soon as possible – I just have to be checked over. And anyway, I've recovered as much as I'm ever going to: I'm almost back to normal. It'll be okay and it's the best thing for me. I'm going nuts here, no offence of course!'

'None taken, my darling brother-in-law, none taken!' Louisa laughed. She walked to the back of his chair and ruffled his hair. 'Now, I'm off to get changed for a game of tennis with Harry. Do you want me to check on your car? I'm sure I can find out about it from Hooper. Knowing him, he's probably put it back together again in his spare time.'

Once again Edward felt bad that he had doubted Louisa because she had been a real friend to him during his difficult convalescence. She had welcomed him being a disabled best man in a wheelchair, and was forever popping over from their side of the house to sit and chat with him. His parents and Harry floated about as happily as they always had, but it was Louisa who had been his greatest support and Edward had eventually realised that she was really a very pleasant and knowledgeable young woman, who genuinely loved Harry despite his lack of focus or ambition.

Despite the passage of time, Edward still couldn't quite get his thoughts away from Gracie. During the darkest moments in the early days of his recovery, he would wake in the night and see her standing at the end of his bed in her wedding dress, looking at him.

He knew it was the madness of painkillers making him hallucinate but in a strange way he missed it when the images of Gracie went away and were replaced by nightmares of the crash itself.

Edward still didn't remember much about the accident or the immediate aftermath, but he did know why he had lost concentration. He had gone to Southend and seen Gracie McCabe get married, and then driven home at speed. He remembered racing along, going faster and faster...

When he had first come out of the coma he had remembered nothing about the accident or the few days either side of it, but as he recovered things came back to him slowly, and as each day passed he remembered something else; mostly little things but he was getting there.

But no matter how hard he tried he couldn't stop thinking about Gracie McCabe. Something was niggling at him, something tucked away in his memory he couldn't grasp. No matter how hard he tried, he just couldn't remember.

He was still deep in thought when Louisa bounced back out into the garden, dressed in her tennis whites and sporting a couple of racquets.

'Righty ho, I'm off to the courts, are you coming to watch?'

'Not a chance!' Edward laughed. 'I've decided I'm going to find Hooper and find out about the car and my belongings. I can't even remember what was in there... Maybe just a few items in the glove box...'

'Oh, talking about that, I've just remembered something; I know you were still in hospital and Pa said there was a letter amid all the debris in the car. He posted it for you...'

The letter. Edward had completely forgotten the letter he had written to Gracie and addressed to the Thamesview. He had decided against posting it and then he had crashed his car...

'Did you see the letter?' he asked, as casually as he could.

'No, but Pa said it was addressed to a hotel on the coast. I think he thought you were planning a dirty weekend with someone. You know what Pa's like, he was quite impressed.' She winked as she laughed. 'I don't know why he posted it, probably because it helped to do normal things when everyone was so worried about you.'

'I don't remember it, so it can't have been important.' Edward didn't look at Louisa.

'I'm sure it wasn't,' Louisa said dismissively. 'Do you want to walk with me if you're going to search out Hooper?'

Edward pulled himself up out of the chair. 'That's a good idea, I need some exercise.'

Although he was almost back to normal in everything else, the events surrounding the actual crash were still a mystery to him. He remembered going to Southend; he remembered seeing Gracie at her wedding but the drive home was a

247

foggy blur.

He thought about the letter and tried to remember what he'd written but it wouldn't formulate in his mind so he dismissed it, knowing from experience that it was the best way for all the snippets of memories to return.

The old stable block on the edge of the property was no longer in use so it had become Hooper's enclave, a place where he stored all the garden equipment and his tools, but it was also a haven for him; it was his own great big personal potting shed.

Edward could sense his reluctance to let anyone else inside his territory but he wanted to see the wreckage of his car. He hoped it would jog his memory about the reason for the accident.

'It's in here, Mr Edward,' the man said. 'We brought it up and it's not been touched apart from hosing the blood off. Nasty accident it was hitting that tree, not like you at all, what with you normally being the sensible one...'

Edward smiled. 'I know. I've got the scars to prove it!'

He had been expecting a wreck, but when Hooper pulled the tarpaulin back he gasped out loud. His beloved MG was barely recognisable as a car at all; but it wasn't that which shocked him. It was the realisation that it was a miracle he had survived at all. As he looked at it, he couldn't quite believe how he had lived.

He walked around the mangled wreckage, staring at every part of it, touching it almost reverently and remembering.

'Oh my dear lord, Hooper, how did I ever survive that? Someone was certainly watching over me that day...'

'Yes sir,' Hooper said. 'You used up one of your lives that day, now you have to make the most of the others.'

'You're right, I was incredibly lucky.' He patted the man on the shoulder. 'And now we have to get rid of this reminder. If you can make use of any of the parts, please do, and then arrange for it to be disposed of. I've seen and remembered all I need to.'

For the first time since he was a small boy Edward Woodfield could feel tears welling up in his eyes. He blinked rapidly and turned away from Hooper, who was still shaking his head at the wreckage.

As he walked out into the sunshine he heard laughter so he walked back across the grounds and stood under the cover of a tree watching Louisa and Harry running around the tennis court. He watched for a while and then headed back to the house. The weight had been lifted, the last memory recalled and it was time for him to put Gracie McCabe right out of his mind and get on with the life he had been given back.

TWENTY-FOUR

'Hello girls, did you have a good journey? Oh, it's so nice to see you both again!' Babs Wheaton was standing on the garden path as Gracie and Ruby got out of the car. She held out her arms for a hug.

'Oh, and you too, Aunty Babs, it's been too long...' Ruby said, rushing forward to hug the woman who had been a second mother to her since the day they met, when she was a ten-year-old evacuee during the war and was billeted with the Wheatons.

'How are you, Gracie? And Fay, where is she?' she asked Gracie as she looked towards the car.

'In her carrycot in the back, I'll just get her out,' Gracie said. 'She's slept all the way – I think the long drive soothed her, or else she was bored.'

Babs Wheaton peered into the carrycot. 'Oh bless her, she's beautiful! Now in you all come. I know you said not to, but I've laid out just a little spread for you. Very little, I promise, and I've got presents here for Fay, just a few little bits.'

The woman laughed and held her thumb and forefinger apart to indicate something very small.

'Oh God, that means the full Wheaton buffet and the table heaving under the weight of food and gifts, doesn't it?' Ruby laughed.

'Well, you've had a long drive, you're bound to be hungry and there'll be five of us to eat it. Six, if we count Fay.'

Gracie took the metal transporter out of the boot, unfolded it and carefully placed the carrycot onto it. 'She's still asleep so we may just get time to catch up before she needs feeding. She does cry a lot, so be prepared.'

'I think they all do that. She'll grow out of it soon enough, Maggie certainly did.'

'Is Maggie here?' Ruby asked as she looked around.

'No, but she will be. She's gone down to the vicarage with George. I thought it would be nice for us to chat for a bit before she flies in like the proverbial whirlwind and dominates the conversation. She's such a chatterbox now and so very clever. She's doing really well at school.'

Although they were not related Babs and Ruby looked as if they could be mother and daughter. Both were tall and slender, with straight-backed confidence, striking colouring and quick smiles. All the time Ruby had suffered problems with her real mother and her errant brothers, Babs and George Wheaton had been there to pick up the pieces. It was having the love and support of the Wheatons that had enabled her to broker the peace and rebuild her relationship with her own estranged family. And now the couple were offering help and support to Gracie at a time when she really needed it.

The three women walked up the path to the back door of the house, which was also the doctor's surgery, and went straight into the kitchen. As Gracie wheeled the carrycot into a quiet corner behind the door, Babs turned up the heat under the kettle, then all three sat down at the well-worn farmhouse table which had been the venue for so many of the traumas in Ruby's life.

Gracie sensed the emotion rising in her friend and touched her hand in support. She knew it was always difficult for her in the build-up to seeing Maggie, her daughter. It was hard and emotional but something that Ruby had to bear for her daughter's sake in the long run.

But this visit had a dual purpose. It gave Ruby the opportunity to see Maggie fleetingly but she was also transporting Gracie to the Wheatons', where she would be staying for some rest and recuperation.

It was just a couple of days before that Gracie had been persuaded that she had to take George and Babs Wheaton up on their offer of a short break. She was struggling with Fay, not because the baby was a problem, but because she herself was becoming neurotic. Fay only had to sniffle and Gracie went into a panic, which was quickly followed by a deep depression at her inability to cope with being a mother, the one thing she'd desperately wanted for so long.

She'd done her best but when the hotel was full and they were rushed off their feet, she just couldn't cope with working and looking after Fay. Jeanette was going out more with her new boy-friend and Ruby was either working in the hotel or helping Johnnie Riordan with the renovations to the house next door. All of them had done their best, but it wasn't enough to take the pressure off Gracie.

Everything had come to a head when she had

been helping Ruby serve breakfast and she heard Fay crying in the distance. Instead of finishing what she was doing and then going to see to her, Gracie had lost concentration. The two full breakfast plates in her hands had plummeted straight to the floor while she'd run to the office, only to find Fay safe and sound in her carrycot, albeit a bit fretful.

If Fay cried then Gracie panicked; if she didn't cry then Gracie panicked, until she felt she was going mad. She did her best to cope but then Ruby had intervened.

'Gracie, you can't carry on like this, you're worn out, and it's my fault for working you so hard. If you don't want to go to your parents for a break then you have to take Fay and go and let Babs and George look after you. They can do much more for you than I can.'

'Are you throwing me out? I can't face going to Mum and Dad's, not while I don't know where Jennifer is and what she's up to. I know Mum has such a soft spot for her, imagine if she turned up?'

'Of course I'm not throwing you out, but you're cracking up and you need some help. It's been a horrible few months for you so I'm not surprised but you need a rest.' Ruby had smiled reassuringly but Gracie was still irrationally suspicious of her motives.

'Look, Babs will love to look after you both and you'll have Uncle George there for Fay, so you can relax. Just go for a week or so.'

Gracie had tried to refuse but Ruby wasn't having it.

'What about Sean?'

'Oh Gracie,' Ruby said, her frustration badly disguised. 'What do you mean, what about Sean? What *about* him?'

'I still haven't told him about Fay. I have to tell him as soon as I can, for her sake.'

'It's you that's important, you and Fay. Sean can just get on with it for the moment. I mean, he's not even bothered to tell you where he is. No, we need to get you well again, we all want the old Gracie back. Please go and stay with them, just for a week or so. A week away from everything that's going on here...'

'But Sean...'

'Stop it! You're going.'

'Rubeeeeeeeeeee,' the sound of Maggie Wheaton's screech echoed ahead of her. She ran in through the door and hurled herself straight at Ruby, the woman she had always known as a big sister.

George and Babs Wheaton had been unable to have children of their own, so when Ruby had arrived to stay for a while as a ten-year-old evacuee from London they had delighted in having her. As a result they became like second parents to her – and then they had adopted Maggie, and the bond had become unbreakable.

'Oh my missy, you've grown so much since I last saw you and that was just a few weeks ago! You're going to be the tallest in the family, I can tell...' Ruby said as she hugged her tight and sniffed her hair. She was convinced that the smell had never changed and it always reminded her of the new-born Maggie in her crib at the hospital, the day after she was born. Ruby nuzzled and hugged her again but the child was already looking over at Gracie.

'Gracie, can I see Fay? Mummy said you're both going to stay here. Will I be able to hold her and take her for a walk?'

'We'll definitely be taking her for a walk together while she's here,' Babs said. 'Gracie is here to have a rest and we're going to help look after Fay. That'll be fun, won't it?' She looked from Maggie to Ruby. 'It'll be nice to have a baby in the house again.'

'I'm still your baby though, aren't I, Mummy?' Maggie said, with her bottom lip very slightly stuck out.

'Of course you are, you'll always be our baby, but Fay's still helpless so we'll have to do everything for her,' Babs laughed, but with her eyes on Ruby, ever aware of her sensitivities.

Maggie looked puzzled. 'She's not staying forever, is she? I don't think we want another baby here forever...'

'Of course not forever,' Ruby smiled and tousled her hair. 'Gracie is her mummy...'

Gracie watched the interaction and, knowing what she did, could easily interpret the hidden conversation, which saddened her all over again. It may not be the ideal situation but at least Ruby could see her firstborn and watch her grow and have a relationship with her.

Gracie's firstborn was gone forever.

Ruby stayed long enough to have some time with Maggie and enjoy the buffet spread before heading off home, leaving Gracie and Fay to be tended and spoilt by Babs and George.

'I'll do the same for you one day, when you have your babies, or even when Johnnie's boys come to stay. I'll run round after you, the same as you have for me...' Gracie said as they walked back to the car.

'I know you will. Now you go and make the most of being cosseted; you deserve it and George and Babs are brilliant at it! I wish I was staying as well.' She hugged her friend. 'Next time we'll come together.'

Gracie reciprocated the hug but she didn't answer, for fear of her over-sensitive emotions taking control of her again.

Gracie was resting in her room and enjoying the quiet solitude that she had had so little of for so long. George had prescribed her a tonic to help her relax so she was feeling calm and a little detached as she sat curled up in the big armchair by the window, flicking through one of the magazines that Babs had given her.

For just over a week all Gracie had done was eat and sleep, and take long walks around the lanes that spiralled out from the small village. Usually she went alone and would take the shortcut across the fields, down to the small tree-edged river that was always dotted with fishermen and picknicking couples. It was so quiet and peaceful that it gave her time to think and get her head into some sort of order, ready for the return to Southend.

She felt so much better that she almost didn't want to go home, but she knew she had to go back to work to earn the living she needed to support herself and her daughter. She couldn't rely on Ruby forever.

Babs and Maggie had taken Fay with them to the duck-pond in the big old Silver Cross pram that used to be Maggie's and George was busy in the village surgery on the other side of the house so she was all alone, and savouring the solitude.

Dr George Wheaton was officially retired, but he still kept his hand in by supervising the new doctor, an affable young man who was living in what used to be the nurse's quarters. Now there was no longer a resident nurse it had seemed the right time to let someone else start taking over, but George found it hard to let go of the reins so he always found something to do to keep him on the surgery side of the interconnecting doors.

Gracie sighed happily, put the magazine down and slowly stretched out her arms and legs like a satisfied cat. She felt so much better, both physically and mentally, from having the break but she knew it was time to get her life back into some sort of order.

Deciding to write a few notes for herself as prompts for what she had to do when she went back to Southend she delved into her handbag and pulled out her diary. But as she did so she also pulled out the envelope that contained the sealed letter from Edward Woodfield, the letter to Ruby, the signet ring and the card with his phone number on it.

She took the ring out and looked at it carefully before rolling it around in the palm of her hand a few times and then, without really thinking, slipped it onto each of her fingers in turn. When she put it on the third finger of her left hand it slid right over the top of her wedding ring. Guilt washed over her and she quickly put it back in the envelope. She smiled as she read the letter addressed to Ruby, which was just a nicely written and very polite note asking her to please give the enclosed letter to Gracie. Putting it to one side, she then studied the envelope of the other while she decided whether to open it or throw it away. The envelope was grubby and crinkled, with a few stains on both sides and a rip on one corner, but it was still well-sealed and she wondered what it might say.

Gracie placed it almost reverently on the small table beside the chair and closed her eyes. She wondered long and hard about what the contents could be, before picking it up and studying it all over again. She looked at the way it was addressed, she studied every curve of every letter, the date and time of the postmark, even the faint dirty fingerprints around the edge of the envelope.

She peered at every detail, until she couldn't put it off any longer and opened it slowly and carefully. She looked at it for another few moments, before pulling the flap right back and taking the note out, all the time trying hard to preserve it as it was.

She read the contents several times; over and over again, interpreting all the words in several different ways.

Gracie wondered how she would have reacted if she had received it before she walked down the aisle to marry Sean Donnelly.

TWENTY-FIVE

My Dear Gracie,
I'm writing this after our meeting to make sure you know that I meant every word I said to you. I saw you in the distance at the funfair, I watched your enjoyment, I envied your joie de vivre and I knew right then and there that I wanted to marry you.

As I write the words down and read them back it seems like madness and so out of character for me. I can't believe I'm saying it, but it's true. Love at first sight may be a cliché but that is what I felt the moment I saw you. I know that you felt the same, I could see it in your eyes, but I could also see that you were torn between the familiar and the unknown and that maybe the unknown, me, was just a step too far.

I can't bear the thought that it's too late, but whatever happens I'll forever remember the day by the sea with Gracie McCabe with much affection. If anything changes in your life then I hope I'll be the person you get in touch with.
With love
Edward

After the letters were safely back in their envelopes, Gracie took the card that Edward had given her that day and went downstairs. She checked that no one was around, then she went through to the hall, closed all the doors, picked up the telephone receiver and, without hesitation, made the phone call. Her heart was thumping and her fingers were crossed as she waited to be connected.

'Can I speak to Edward Woodfield, please?' she asked when the phone was answered by someone who she assessed to be an older woman. She wondered if it was his mother.

'Who shall I say is calling?'

She thought quickly. 'Miss McCabe.'

'One moment please.'

'Hello. Edward Woodfield speaking'

'Hello. I don't know if you still remember me, it's Gracie from Southend? We met on the beach...'

'Of course I remember you. How are you?'

At the sound of his voice she was back on the beach, still single and optimistic about her future. It seemed a lifetime ago and when Gracie thought about it she found it hard to believe that it was only a year and so much had happened.

'I'm well...' she paused. 'And you? I wasn't really expecting you to be in England, I just phoned on the off-chance.'

'I'm here and yes, I'm well also...'

The silence that followed seemed to last forever, with neither knowing what to say next.

'I don't know why I phoned you. I probably shouldn't have, I didn't think properly,' Gracie said nervously, wondering for the first time if Edward was also married. It was quite possible.

'But you did telephone me, so let's talk. Are you still living in Southend?' he asked.

'Yes, but at the moment I'm staying with Ruby's relatives in Cambridgeshire for a few days.'

'That's not too far from me. I could drive and

260

meet you. We could catch up. Just as friends, of course.'

Her head said '*I can't do that, I'm a married woman...*' but her mouth refused to cooperate. She wanted to see him again. 'Yes. Just as friends,' she replied.

It was a short and superficial conversation that didn't touch on anything remotely personal, but by the time Gracie ended the call she had arranged to meet Edward the next day on the outskirts of the village to go for a drive into the nearby town for lunch.

That night, despite the peace and quiet of the village and Fay fast asleep beside her, she couldn't sleep. It wasn't just excitement that kept her awake; rather it was a gnawing guilt that was nibbling away at her, telling her she should not be meeting Edward Woodfield. She had made her decision at the time and she knew she should stick with it, despite everything that Sean had done.

Gracie lay warm in her bed, hands clasped under her head, looking at the ceiling and wondering what the meeting would be like. A part of her felt as if she knew Edward Woodfield really well and yet, when she really thought about it, he was a stranger and they had simply spent one afternoon together on the beach. Now she was married to Sean and he could also be married for all she knew.

It was crazy.

By the time morning came she was exhausted but as soon as breakfast was over she ran back upstairs to get ready.

261

Gracie walked down the stairs and into the kitchen. She'd tried to make herself look nice without going too far, and without raising any questions from Babs Wheaton about exactly why she was going into town again. She felt guilty that she was going and guilty that she was lying to the Wheatons but she couldn't help herself. She wanted to see Edward again.

But as she walked into the room to say goodbye Babs was waiting for her.

'Gracie darling, I was just coming up to see you. I have to tell you something. Now, I don't want you to get stressed but Ruby has been on the phone...'

'Has something happened?' Gracie asked quickly.

'It has. I did call up to you but you were in the bathroom and it was a brief call. It's all gone a bit mad there. She said Sean has found out about Fay and is at the hotel demanding to see you, he's made a bit of a fuss...'

Gracie felt sick.

'Oh God, this is what I was dreading. How did he find out?'

'It seems Jennifer is also back from wherever she was. She found out somehow and told him; the story was brief and garbled but Ruby thought you should know.'

'Jennifer again. He told me it was all over. I knew he was lying, I knew it...' she said resignedly.

'Don't get upset. You have to ring Ruby in half an hour, she's trying to deal with him at the moment.' Babs smiled. 'Which she will. We all know how good Ruby is at being calming and

262

Johnnie's there as well.'

Gracie couldn't move; she just stood on the spot and shook her head.

'I knew something like this would happen. I should have told him about Fay, that was mean and nasty of me and now Ruby's getting the brunt of it.'

'It was a reaction; the wrong reaction I absolutely agree, but an understandable one given the circumstances,' Babs told her gently. 'You just need to explain to him...'

'You know it always comes back to Jennifer,' Gracie continued. 'I don't understand why my own sister hates me so much. I mean, Sean is hardly her type – she always liked them intellectual.'

'From what you and Ruby have both said, she has a jealousy problem. She wants what you or Jeanette has – even if she doesn't want it, if you see what I mean.' Babs smiled. 'This probably wasn't about Sean, or even about you, it was about *her* personality. I'm not a psychiatrist but I understand people after all these years as a doctor's wife.'

'But what is there to be jealous about?' Gracie asked. 'Jennifer had her own fiancé, a nice job and she could twist Mum around her little finger. She was always Mum's favourite; she had nothing to be jealous of, especially with me, the black sheep. Yes she's always been sly and sneaky but lots of kids are.'

'Maybe she was just the deceitful one who always got away with it? I don't know, but I do know that you have to not let this set you back.'

Gracie forced a smile. 'It won't. I just feel bad for Ruby in the firing line. I should be there...'

'Well, don't. She's got Johnnie there and he's more than capable of dealing with Sean, but we both thought you should know what was going on. You're not a child who needs to be shielded.'

'Thank you. I'm just a bit shocked...' Gracie shook her head gently as if to get it clear. 'It's not even Sean really, it's my sister. It's so wrong.'

'Well, there's nowt so queer as folk, as they say. It's a shame if Jennifer is back in Southend – it would have been good for her to build her own life. She must be a very unhappy young woman inside.'

Gracie thought about what Babs was saying and knew she was probably right, but it didn't make any difference.

And then her brain clicked and she remembered where she was supposed to be.

'Do you mind if I go for a walk? Just to think about it all...?'

'Of course I don't mind, shall I come with you?'

'No, it's okay but can I still leave Fay?'

'I was expecting to have her anyway while you went into town,' Babs smiled. 'It's a shame you're going to miss your shopping trip though, the bus will have gone by the time you get there.' Babs paused for a moment. 'I could run you into town in the car after you've spoken to Ruby? Or maybe you can go tomorrow?'

'No thanks, it's too late now. I'll have to go back as soon as possible to see Sean so shopping will have to wait!'

Not wanting anyone to see her panic, Gracie

casually picked up her handbag and strolled off down the path until she was out of sight, then ran to the telephone box, hoping against hope that Edward hadn't already left.

'Can I speak to Edward Woodfield, please?'

'He's not here ... who's calling?'

Immediately Gracie recognised the voice as Louisa's. She doubted for a moment that she would remember who she was, but she didn't want to give her name just in case.

'When he comes back would you tell him I'm sorry, something came up...'

'Who is this?' Louisa asked curiously. 'And sorry for what?'

'He'll know. Please tell him.'

'Is that Gracie from Southend?' Louisa's tone was gleefully curious.

Gracie didn't answer, just gently replaced the receiver and went back to the Wheaton's house knowing she had to pack. It was time to go home.

'Is it okay to phone Ruby now?' she asked George, who was in the kitchen tucked in his usual corner beside the boiler holding Fay, and rocking her back and forth.

'Of course it is. Help yourself.'

Gracie made the phone call to Ruby and it was arranged that Johnnie Riordan would drive to Melton the next day and take her and Fay home.

She went back upstairs to her room, walked over to the window and looked out. The window was at the side of the house and looked out over the fields. She remembered Ruby telling her about life in Melton, about her friends and their free and easy lifestyle. Ruby had wanted more excitement in her life than a village could offer but Gracie could imagine living there quite happily with Fay.

She stared for several minutes before she realised she was imagining life in the country with Fay, but she hadn't even thought about giving Sean, her husband, a place in the scenario.

It saddened her to accept that her marriage to Sean Donnelly was dead and buried but she knew there could be no going back despite their marriage vows made barely a year before.

TWENTY-SIX

On the drive back to Southend Johnnie explained to Gracie exactly what had been going on. Whereas Ruby would have been gentle and a little evasive in telling her the details, Johnnie was far more forthright. He wasn't tactless, he simply thought Gracie didn't need to be protected from the facts of the event and she in turn appreciated it.

'Sean turned up out of the blue, really drunk, which was a shock because I'd never seen him like that before. He was shouting and swearing in the lobby like a navvy. I mean, he was disrupting the guests, threatening to beat the hell out of anyone who was in his way, so I had to remove him...'

Gracie managed a smile. 'I can guess what you mean by that.'

'I was very restrained, I'll have you know.' Johnnie grinned. 'I simply had a word in his ear, took him by the arm and led him outside, but he'd already caused havoc for Ruby before I got there. It was daytime so there were lots of people around.'

'I suppose he thought I was there. Jennifer probably fired him up, she seems to have that power over him, but he shouldn't have done it...'

'We told him you weren't there but he didn't believe us, which was fair enough, but to carry on like that in the hotel was bloody ridiculous,' Johnnie said firmly. 'If you want to know what I think, Sean is making a fuss to put himself back in the right. It was such a childish temper tantrum. I was shocked but I could see what you meant about him being a mummy's boy; that was a really spoilt child in action.'

'But he's getting good at that, turning the tables. I think Jennifer must have taught him – the bitch!' Gracie let out a short burst of humourless laughter before continuing. 'But I still don't really understand what the hell's going on and I don't want to blame her for everything, even though I do hate her guts. Any idea about what he knows, doesn't know? How he knows?' Desperate to find out what was going on she fired the questions at him.

'Not really, he was so drunk. But I got his new address from him. I told him it was either that or I phoned the police and had him nicked then and there, and he understood,' Johnnie said with a slight nod of his head. 'Why not go and see him without Fay and get the lay of the land? Seems he's living in a room in a house in Westcliff and working in a seafront café.'

Gracie looked sad. 'That's a shame, he had such high hopes with his job and we loved our flat. It wasn't Buckingham Palace but it was a first proper home for both of us. Now everything is gone. Stupid idiot that he is. And me... *I* was stupid...'

She looked out of the car window. A year ago they had everything going for them: good jobs, a nice place to live and a baby on the way. Life could have been good but it had been snatched away because of her stupid deceit, his intransigence and her sister's total lack of family loyalty.

'Seems he blew his chances at the Palace when he left without a word,' Johnnie continued. 'He was at work one day and then disappeared the next. Or so one of the Palace girls told Ruby. Not the way to be Mr Popularity!'

'I know you don't like to agree but this whole situation, all of it, is my fault. I wish I could go back to just before the wedding, I really do...'

'But if you'd told Sean he probably wouldn't have married you, and if you hadn't got married you wouldn't have Fay so there are two ways of looking at it. I'd go for the positive view myself, as someone who has cocked up so many times,' Johnnie said quietly. 'I mean, I feel so bad about Sadie, God rest her soul. I did that all wrong but I have my sons and I couldn't wish them away.'

Gracie reached over and touched his hand on the steering wheel.

'Thanks Johnnie, and thanks for coming to collect me. Babs said she'd bring me back but I didn't want to put on her any more than I already have and I didn't fancy the train with the carrycot.'

'Can you imagine Ruby letting that happen? No, it's my pleasure, my dear. And anyway it's nice to have a drive out sometimes.'

Gracie looked at him and smiled.

Johnnie Riordan was tall, fair and slender in a fit, muscular way. Leaning back in the car seat one hand relaxed on the steering wheel, his elbow on the armrest of the door and the other hand on his knee, he looked completely comfortable with himself and was happily driving slower than usual, aware of Fay in the back of the car.

When he'd arrived to collect her from the Wheatons, Gracie had watched him say hello to Maggie as if she was just a child he knew. She had been overwhelmed with admiration for both him and Ruby at the way they could brush their own feelings aside in the best interests of their daughter.

When Gracie had first met him, all those years ago, she had been defensive of Ruby and naturally wary of him, because it was no secret that Johnnie Riordan had been a bit of a lad in the past, and he was also married.

At that time he worked in a public house in Wanstead but he was also a self-proclaimed businessman, an ambitious wheeler dealer who mostly operated on the very edge of legal, occasionally slipping over into the really dodgy territory of London's gangland.

Everything she knew went against him but Ruby loved him and Gracie had soon been won over.

Ruby had been barely sixteen when they'd met and he was a few years older but much more streetwise; they had instantly clicked but it had all gone wrong when Ruby left Walthamstow and didn't return. It was several years later he had found out that she had run away because she was expecting his baby.

'What was Sean saying?' Gracie asked, getting back to the present. 'I mean, what was the gist of it through the drink? I just need to know how he's thinking.'

'I think you have to ask Ruby when we get back, she got the brunt of it. But for now you just relax and enjoy the rest of the journey. There's plenty of time for the other stuff when you get back to the madhouse that is Thamesview!' Johnnie laughed. 'So tell me, how are you feeling now? I bet you enjoyed your holiday. George and Babs always push the boat out for guests...'

'Nicely put, Johnnie!' she laughed. 'We both know it wasn't a holiday, I was packed off to stay at the Wheatons before I went really doolally and ended up in the loony bin ... but yes, it was just what I needed. Everything had built up inside me, it was just too much, but I had a lot of time to think and I feel as if I know what I'm going to do.'

'Thinking can be good and bad,' said Johnnie.

'I know, but this was mostly good!'

Gracie looked sideways at the young man she had come to think of as a brother; he was good company and had a good business head on him but mostly she liked and envied the way he unconditionally loved Ruby. It was how she had wanted her husband to be, but she could see that Sean simply hadn't loved her enough.

'How are the boys? And your sister?' she asked, to deflect the conversation away from herself.

'They're fine. Betty is doing a great job with them, especially after the Sadie tragedy, but they need to be with me now. She's still hostile to the idea of me and Ruby having them but she knows it'll happen. It has to. They're my flesh and blood, and should be with me. And with Ruby; she'll be a fantastic step-mother.'

'Are you still planning to live in the house next door?' Gracie asked.

'Probably in the basement flat when it's finished, though we have talked about making the basement of the hotel into a flat as well. Depends where we can find most space. It's hard when there has to be some staff accommodation...'

'I'm sorry, I know I take up too much room now I have Fay. I need to find somewhere else for us.'

'Don't be daft, I didn't mean you! You're not staff, Gracie, you're family and you earn your keep. Ruby couldn't have managed in those early days after Leonora died without you.'

Gracie felt a blush rise up over her face but it was a pleasant glow, brought on by the welcome compliment. After all the bad things that had happened it was just what she needed.

The journey continued in companionable silence. Gracie watched the passing countryside and towns with half an eye while at the same time thinking about her imminent confrontation with Sean.

She also wondered about Edward, but common sense told her it was for the best that their meeting had been thwarted. Regardless of Sean's behaviour, she was still a married woman with a baby. It would have been wrong to even think about meeting him again. Two wrongs never make a right and Edward Woodfield would have to be put back in the box of memories; the ship that sailed without her.

As they pulled up at the Thamesview Gracie felt the nausea rising all over again, and she hoped against hope that Sean wasn't hanging around watching. She needed to get inside, get Fay settled and then hear the whole story from Ruby before she decided what she was going to do next.

That evening, after hearing all the details about Sean's crazed visit, Gracie had gathered herself together emotionally and, going against everything Ruby and Johnnie counselled, she left Fay with Jeanette and went to see Sean. She wanted to see him on her own terms and she also wanted to visit without telling him so she could see if Jennifer was there with him.

Gracie felt really uncomfortable as she knocked on the door of the rundown old house in nearby Westcliff, which had been converted into several bedsits with a shared bathroom and kitchen on each floor. The paint was peeling off the whole building, there were cracked panes on some of the windows and the front garden looked like it was a dumping ground for the whole street. As she waited, a mangy dog appeared from the overgrown hedge at the side of the house, her teats hanging low. She had three small puppies around her feet. Gracie remembered the piece of cake that Babs had given her for the journey and pulled it out of her bag just as the door opened. She threw it quickly towards the hedge.

'Which is the door for Sean Donnelly?' she asked the angry-looking old woman who pulled the door back.

'Is he the Irishman? Upstairs, first door on the left.'

Gracie started to thank her but she disappeared

straight into the nearest door and slammed it hard. She walked into the darkness of the hall and then gingerly made her way up the decrepit staircase to the next floor.

She found the door and tapped gently on it. When there was no answer she knocked properly. It was a good minute before it was opened and she found herself face to face with Sean.

'Gracie! What the fuck are you doing here?' His voice was flat and she could smell the alcohol on his breath.

Glancing over his shoulder Gracie quickly scanned the room; she had been so convinced that Jennifer would be there she wasn't sure if she was relieved or disappointed to see the room behind him was empty. But regardless, she was mortified to see what he had gone down to.

The room was noticeably damp and dingy with just a single bedstead, a battered old armchair that looked on the verge of collapse and a chest of drawers; a heap of his belongings were strewn around an open suitcase and he had a candle burning precariously in an old saucer. On the floor beside the armchair was an open bottle of whisky but no glass and it was obvious he'd been drinking straight from the bottle.

'Ruby said you wanted to see me so here I am,' she said, trying to ignore the state of the room. 'I didn't think the hotel where I work was the right place for this, not after what you did. Are you going to invite me in?'

'No, I'm not,' he slurred.

'Oh Sean,' Gracie sighed as she stared at him. Despite everything, she wanted to reach out and hug him. He was still her husband and it upset her to see him like this. 'You don't have to live like this, Sean. There's stuff from the flat stored in the shed at the hotel, you could get another place better than this...'

'Fuck all of that, and fuck you, slut...'

He slammed the door in her face so hard it rattled on the hinges.

'Sean...' she said through the door. 'Sean, please let me in...' She rattled the handle and knocked harder but the door was locked from the other side and there was no response, other than a loud 'Shut up' bellowed from behind a door further along the hallway.

Gracie's hands were shaking as she fumbled in her bag for her diary and a pencil. She tore a page out and wrote a short note which she pushed under the door.

He seemed to have completely forgotten that he had wanted to see her because of Fay. In the fug of drink he had probably forgotten she existed the moment the door closed.

As she walked out of the entrance to the building she saw the dog again; she was sitting on the step looking sad while her pups hung on teats from underneath, desperately trying to feed. It was the final straw for Gracie; she sat down beside the dogs and burst into tears.

TWENTY-SEVEN

Sean was trying to focus on the words on the scrap of paper when there was another knock on the door. He ignored it.

'Come on, Sean. It's me, open the door...'

He turned the key and walked over to his bed, leaving Jennifer McCabe to let herself in.

'Ooooh, pigsty!' She laughed and turned her nose up as she picked her way through the débris on the floor, then sat down carefully on the edge of the sagging armchair to avoid falling down the dip in the middle.

'No worse than yours,' he slurred.

'What did she want?'

'You heard. I saw you hanging over the banister like an ape, you're lucky she didn't see you as well.'

Sean was already lying flat out on the bed; fully clothed but very dishevelled. He still had the note in his hand.

'I'm far cleverer than that! I also saw her write you a message. How cute of her, slipping love notes under the door.' Jennifer waved her fingers at him. 'Hand it over, lover. No secrets, remember?'

'How did you know she was here?' he asked.

'I was in the kitchen and I heard her. She's my beloved sister, I'd know that sweet voice anywhere. Now, give me the note.'

276

He held his arm out and she reached over and snatched it from him.

'You're not going to meet her, are you? Actually, let me say it this way: you're *not* going to meet her. You'd better not, I've told you to stay away from her – she's a slut.'

'I've got a daughter and I want to see her, and you can't stop me...' he rolled over on the bed as he spoke.

'How many times do I have to say this?' Jennifer said coldly. 'Her or me. You can't have both...'

'But the baby...'

'...probably isn't yours,' she interrupted, finishing the sentence. 'We've gone over this so many times, you idiot, so why are you bothering? To appease my dear sister Gracie? Or to keep your precious mammy happy? What about me? I love you the way none of the other buggers ever will. I've given up everything for you...'

But as she looked over at him she realised he wasn't listening. Sean had fallen into a drunken stupor.

As the snoring started she stood up and went over to him. She stripped all her clothes off, climbed over him into the narrow bed, snuggled down in the curve of his back and pulled the covers up over them both. When he woke she would be ready to convince him that he wouldn't be going to visit Gracie under any circumstances.

What had started as a bit of spontaneous amusement had quickly turned into something much more serious for the slightly unstable Jennifer McCabe. All she had really intended was to have some fun at her sister's expense, exert a bit of power and cause a few problems between them. She hadn't intended to actually have an affair, she hadn't even liked him very much, but then it had all got out of control and she had quickly and illogically ended up obsessively in love with the man who was still her brother-in-law.

Although they had always been lumped together as 'the twins', Jennifer had spent her childhood in the shadow of her much prettier and more exuberant twin sister. From babyhood she had been the Plain Jane of the family and the older she got, the more it rankled that no one seemed to look beyond that. She hated the way that she and Jeanette were always being compared because Jennifer knew without doubt that she was by far the smarter of the two but no one seemed to care about that.

Her sister Jeanette was always the popular one who had a roaring social life and a steady stream of boys chasing her, and her older sister Gracie had landed on her feet with Ruby as a friend and a cushy job for life.

Jennifer meanwhile was the one at home all the time with just her mother for company, and nothing to do but read and fantasise about being a different person in a different life. She had always spent hours gazing into space, weaving stories in her head with herself as the beautiful and popular girl who everyone wanted to be with.

Jennifer resented every single one of her family, and had been looking for an escape route when a boring old bachelor from her office had warily asked her out and then quickly proposed. She had accepted, not because she loved him – in fact she didn't even like him – but because she wanted the validation of an engagement ring on her finger and a virginal white wedding. She wanted to show everyone that she wasn't the plain Jane they all thought she was.

She was bored and unhappy but then she'd overheard her parents talking on the day Gracie had been to visit them and discovered her sister's shocking secret. But instead of using the knowledge straight away she had savoured it and tucked it away for future reference.

It was during her engagement that Jennifer McCabe had discovered the power of sex and seduction. It wasn't that she enjoyed sex, she didn't, she hated it, but she enjoyed the power it gave her so she had approached the subject in much the same way as she had passed all her school exams. She had managed to get hold of a copy of the *Kama Sutra* and she studied it, remembered it and where necessary, practiced it and discovered that it worked.

The seduction of her brother-in-law was meant to be just another feather in her hat, a recognition of her power and a point-scoring exercise over Gracie. But then it had all gone wrong, because she had actually fallen for Sean.

As she lay awake tucked behind him and savouring the warmth of his body on hers she started to plan her next move.

The goal posts had moved but she was still enjoying the game.

When they had both been fired from the hotel in Brighton for being late for work two days in a row they had decided to go back to Southend in the hope of getting their old jobs back but neither of them had succeeded. Sean had got a seasonal job in a seafront café and Jennifer was doing filing in the back room of a High Street department store. Even worse, they were living in separate rooms in the decrepit boarding house which, despite its disgusting living conditions, didn't allow unmarried couples to share. But Jennifer was optimistic that given time they would be married, have a fabulous home and their own baby.

Silent patience and a good imagination had always been her strong points.

'I said, you're not going to go and see her, are you?' she asked the next morning, when Sean was awake and trying to pretend he hadn't got a hangover. It was the fourth time she'd asked and he was doing his best not to lose patience with her.

'I said I'm not, I'm going to work. Now are you going to be getting yourself ready for work? We need to be gathering some money together so we can get out of this dump as soon as we can.'

'Just before we go to work...' she murmured and reached under the covers, determined to continue to exert her control over Sean Donnelly.

Although Sean did exactly as he had told Jennifer he was going to do and went to work, he quickly pleaded a family emergency to get some time off from the café, and caught the bus to Thorpe Bay to meet Gracie as she'd asked in her note. But to be safe, he had telephoned her at the Thamesview first to make it a much earlier time because he knew without doubt that Jennifer would be checking up on him.

When Sean had phoned to rearrange the time, Gracie had then changed the venue and arranged to meet him at the newly-acquired house next-door to avoid any more disruption to Ruby in her hotel.

The initial meeting up on the doorstep had been embarrassing for both of them after the events of the night before but Gracie had already decided not to mention it. She was there with him only because of Fay.

The house itself was still uninhabitable and there was nowhere other than the orange boxes to sit so Gracie had led him through the house to the walled garden at the back that had already been given an archway through to the Thames-view garden next door. She signalled for him to sit on the bench that was centered amid the rubble, confident in the knowledge Johnnie Riordan was working in the house, out of earshot of their conversation but still there if she needed him.

'The Blakeley bandwagon is well and truly rolling now,' Sean said, looking at the extensive repairs on the house. 'You hitched yourself to the right one, didn't you now?' he added, and Gracie instantly recognised the old envy in his voice. 'And Johnnie boy working here as well? *Very* cosy. It's a pity I never made the mark or we'd all be doing just fine. I could have been the chef but no, not good enough for the Blakeleys and Wheatons.'

'You threw *me* out, Sean; when I was expecting,

you slept with my sister. You made your choice, it had nothing to do with anyone else.' Gracie tried to keep her tone calm as she answered. Because they were sitting side by side and she didn't have to look at him she found it easier.

'You lied to me twice. You lied about my baby...'

'Look, I'm sorry, Sean. I keep saying it and I mean it. It was cruel of me and I shouldn't have done it but I just wanted to hurt you as you had hurt me. I shouldn't have done it.'

'That's no excuse...' he said, his anger starting to rise. 'No excuse at all.'

'I know...'

'But if you know, then why is this happening, Gracie? Why haven't I seen my daughter?' he looked genuinely bewildered and she wondered if he was faking it or if he really couldn't comprehend how much he had hurt her in believing her sister over her, by trying to claim that Gracie, his wife, was having an affair and was pregnant by someone else. All she could do was shrug and shake her head.

'I said I'm sorry...'

'A lie is a lie, however you look at it.' He continued to berate her, as if he hadn't heard her. 'I have a daughter and I didn't know. I thought my baby had died, how wicked could you be?'

'Your baby did die, Sean,' Gracie said sadly. 'Phillip died but Fay survived. Just. You were nowhere to be found, you denied you were the father – don't you understand that, Sean? While I was giving birth and then having an operation which robbed me of my chance to have any more children, you weren't anywhere to be found.

Don't you understand?' Gracie was crying but it was with tears of frustration rather than sadness. 'You weren't there...'

Sean remained unmoved. 'It's not the same thing at all and that's twice you've lied. You're a liar, Gracie. A LIAR!' he spat the words at her. 'Now where's my daughter?'

Gracie was trying to be logical, to see it from Sean's point of view and to apologise for what she'd done. She knew she had been in the wrong but she wasn't prepared to take all the blame nor was she willing to trust him.

'It's not as simple as that. I need you to explain. You sat here bold as brass and said Jennifer was out of the picture, you wanted us to try again and then...'

'And then you threw me out without even telling me I had a baby who was alive,' he said with venom. 'What was I supposed to do? Sit on the step outside Ruby Blakeley's hotel and cry for all to see?'

'So you *are* with Jennifer. Does your mother know?'

'That's neither here nor there. I just want to know about the baby.'

'You said the baby wasn't yours. Either you believe my sister or you don't, you're with her or you're not.'

'Oh, stop going on and on, Gracie,' he said before she could finish. 'You've turned into such a moaning minnie! Jennifer is none of your business now. I tried to make amends with you, to do the right thing but you told me to go. And I went and then I found out you'd lied once again. There's

283

something wrong with you. I swear, you're a compulsive liar.'

He stood his ground and stared her down until she looked away, then he continued.

'But even then I thought maybe you and I had a chance to sort this mess out, but knowing how you've deceived me again...' he broke off and looked away.

Gracie found herself caught up in the middle of it all again. She wanted to hurt Sean so much but she also wanted to do what was best for her daughter, who had not had the greatest start in life and had an uncertain future ahead of her.

Gracie loved her baby with a passion that had engulfed her the first moment she set eyes on her, a passion compounded by the loss of Fay's twin brother Phillip. She hadn't seen her when she was born or even straight after the surgery, and when she had seen her she hadn't been able to hold her; her introduction was simply looking at her through the wall of the incubator.

The baby was small and silent but as she watched and waited Gracie was sure she knew her mother was there and that she always would be, whatever happened.

She prayed silently and willed her to live because she couldn't imagine any other scenario, but then as time went on, and the worrying should have lessened it had increased, because she knew she would never have another baby.

It was that worry that had threatened to tip her over the edge but the calm reassurance of George and Babs Wheaton had pulled her back from the brink.

'Does she know you're here?' Gracie suddenly asked. 'I bet she doesn't, else she'd be hanging around as well. Perhaps she is. Oh look, I'm not going to go over this anymore, Sean. Two questions, do you want to see Fay? And are you with Jennifer?'

'Jennifer is nothing to do with you...'

'Then you won't ever see Fay. As long as that cow is around you're not having anything to do with Fay. I don't trust her, she's mad.'

She stood up and straightened her clothes as if to walk away but Sean didn't react as she expected. Instead, he was leaning back and smiling.

'Gracie darling, there's nothing you can do about that. Is it my name that you put on the birth certificate?'

Gracie knew then and there that he had won. That Jennifer had won. She didn't have the energy to fight anymore.

'Johnnie...' she shouted. 'I'm going to get Fay! I'll come back through the garden.'

He walked through into the room. 'Okay, I'll stay here.'

As Gracie left, so Johnnie went and sat on the bench beside Sean. She could hear him talking to Sean as she left the house.

'Just a few words, Sean. You and me got along okay and I don't want to take sides but I love Gracie like a sister and Fay like a niece. If you make one wrong move towards either of them, if you hurt them or do them down in any way, then I'll break your legs and arms very slowly and then I'll bury you alive. Do we understand each other?'

'Are you threatening me, Johnnie? I thought we

285

were friends...' Sean asked with fake bravado.

'Of course I'm not threatening you. I'm just giving you some friendly advice.' Johnnie patted him on the arm as if he was a good friend. It was a gesture that could be interpreted either way depending on which side of Johnnie Riordan was to the fore.

Johnnie was still smiling when Gracie put her head through the arch in the adjoining wall.

'Sean? I don't want Fay to be around all the dust, you'll have to come through into the hotel garden.'

'Remember what I said, Sean. One wrong move...' Johnnie said as he stood up. He started to swing an imaginary bat. 'Just remember.'

TWENTY-EIGHT

As Gracie watched Sean walk through the archway from the garden next door to the hotel her heart was thumping and she felt strangely detached. So much was resting on the meeting between him and his daughter, but she still wasn't exactly sure what it was that she wanted.

All she knew for certain was that she wanted Sean to acknowledge that Fay was his daughter, regardless of anything else, and to accept her.

She stood bolt upright in the middle of the garden, grasping the handle of the carrycot with both hands, and waited for Sean to walk across the lawn and go up to her.

Gracie felt nervous and scared; she wasn't scared of Sean himself but of how he was going to react to the tiny scrap of a person she was so protective of.

The hotel garden was mostly lawn with a path down the middle, leading to the tool-shed tucked away at the bottom. It was well established with shrubs in the borders and a vegetable plot in front of the shed and there were three new wooden benches carefully placed at different angles which were for the guests. There was also the new archway which had been cut into the dividing wall between the hotel and the house next door and fitted with a wooden gate.

'She's asleep at the moment but she'll wake

shortly, if you want to wait. She's due for a bottle,' Gracie said as Sean folded the hood down and looked into the carrycot. With the confidence of someone who had been brought up around babies, he reached out and moved the crocheted blanket to one side so he could see the face of the sleeping infant.

Gracie watched his face, trying to assess his reactions. She still wasn't completely convinced that he believed one hundred per cent that Fay was his, that Phillip was his, but his expression as he looked at the sleeping infant told her nothing. He looked like any other man gazing into the pram of any other baby. He stared for what seemed like an age.

'She looks like you,' Gracie said. 'Can you see that? Look at her hair and colouring...'

He stared down at Fay. 'She's very small. She looks like a newborn...'

'She's small because she was born very early. She's doing well though, especially as they said it was touch and go at the beginning, but no one knows yet how she'll be affected in the long term...' The words tumbled out as she tried to get all the information across to him before he said the wrong thing. She said a silent prayer as she waited for his reaction. *Please God, don't let him say the wrong thing; please don't let him deny her...*

'I thought you said she was okay? What do you mean by *affected in the long term*? I don't under-stand what you mean.'

Sean stared at her. For the first time he seemed to hear what Gracie was actually saying instead of focusing on berating her.

'It's cos she was born so early and tiny, and she spent her last few weeks in the womb alongside her dead twin,' Gracie said sharply. 'Didn't Jennifer share that bit of news with you?'

Sean looked shocked. 'That sounds horrible ... how did that happen?'

'No one knows why Philip died when he did, he was born first and no one realised there were two babies and then Fay had to be resuscitated. She's lucky to be alive after all that and we're lucky to have her but she may be handicapped. She probably will be handicapped, but they can't say how much.'

Gracie's tone was factual because she could never talk about it any other way; it upset her too much to think about her daughter having problems.

When the doctor had spoken to her in the hospital she had been shocked and angry but at the same time she had been grateful for his calm assessment and honesty in telling her the truth.

As you know Mrs Donnelly, Gracie, it was a very difficult birth and the lay of the babies meant a twin pregnancy wasn't suspected. Your baby suffered from a lack of oxygen when she was trapped in the birth canal behind the stillborn baby and as you know, she had to be resuscitated. She will suffer consequences; it's just a question of assessing her level of handicap. I'm sorry but there's no way that we can know about long-term damage until she's older. You should hope for the best.

'Handicapped?' Sean stared at her.

'Yes, that's what I said. Fay may not develop properly. I was going to talk to you about it last

289

night but you were so badly in drink you wouldn't talk to me.'

Sean backed away and leaned against the wall that divided the two gardens.

'I hadn't thought about anything like that. Are you saying she won't be normal?'

'I suppose that is exactly what I'm saying.' Gracie knew she was laying it on the line so he knew exactly what the future could hold for Fay, but all the while she was hoping Sean wouldn't walk away.

'But she's still our daughter,' Gracie continued. 'She's going to need lots of help from us, and probably a special school. Who knows what the future holds for her...'

'A retarded child? Is that what you're saying?'

As the full impact of her words hit him, she saw him recoil from the carrycot, away from his daughter. She knew he didn't intend to do it, that it was a reaction, but all the same he looked horrified as he took several steps backwards.

'Have you lost interest now, Sean?' Gracie calmly asked him. 'Because if you have, then now's the time to walk away and stay away. It's not her fault that it happened and it's not her fault that her brother died.'

'That wasn't what I meant. It's a shock. I don't know, I mean, if she's going to be handicapped, why did they do everything? Wouldn't it have been kinder to let her go and be with her brother?'

Gracie could feel a disappointed anger building inside and she had to force herself not to go for him.

'Look at her, Sean. *Look* at her! Are you saying

she'd be better off dead?'

'No, but...' he looked genuinely bewildered.

'Well, I tell you what, you let me know when you've decided – because Fay doesn't need someone who'll step away just at the possibility of her being, as you put it, *retarded*.'

Sean looked into the carrycot again, and then, shaking his head in despair, he turned and walked away.

'I can't be doing with this...'

'Have you accepted that she is your baby?'

He carried on walking away.

'She's your daughter, you ignorant bastard, *your* daughter...'

Sean Donnelly didn't turn around.

'Johnnie,' Gracie shouted at the top of her voice. 'See Sean out, will you? And don't let him back. Ever.'

'What happened out there?' Johnnie Riordan asked him as they walked back through the old house to the front door.

'She told me the baby's not normal.'

'Did she? And what did you say?' Johnnie asked.

'The wrong thing as usual and then Gracie just switched off. I was shocked, that's all. I mean, what if someone told you one of yours might be affected, what does that mean? I don't understand...' Sean said obliviously.

'I'm sure she explained it,' Johnnie said, still with a smile on his face. 'What are you going to do?'

'I don't know; it's all such a shock. Gracie

291

warned me in the garden that the baby might be having problems but I never thought that it might be serious. I expected her to be small but handicapped? I didn't realise what she meant... Jesus, what would *you* do?' Sean looked at him intently.

'It's what *you're* going to do that counts, me old mate. And if you're not going to do what's right for a father to do, then just get out of here and out of their lives.'

'That's for me to decide. Gracie's my wife and that's my daughter, they're my business and you should be minding yours...' Sean pulled his shoulders back and looked Johnnie in the eye.

'So you're going to do the right thing then?' Johnnie asked. 'You're going to provide for your wife and baby? Because if not then I'll...'

'You'll *what*? Go on, tell me. You threaten away, big man – you don't fucking scare me!' Sean interrupted him with a dry laugh. 'You're not one to say anything after what you drove your own wife to. You did her wrong and she's dead and buried now so don't preach to me from on high! I'll decide what I'm doing and when I'm going to do it.'

He walked away and out of the building without a backward glance. Johnnie Riordan watched him go. He wanted to batter him into the ground but instead he leaned back against the wall and thought about the whole messy situation, about what had happened to both of them and he wondered how he himself might have reacted.

He had never been unfaithful physically to Sadie, his wife, but he had never loved her the way she had wanted to be loved and it was only after the event that he had realised he had done her a huge disservice in marrying her.

As he thought back to his own ill-fated marriage he felt a small twinge of sympathy for Sean Donnelly.

Gracie and Sean had drifted together over a long period of time and everyone had assumed they were right for each other, but now Johnnie could see the parallels with his own mistakes.

He rushed out and shouted, '*Sean*! Sean? Wait a minute. Fancy a snifter in the pub? I'm due a lunch break...'

Sean looked at him cautiously. 'Just now you were going to be smashing all my limbs to smithereens...'

'I know I was, but you're right. There are two sides and no one looked at the other side with me. I had so much unfair stick over Sadie. Go on,' he grinned and playfully punched Sean on his upper arm.

'I can't now, I have to get to the café. I'm already late – but this evening?'

'Okay. In the Castle at seven?'

'That would be grand.' Sean paused and smiled. 'Thank you, Johnnie, I appreciate it.'

As he went back into the house Gracie came through from the other way.

'Was he okay?'

'He was. He's gone to work now.'

'Did you say anything to him?'

'I just suggested he thought about how he was going to deal with all this. Hopefully he'll make the right decision.' Johnnie put an arm around Gracie's shoulder and hugged her. 'I think he will but it depends on what you think is the right decision.'

'Are you feeling sorry for him?' Gracie asked suspiciously. 'Are you taking his side? Because I think I've been more than fair to him...'

'Gracie, I'm not taking sides. I was just wondering what's best if he's going to be with Jennifer. Do you want him to be a father to Fay under those circumstances? Or would it be better if he and your sister were both out of your life? You need to think about it before you push him to do something neither of you want.'

Gracie looked at him. She had grown to love Johnnie like the brother she'd never had and she knew he felt the same sibling affection for her, but at that moment she wasn't sure if he was actually feeling sympathy for Sean.

'So what do you think I should do?' she asked curiously.

'Oh, no, no, no! I'm not answering that, any more than Ruby would. You have to figure it out for yourself. Now I have to get back to this heap of rubble that needs shifting or I'll be here all night.'

TWENTY-NINE

Gracie, Ruby and Jeanette were all up in the flat at the end of a long hard Saturday of check-ins and check-outs. Henry the night porter was already on duty at the reception desk and Johnnie was closeted in the office with a pile of paperwork and a glass of brandy, so it was a rare evening off for Ruby and an opportunity for the three young women to catch up and have a lazy fish and chips supper together.

Jeanette had volunteered to go out to get it from the fish and chip shop along the road and, once she got back, they had all settled round the small oval table under the window eating it out of the paper while at the same time chatting, laughing and enjoying a port and lemon each.

Ruby had made some superficial changes to the flat during the previous weeks, altering the layout of the furniture, putting new pictures up on the walls and hanging some different curtains. It was just enough to modernise the room a little, without altering it too drastically. It was comfortable and cosy without being as old-fashioned as it was, but it also meant that the character of Leonora Wheaton hadn't been completely erased.

After they'd finished eating they cleared the table and Ruby sat back down to go through her backlog of mail, while Jeanette sat opposite her with a mirror, a bag of rollers and pins in front of her. Gracie was on the sofa, crocheting a jacket for Fay, who was fast asleep in her cot in Gracie's bedroom.

'Have you got a start date yet, Jeanette?' Ruby asked.

'I know it's going to be in September, but not the actual date. Just think, that's when you'll be shot of me! I'll be living in the nurses' home at the hospital, don't know which yet, and behaving like a nun apparently. They keep their student nurses under lock and key.' Jeanette laughed. 'When they showed us round I thought it looked just how I imagined St Angela's...'

'Nothing could ever be like St Angela's,' Gracie said. 'Unless you're in the workhouse, or prison, or down in hell.'

'Sorry, I shouldn't have said that – I forgot. We always used to say that at school, it's a habit. I didn't mean it like that...' Jeanette clasped her hand over her mouth.

'Oh I know you didn't, you daft mare,' Gracie smiled quickly. 'I'd say it myself if I wasn't so bloody scared of everyone finding out I'd actually been there. Mind you, they will find out soon. I can't see Sean and Jennifer not broadcasting it across the town. But never mind that now, tell us some more about your interview.'

Jeanette jumped up from her seat and bowed.

'It was nerve-wracking but, *hold the front page*, Jeanette McCabe passed her nursing exam. How about that? I did something clever for the first time in my life, and I did it of my own accord.'

'You're being modest now; you always were clever, you just didn't *apply yourself* as your report cards always said. But this is so exciting. Imagine, Jeannie becoming a nurse! Even Mum's impressed and that takes a lot to do.' Gracie grinned at her sister.

So many times over the previous few months she had felt both amazed and guilty at how little notice she had really taken of her younger sister. Both of her sisters, in fact. She had always thought of them as 'the twins' and assumed they were content with each other but now she realised that was only how they were when they were small. Everyone had always lumped them together as one unit, whereas in fact they were two very separate people.

'It's been good for Mum actually, something to boast to the neighbours about,' Jeanette said. 'And it's been a distraction after her distress at what our mad sister's done and all that. Poor cow, she can't quite get over Saint Jennifer's amazing leap off the perfect daughter pedestal into the fires of hell...'

'There's none so blind as those that won't see, as Mum herself always says!' Gracie said. 'It would be funny if it wasn't so bloody tragic. Though to be fair to Mum even I hadn't realised quite what a bitch Jennifer was, I really hadn't.'

'When you went for your interview did you spy any of your hunky doctors roaming the corridors, looking lost and in need of some tender loving care?' Ruby asked as she shuffled and sorted the papers in front of her.

'Not a single one, they were probably all doing doctorly things somewhere. But I did meet Matron and she is a very frightening woman, far more scary than Mum in full flow. She marched

297

into the room like a Major General and we all automatically jumped up. Someone said she's really nice underneath but I can't see it!'

'I wonder if she's got a doctor to keep her warm?'

'I've told you already, there's a single hunky doctor in the house at Melton. He's ready and waiting for you, perfect husband material and ready to be snapped up...' Gracie said to Jeannie, laughing. 'We'll have to fit in a visit so you can meet him.'

'And I told you ... anytime! Now, who's for another drink?'

Out of the blue, Gracie felt a huge wave of affection for the sister who had not only supported her in her hour of need, but had done so with subtlety and humour. Especially as she could easily have sided with her twin and left Gracie completely out in the cold.

The previous year had been hell but it had helped Gracie to have her sister there and the drama also brought her slightly closer to her mother. There would always be a chasm between Gracie and Dot McCabe but it was narrower than it had been over the years since she had been packed off to St Angela's, and for that she was grateful.

It meant her daughter would have at least one set of grandparents in her life.

'Oh, for heaven's sake,' Ruby suddenly said as she opened another letter from the pile in front of her. 'I don't believe it, your mother-in-law wants to come and stay here! For nothing. She wants a free room here for two weeks...'

She peered at the letter as if she might have got it wrong first time, and then read it aloud to Gracie and Ruby.

Dear Miss Blakeley,
I'm sure you remember me. I am Sean Donnelly's mother and the grandmother of the baby Fay Donnelly and I stayed at your establishment when the ill-fated marriage between my son and his wife Gracie took place.

I am hoping to be visiting my son and grand-daughter but, because of the circumstances of which I'm sure you are well aware, my son is staying in a place which is unable to accommodate me.

As a friend and employer of Gracie, my daughter-in-law, I am hoping you will see your way to letting me stay in your hotel at no charge. I want to meet my granddaughter and also pay my respects to my late grandson but I am unable to find the funds for any-thing other than the fare for the boat and trains. Because of his hard times Sean cannot help me.

I will be accompanied by my close friend Yolande Hall as I'm unable to travel alone and we will stay in the same room but in separate beds.

If it is acceptable to you I shall be arriving on the twenty-third and staying for two weeks exactly.

Please don't mention this to Sean as I don't want him to feel obligated and I also want my visit to be a surprise for him.

I look forward to hearing from you as soon as possible.
Yours sincerely,
Rosaleen Donnelly

'Well, bugger that for a game of soldiers...' Gracie said. 'Who does she think she is? And as for the awful Yolande, I met her in Ireland when Sean and I got engaged. She's a neighbour of the Donnellys, and she makes Hitler look like a kindly old soul in comparison.'

Ruby and Jeanette both laughed at Gracie's words as Ruby passed the letter over for them to read for themselves.

'Maybe she really does just want to see her grandchild. Sean *is* her precious only son, she's bound to. I feel a bit sorry for her, like I do for our mum. Another one fallen off the pedestal of the idolised child,' Jeanette said after reading the letter for herself. 'Have you noticed I'm learning to be nice now that I'm going to be a nurse...'

'We noticed...' Ruby said. 'You're quite good, you nearly had me convinced.'

'I'm sure she does feel bad, but to ask for a free room? Blimey, that's cheek for you! And anyway, I don't trust her.' Gracie shook her head. 'And why isn't she writing to me? I'm Fay's mother, she lives with me...'

'She knows you live here so she'll know I'll tell you. I don't know about trusting her but I suppose I do feel a bit sorry for her as well,' Ruby said. 'But it's up to you, Gracie: yes or no?'

'It's not up to me, it's your hotel but if you both feel so bloody sorry for the old battleaxe and her miniature sidekick...'

'How about I agree to one room for both of them but only for one week? I'll tell her we're booked up for the other week, like it or lump it. We can do that, but if you really don't want her here then that's up to you.'

'She's a witch and I think she's up to something but I still feel a bit sorry for her,' Gracie said, her words tailing off as she thought about it.

'At least if she's here you can keep an eye on her. She can see Fay without the risk of Jennifer worming her way in.' Ruby smiled. 'And then if she plays up when she's here we'll drag her off to the ducking stool!'

Ruby and Jeanette both laughed but Gracie didn't join in.

'I wonder how much Sean has told her about Fay? I would hate it if she didn't know, but I can imagine her reaction if she does. She won't be happy, that's for certain.'

'I hadn't thought of that,' Ruby frowned. 'But surely Sean has told her and if it was a problem for her she wouldn't be coming over.'

'I wonder what he's told her about us? I mean, she's not going to be happy at the break-up, even though she couldn't stand the sight of me in the first place. Marriage is forever in her eyes and we barely managed a year!' Gracie rolled her eyes at Ruby and Jeanette. 'Shame on us.'

'Well, as I said, it's up to you. I can just write and say we don't have any rooms and that'll be the end of it.'

Gracie leant back and closed her eyes. 'No, let's get it over with. She can stay, but no sea view for the old crones. And it'll be interesting if she hasn't told Sean she's coming, won't it? Imagine if she turns up and finds him and Jennifer in that disgusting bed together in that crummy, smelly room?'

Again the three women sniggered. After three port and lemons each everything was suddenly funny.

'Are they still there? I can't believe it, how the mighty have fallen. I can't believe Jennifer has sunk so low. She must be off her head ... they both must be,' Jeanette said with a laugh but Gracie knew that regardless of everything that had happened, she was sad at the loss of the twin sister she had shared her life with for so long.

'In a strange way I suppose I hope they'll be happy together. Preferably not round here, though...'

This time when they laughed, Gracie's laughter wasn't quite so loud.

For the first time since Sean had thrown her out she had started to feel settled. She had got into a routine with work and Fay, and her life was calm. Sean had been back to see Fay just the once and although he had been less confrontational, Gracie could tell he just didn't want to be there. She knew instinctively that he wouldn't be part of Fay's life and it saddened her but she accepted it.

She just hoped that her mother-in-law would accept it also.

THIRTY

Gracie remained resolutely out of sight as Rosaleen Donnelly, Sean's mother, and her friend
Yolande Hall arrived at the reception desk of the
Thamesview Hotel. They were both dressed from
top-to toe in dark clothing, each had one small
suitcase and a handbag, and both looked as
mournful as if they were about to attend a fun-
eral, serious-faced and straight-backed.

Johnnie had collected them from the station in
town and was busy trying to charm them as they
waited for Ruby to check them in at the desk but
it made her smile to see that he was fighting a
losing battle. They were both looking ahead and
she could see they were resolutely determined to
ignore him, despite his best efforts.

As they stood side by side in silence, looking
uneasy and uncomfortable, Gracie continued to
watch surreptitiously from behind the sliding glass
windows of the hatch between the outer and inner
reception area. The area that was out of sight was
small and airless with just enough space for two
chairs and a tiny table which wobbled and was
covered in stains and burns from cigarettes that
had fallen from the small Bakelite ashtray. The
room was mostly used as somewhere to sit and
have a drink and a cigarette when the reception
desk was quiet, but because of the small hatch, it
also served as a useful spot to secretly watch what

was going on.

Rosaleen was a buxom woman who was tidy and well-turned out, despite the long journey she'd just endured, but her clothes and shoes told a story of hardship and make do and mend. Her friend was small and wiry and equally neat and tidy, but her clothes were noticeably newer and classier. Rosaleen was standing perfectly still, but Yolande Hall was moving from foot to foot impatiently. It was obvious neither woman wanted to be there, cap in hand at Ruby Blakeley's hotel, but Gracie could see the situation would be harder for her mother-in-law to bear. Gracie didn't like Yolande at all; she had found her mean-spirited and spiteful, but she respected her for supporting her friend Rosaleen in her hour of need.

Without moving a muscle, Gracie stayed put behind the glass, watching and waiting for Ruby to do her bit. When she'd discussed their arrival with Ruby they had decided that the women would be given time to rest and then they would be offered tea in the lounge at a time when no other guests were around, so that Gracie would join them there.

Over and over again Gracie had told herself that Rosaleen Donnelly's opinion wasn't important now she and Sean were no longer together, but still she was nervous of the initial face-to-face and the inevitable inquisition. She felt so defensive of her fragile daughter and she didn't want anyone maligning her.

Fay was growing and thriving, and Gracie was even more besotted than ever. The tiny girl was wide-eyed, dark-haired and contented. She took her bottle happily, slept well and rarely cried nowadays; she was perfect.

Gracie knew that it was the perfection that worried everyone but it didn't worry her. She saw her contentedness as a sign that Fay was cosseted to the point that she didn't need to cry and she interpreted her baby's wide-eyed observation as a sign that she was intellectually sound. She didn't want to hear that there might be something wrong with her daughter until it was proven beyond all doubt so she had pushed it to the back of her mind and carried on doing what she was doing.

She hadn't seen or heard from Sean since his second fleeting visit and although Gracie was sad about it, she was able to be pragmatic. She knew that, thanks to Ruby, she was in a position to provide for her baby without Sean, but she was sad for Fay that her father didn't want to know her.

In the quiet of the night she often thought about her own gentle father who, unlike her mother, had always loved all his daughters without favouritism. He had been away during the war but never spoke a word about it once he came back, he just went back to work and it was as if he had never been gone.

She had wanted a father like that for her children, for Fay, but it wasn't to be. Gracie now accepted that Sean wasn't the one. She had made the wrong choice.

The atmosphere in the lobby changed when Ruby appeared, apologising profusely.

'Mrs Donnelly, Mrs Hall, welcome to the Thamesview Hotel. I'm so sorry I wasn't here to greet you but the laundryman arrived early and I had to go through the list...' Ruby looked from one to the other, her professional smile plastered on. 'I hope you had a good journey? The weather's been good so I hope the Irish Sea didn't cause too much sickness – I've heard it can be a cruel sea at any time of the year.'

'The journey was just fine,' Rosaleen said. 'If you could show us to our room and tell Gracie that we're here...'

'We thought you would like to have a rest after your journey...'

'No, I want to see Gracie as soon as possible. I can't be worrying about this any longer. I want to hear from her what's been going on these past few months.'

'If you could fill in this card I'll go and find her but she may have gone to the shops. We're very short-handed here and we all have to do what needs doing.'

Ruby continued to smile and she then turned away and winked at the glass window, knowing Gracie was watching.

As Gracie looked at her mother-in-law so her feeling of dread started to fade. Although she was trying to hide it, Rosaleen Donnelly looked sad and lonely standing there with just a friend to support her.

Gracie didn't wait any longer. She took a deep breath and walked through to greet them as professionally as Ruby and Johnnie had done.

'Good day to you Mrs Donnelly, Mrs Hall. Johnnie here will show you to your room and I'll be waiting for you in the lounge...' Gracie smiled politely and shook hands with them both.

'Hello Gracie,' Rosaleen and Yolande said in unison.

'This way, ladies.' Johnnie smiled as he headed to the stairs. 'Let me carry your bags...'

A few minutes later Rosaleen Donnelly was back downstairs and walking through to the residents lounge to meet Gracie for the first time since the wedding, with Ruby just a step behind, carrying a large tray carefully laid with tea and an assortment of biscuits and cakes.

'Please have a seat,' Gracie said as she indicated an armchair. She waited for the woman to sit down before sitting in a nearby armchair that was neither too close to be uncomfortable nor too far from the woman to be rude. She wasn't trying to cause discomfort, she simply needed a little space between them to feel emotionally safe.

Ruby laid the tray down and then quickly left the room, leaving them to it.

Gracie poured the tea, offered her mother-in-law a cake and then sat back and waited.

'This is very difficult for me, Gracie...' Rosaleen said after a few minutes' awkward silence. 'I don't want to be here with you after what you did to my son but I want to see my granddaughter, Sean's first-born, and to pay respects to my only grand-son, God bless his soul. Poor little thing.'

Gracie chose to ignore the barbed comments. 'Does Sean know you're here?'

'Not yet. We're going to visit him this evening. I have his new address.'

Gracie wanted to smile. She could just imagine her turning up at the dilapidated house and finding Sean living in drunken squalor with his sister-in-law.

'Mrs Donnelly, there are so many things you need to know. I don't want to criticise Sean but there are two sides to the story...'

Rosaleen held her hand up as if she was stopping traffic.

'Please don't try and blame my son, Gracie. You gave birth to an illegitimate baby and didn't tell him. You married my son under false pretences and that invalidates the marriage in anyone's eyes. Now, just let me see my grandchild. We don't need to be having a conversation.'

Gracie stood up. 'I suppose that's true in a way so if you're not interested in my side, I'll just go and get Fay...'

She went through to the kitchen first. 'That woman will drive me to drink before the end of the week! I was going to warn her for her own sake about Sean and Jennifer and their hovel but now I've decided she can lump it. Imagine her and Yolande on the doorstep...'

Gracie and Ruby both laughed as Ruby handed Fay to her mother and then Gracie paused for a moment, flexed her shoulders and took a deep breath. 'Into the lion's den, we go. I don't want to do this but I suppose I have to.'

'You don't have to do it but you'll do it because you're a very nice person... Good luck!' Ruby said.

Gracie held her precious baby close and reluctantly went back to the lounge, where Rosaleen Donnelly was still sitting in exactly the same position, wearing the same expression.

'This is Fay, your granddaughter...' she carefully handed her sleepy daughter out for Rosaleen to take.

Still in her seat the woman took Fay in her arms and laid her across her ample lap. Gracie was braced for a comment but instead Rosaleen just stared silently and without expression. Gracie sat back down herself and watched and waited. It wasn't panning out the way she had expected.

It was several uncomfortable minutes before Gracie spoke. 'She looks like her daddy, don't you think? Her colouring is his.'

'I do think she looks like him, yes...' Rosaleen said, with a grudge in her voice. 'He was such a beautiful baby was my Sean. So loving and easy to care for after all the daughters. I'd waited so long to have a son and then sure enough, God gave me the perfect one. Or so it seemed.' She was still staring down at the baby on her lap.

'None of us are perfect.'

'No, we're not. I'd like to take her for a walk tomorrow...'

'You can't take her round to Sean, I won't allow that.'

'He's her father!' Rosaleen snapped.

'He lives in a hovel with his girlfriend – it's filthy there...' The words were out before she could stop them and for one moment Gracie thought that Rosaleen Donnelly was going to throw Fay across the room. Her face reddened dramatically and she stood up, clutching Fay, and hugged her fiercely, making her whimper.

'Don't you talk about my son like that; don't you dare, after what you did to him! I told him to forgive you and let sleeping dogs lie, that the marriage vows are sacred, but now I see he was right. You are wicked, wicked, wicked! He deserves better.'

Gracie was not surprised at the woman's reaction and in a way she admired her for sticking up for her son regardless, but her total denial told Gracie that she couldn't be trusted.

Gracie stood up also. She was determined to keep the peace, especially while Rosaleen was holding Fay in her arms.

'I don't think I am wicked. I was wrong, but what Sean did was a million times worse.'

'Nothing could be worse than what you did.'

'Would you like to give Fay her bottle? Here, let me take her while you sit down then I'll go and get it.' As a distraction Gracie forced a smile. 'I don't want to fight with you, I know you don't care for me and I don't mind but I do want you to care about Fay. Now shall I go and get Mrs Hall so she can meet Fay also?'

Rosaleen handed Fay over and sat down again but she kept her arms folded to ensure Gracie didn't pass her back again. 'Yes, go and get Yolande. I want her to see the baby before I go and see Sean. But I won't be taking Yolande with me, I have to see my son alone.'

Gracie watched the fight drain out of the woman and she felt sad for her.

Jennifer McCabe, her own sister, had destroyed so many lives in such a short space of time.

'How did it go?' Jeanette asked her that evening when she got home. 'Ruby said you were so controlled, she said you didn't even hit her!'

Gracie forced a smile. 'I feel sorry for the woman but she is so hard to like. Still, she's going to see Sean tomorrow, to surprise him. That'll be funny! I almost want to tag along and see what happens... Then next week she'll be gone and we can get back to normal.'

Gracie waved her arms in the air and wiggled her hips. 'Think we'll have to celebrate. We should all go to the Kursaal...' she stopped and opened her eyes wide. 'Bugger bugger, Ruby and I have missed our date on the roller coaster...'

'What date's that?' Jeanette looked bewildered as she listened to her sister grumbling away and berating both herself and Ruby, even though Ruby was downstairs.

'Never mind, for one year only we'll have to change the date to next week when the dragon has flown.'

THIRTY-ONE

Gracie was walking through the hotel, holding Fay's heated bottle, when she saw Henry dragging a trunk down the stairs.

'Hey, you shouldn't be doing that, Henry! Where's Johnnie? That's his job...'

'Oh I don't mind, it keeps me fit.' Henry flexed his muscles and picked the trunk up by the handle on the end. 'See? Easy, it just bounces down the stairs but don't tell Mrs Skinner that's how I do it!' He looked around. 'Now, where's my favourite baby?'

'She's outside in her pram, I just came in to get this. It's such a lovely day I thought I'd feed her under the porch.'

'That's right, dear – a bit of fresh air is just what a baby needs...'

Gracie put the bottle down and helped Henry get the trunk up to the desk.

'We've just been to the shops up the road to pay some bills and now she's dozed off. I might have to wake her for this.' Gracie waved the bottle. 'She needs all the help she can get if she's going to catch up.'

'Listen to me, young Gracie. I know babies – we had enough of them, me and the missus – and I can see there's nothing wrong with that little 'un that a dose of Virol won't fix. A bit of building up and she'll be right as rain, mark my words.'

Gracie smiled to herself as she walked outside. Henry had reiterated what she herself had been thinking: Fay was going to be just fine.

She pushed the canopy back and stood for a moment looking at the pram, trying to get her brain to process what she could see.

The pram was empty.

Gracie looked all around but there was no one with a baby. And then she screamed and started to run.

'Where's Fay?' Gracie shouted as she flew into the hotel and ran through the lobby into the kitchen. 'Who's picked Fay up? I left her in her pram outside. I went to make up her bottle and she's gone! The pram's empty, her blanket's gone...'

'Calm down,' Ruby said as she ran through from the office. 'Someone's probably picked her up. Where was she?'

'Just under the window in her pram. It's a nice day, I was going to feed her out there on the bench. Ruby, she's gone, the pram's empty...' Gracie could barely breathe, she was hyper-ventilating so badly.

The two young women ran back outside together and looked in the pram, more in hope than expectation – and then realisation hit and all hell broke loose.

'Where's my baby?' Gracie screamed at full volume. 'Where is she?'

Word of Fay's disappearance spread like wild-fire and people ran back and forth between the two properties, looking in all manner of unlikely places around the hotel. Gracie's screams had alerted some of the guests and a few neighbours, and within minutes the area was alive with those who wanted to help, and those who just wanted to know what was going on.

'We have to call the police,' Ruby said, 'and we need to ask around properly. Shouting isn't getting us anywhere. I saw Sean and his mother outside earlier, maybe they saw something.'

'Sean was here?' Gracie's brain started ticking.

'He didn't come in, Rosaleen went out to him. It looked like they had arranged to meet and he didn't want to see any of us...'

'Oh God, they've taken her! Don't you see? That's what Sean was doing here. They've taken Fay, they've taken her away from me...'

Despite Ruby trying to hold her back Gracie ran into the road, screaming hysterically. 'They've taken my baby, they've taken my baby. Help!'

As Gracie ran back and forth so Jennifer McCabe watched, listened and smiled from her vantage point behind the nearby breakwater. She could see them, but they couldn't see her unless they ventured down to the water's edge. Although the sun was breaking through it was still a cool day so the beach was almost deserted and she was well tucked in behind one of the struts.

When Sean had cautiously told Jennifer that his mother had refused to meet her she was steaming mad. She had told him she wasn't prepared to accept it but he didn't take her seriously and so, after he had gone off to work at the café the next day, she had not gone to work but had instead gone to the hotel to try and force a meeting with the woman.

It wasn't that she cared about Sean's mother; she didn't at all. She was simply furious that Rosaleen Donnelly was happy to be with Gracie and Fay in Ruby's hotel, yet she was refusing to have anything to do with her. Jennifer was determined that the woman would speak to her.

When his mother turned up on the doorstep Sean had nearly had a heart attack on the spot. In panic he had carelessly bundled Jennifer down the side of the single bed, and thrown the grubby bedspread on top of her. She had laid there, imprisoned between the bed and the wall, for as long as it took him to chivvy Rosaleen away again by offering to escort her back to the hotel.

As Jennifer crawled out of the space she couldn't believe that Sean had done that to her but she was more furious with herself for letting it happen. She should have stood up to him, to his mother, and demanded that they stop going on about bloody Fay Donnelly. The baby who was causing her more problems than even her sister had.

It wasn't often that Jennifer McCabe admitted she had made a mistake but this time she had. She had allowed Sean to put his mother, and Gracie's baby, first.

The more she thought about it, the more it rankled her that the woman had turned up unannounced and uninvited. It rankled that she had then scolded him like a schoolboy for the state of his living accommodation and it rankled that she had had to listen as Sean had initially denied her to his mother. 'Jennifer is my sister-in-law. Gracie is just making this up to justify herself.'

But worst of all, it had hurt her because despite her original intentions, she really did love Sean.

She had always been the negligible twin, the one no one noticed or was interested in; the attention always on the little blonde poppet who was her twin sister. When she was a child Jennifer had hated being disregarded but then the lightbulb moment had come when she had discovered exactly how to use it to her advantage.

Jennifer had soon learned how to lie with wide-eyed innocence and let others take the blame for her misdeeds. She cheated at school with ease because no one expected it of her, and she could steal sweets from the shop on the corner and pencils from Woolworths and get away with it every time. Whatever she did she had always been able to deflect the blame onto someone else, because no one ever noticed she was there.

Just like her sister had never noticed she was there, inside her marriage.

The moment Gracie had refused to have her and Jeanette as bridesmaids at her wedding was the moment she had set Gracie in her sights.

Jennifer McCabe had never taken well to being snubbed. Jeanette had grumbled and stamped her dainty little feet but Jennifer had shrugged, feigned disinterest and bided her time.

She was a firm believer in *everything comes to those who wait*.

It was her ability to blend into the background that had made her feel quite secure sitting quietly in a deckchair a little way along the promenade, waiting for the right moment to ambush Rosaleen. She didn't want to go into the hotel and be thrown out but she was determined to talk to the woman, to make her see that she was the right person for Sean. She wanted Gracie to be dismissed and she herself accepted in her place.

So she had watched and waited.

But as she was thinking about what she was going to say, Jennifer spotted Sean in the distance, walking along the promenade with his mother. She had been incensed to see the two of them strolling along the seafront deep in conversation and looking far too comfortable with each other for her liking.

But worst of all, Sean had told her he was going to work and had instead secretly gone to visit his mother. Sean had lied. He had put his mother first once again.

It was as she focused on them, analysing their every movement from a distance, imagining the conversation and wondering what to do next, that she had seen Gracie out of the corner of her eye. She was wheeling a pram along the road, a pram that Jennifer knew contained the baby, who was a stumbling block to her complete ownership of Sean Donnelly.

Jennifer watched from her hidden position as Gracie carefully pushed the pram into just the right place under the overhang of the porch; she watched her turn it around so the sun shone down on the tasselled canopy and not the baby, and then she watched her sister go back inside.

Jennifer stared across the road, taking in every detail.

It was a big and bouncy coach-built pram with huge wheels and a cream and silver body that caught the weak sunlight as it filtered down and magnified it. As she watched the canopy's fringe flutter gently in the breeze the picture postcard image of domesticity and motherhood infuriated her.

Without planning or formulation Jennifer had instantly known what she was going to do – and at that moment it seemed like the best idea in the world.

One that would teach them all a lesson.

She had left her deckchair and strolled over the road, her head down and the collar of her jacket up. She walked quietly up the path and then, ducking down just enough not to be seen through the windows, she swiftly lifted the baby out of the pram, pulled out the blanket and strolled casually away with the child in her arms, hoping no one had seen her.

And no one had. The whole exercise had taken seconds.

Jennifer walked along the pavement a short way then crossed over, went down to the beach and settled on the far side of the breakwater, which was out of sight of the hotel. She swaddled the baby up tightly in the expansive crocheted blanket, tucked her up against the seaweed-clad panels, out of sight, and then waited expectantly for the furore.

'But she's sickly, she needs to be here with her mother...' Gracie screamed as the implications of what had happened hit her. 'How can they do this? *How* can they? Where's Sean?'

Gracie was running back and forth in the middle of the road like a mad woman.

'Come here...' Ruby pleaded as she tried to catch her. 'This won't help. We have to go inside and think, and decide whether to phone the police.'

But Gracie wasn't listening. She just kept repeating herself over and over. 'They've taken Fay...'

'*Who* has? Who do you think has picked her up?' Ruby grabbed Gracie by her upper arms and gently shook her. '*Who*?'

'Sean and his sodding mother of course! You said he was here and now Fay's gone; they've taken her.'

'But Sean and his mother are over there. Look, they're over there walking this way, they haven't got Fay...'

Gracie looked over to where Ruby was pointing and saw them walking in her direction. Rosaleen had her arm hooked through her son's and both had their heads down, engrossed in their conversation.

'I don't understand, where's Fay then?' Her hand flew up to her mouth as she tried to block the scream. 'Oh my lord, Jennifer ... this is the sort of thing she'd do when she's having one of her jealous turns!'

She ran over to them.

'Have you got Fay? Where's my baby? Has Jennifer got her?' Gracie pummelled Sean's chest with her fists as she screamed questions at him.

'What are you talking about?' Sean asked as he

grabbed her wrists to stop the attack.

'Someone's taken Fay out of her pram! She's gone, my baby's gone...'

'And you're thinking it was us? That we have Fay?' Rosaleen Donnelly's shock was so apparent that Gracie knew it wasn't them. It had to be Jennifer.

'Does she know you're here?' she screamed at Sean, her face inches away from his. 'Does Jennifer know?'

'What's that got to do with this?' he asked, but Gracie knew he was being evasive. She also knew from the guilt written all over his face that Sean had gone to see his mother without telling Jennifer.

'Jennifer has her.' Gracie took a deep breath and looked around, her eyes taking in every person she could see and then she looked further, desperately scanning the beach.

'She has her, I know she has, and she's watching this and enjoying it. This is for your benefit...'

'Are you mad, Gracie? Why in heaven's name would she do that? She doesn't want anything to do with that baby.'

Gracie vaguely registered Rosaleen Donnelly as she took a step away from her son and turned to look at him.

'That baby? Did you just say *that baby*? That's your daughter and she's missing, and all you can say is *that baby*? Now get yourself together and find out what's going on, Sean Donnelly! Be a man!'

Sean looked at his mother, put an arm around her shoulder and pulled her in to him.

'I didn't mean it like that, Mam.' He looked at Gracie. 'Where shall we start?'

'With Jennifer.'

'I'll drive Sean to find her,' Johnnie said.

Jennifer watched the scene unfolding with delight. She loved seeing the friction between Gracie, Sean and Rosaleen.

That'll teach them, she thought as she savoured it all, but then the baby started to whimper.

'Shut up, they'll hear you.' She put her hand on the baby and half-heartedly pushed her back and forth, rolling her in the sand, while still keeping an eye on the chaos around the hotel.

But then the whimpering turned into a full-blown cry and, despite Jennifer's efforts to stop her, the volume increased.

Jennifer peered over the top of the breakwater and again smiled at the chaos she had caused.

She had wanted to teach them all a lesson and she had succeeded, but now she had had enough. She was bored.

As she watched everyone in deep conversation she took her chance and ducked off in the other direction, leaving Fay alone and crying, tucked out of sight behind the breakwater strut, with the tide slowly but surely coming in.

'Excuse me,' the woman said as she approached one of the guests standing on the edge of the group outside the hotel. 'I heard someone say there's a baby missing. There's a bundle down at the water's edge over there that my dog was sniffing... I didn't take any notice but maybe...'

As she pointed her voice trailed off because everyone started running.

'She's here, we've found her...'

Gracie ran down to the spot with Sean alongside her. She was scared as she had never been scared before but then she heard the cry.

'See? I told you it wasn't Jennifer...' Sean said.

'Then who do you think it was, Sean?' She screamed at him. 'Who else would have dumped Fay on the beach?'

'I don't know, I don't understand it – but Jennifer isn't here and Fay is safe.'

Gracie held Fay to her. 'Listen to me, Sean; *listen* to me! As long as you are with Jennifer you will never see Fay again. She's dangerous, and so are you when you're with her.'

Sean shrugged and walked off, oblivious to the look of horror on his mother's face.

THIRTY-TWO

'Hello Gracie,' the man said as he approached her on the pavement. 'Fancy a spin on the roller-coaster and an ice cream?'

Gracie was just going into the chemists on the Broadway in Thorpe Bay when Edward Wood-field appeared in front of her. For a moment she didn't recognise him. The voice was familiar, with its gentle tone and perfect enunciation, but his whole appearance was so different. She was momentarily thrown as she realised who it was, and she looked at him with a mixture of shock and curiosity.

'Edward? Blimey! What are you doing here?' Gracie looked around nervously.

'I'm sailing back to Africa next week and I wanted to let you know so I decided to drive down and tell you face to face...' He paused and grinned. 'Don't look so shocked, I didn't just turn up at the hotel. I telephoned when I arrived in Southend and Ruby told me you were at the shops. Luckily she gave me directions.'

'She shouldn't have done that,' Gracie said, trying to compose herself and pretend nothing out of the ordinary was happening.

'Don't blame her, she was just trying to be nice. Did you tell her we'd spoken the other week?'

'Yes, I did. Ruby is the only person who knows everything about me, the only person I trust with everything. And it works the other way, of course...'

'It must be nice to be close friends like that. I don't think men do that sort of thing... Look, can we go somewhere to talk? I'm not trying to pressure you, just a chat, as old friends. I know your situation and I'd never compromise you.'

'I don't think it's a good idea, even if you are going back to Africa. I'm still a married woman,' Gracie said, edging away. She didn't want to be that close to him, she didn't want to remember their kiss.

'You're probably right, but you did phone me and then you stood me up so I thought it would be nice to have the catch-up we didn't have in Melton.'

'I'm sorry about that. I had to get back to Southend straight away. But Louisa guessed who it was, you know. You remembered me.'

She started walking but he fell into step beside her.

'Louisa is the nearest thing to a Ruby that I have. But I don't tell her everything, because she's my brother's wife, and if it came to the wire that would be where her loyalties lie.'

Gracie started laughing. 'Sibling loyalty? Wish my sister had heard of it...'

'Why do you say that?'

'Never mind, it's a long story and I have to get back to work...'

'Well, as I'm here we might as well have that chat, don't you think? I won't be back in England for another three years. Let's go and sit over there and talk.'

As Edward looked at her she could feel herself weakening, in exactly the same way she had when they'd met. But there was something different about him, and it took a moment for her to realise that beneath the beard there were scars and he didn't lope along as he had before. And then she remembered that he'd told her on the phone that he'd had an accident. *An altercation with a tree.* She realised, looking at him, that he had made light of it. It had to have been far more than an altercation.

'Look, you can come back to the hotel with me if you wish,' Gracie said, softening. 'We can talk there but I can't be seen with you, not at this moment. I don't want anything to go wrong with...' She stopped herself. 'I just don't want to be seen doing anything untoward.'

'Look, I've borrowed Harry's car – I'll give you a lift,' Edward said quickly, indicating a vehicle parked a little further up the road.

'Nice car...' Gracie smiled as she lowered herself into the passenger seat of the dark green sports car and stretched her legs out. She tucked her shopping bag down by her feet and rested her arm on the cutaway door.

'It's a Triumph,' he said.

'I know, I can read. Now no trees this time, please,' she said and Edward laughed.

'Definitely no trees, especially in Harry's car.'

Under Gracie's directions, he drove the long way back to the hotel through the country lanes of Barling and Wakering, and then from end to end of the seafront, with Gracie holding onto her hair which was trying to stand up on end.

When they finally arrived at the hotel, Edward parked a little way away and let Gracie go on ahead before following her.

Gracie was in the lobby when he entered. 'If you'd like to come this way, Mr Woodfield, Miss Blakeley is in her office'

He remained straight-faced and as they walked into the office Ruby jumped up from her chair.

'Oh my, oh my, whatever happened to you?' she asked by way of greeting.

'I had a car accident a while ago...'

'Well, the beard suits you, you look very distinguished but I can't say the same for Gracie. Your hair ... have you looked in the mirror?'

Gracie blushed and tugged at her hair with her fingers. 'Oh well, can't be worse than the roller-coaster.'

The three of them laughed at the shared joke and it eased the awkwardness of the situation.

'Well, I have to go and do something or other so I'll leave you to it,' Ruby said, still smiling. 'But don't forget dragon lady and satanic friend are leaving this morning. Johnnie's taking them to the station in about an hour.'

'Praise the Lord and bang the tambourine, I'll be there to wave her off with streamers,' Gracie smiled.

'I'll bring you tea. I'm getting good at handing out tea trays to you, aren't I? Aunt Leonora taught me well!'

Ruby grinned as she left the room and pulled the door shut behind her.

'Did you have the accident in Africa?' Gracie asked, not only to break the ice but also because she was curious. If he hadn't come up to her at the shops she doubted she would have recognised him, he looked so different.

'No, near home. I was on the last bend before the drive when I had an encounter with a very large aged tree. The tree survived.' He laughed. 'And so did I. Eventually. The car didn't make it, though! I've not been back to Africa yet. Saffron Walden has been my prison since the day of...' he stopped and looked away.

'Since the day of what?'

'The accident, since the day of the accident. But that's unfair of me. My family have been wonderful, especially Louisa. She's turned out to be such a gem during my time out of action. I feel really embarrassed about how dismissive I was of her previously.'

Gracie felt a strange twinge of jealousy but quickly brushed it away.

'How is Louisa? I know it was she who answered the phone when I rang to tell you I couldn't meet you. And she recognised me. I can't imagine how she did that after one brief meeting on the beach...'

'I confided in her just a little. She's been good to me.'

Again, Gracie felt an odd jealousy.

'I'll go and chase up the tea. Ruby's rushed off her feet so she'll probably forget.'

'Is it okay for me to be in here? I don't want to upset anyone, especially your husband...'

'How much did Ruby tell you?'

'Only that you and Sean weren't together and that you were having a bad time.'

'Did she also tell you that Sean and I have a baby? A daughter?'

'No, she didn't, I had no idea.' The expression on his face was hard to read but Gracie had immediately decided she was going to be open and honest.

'There are a lot of things about me you have no idea about.'

As she looked at him she remembered the day they had gone to buy the ice creams. It was a memory that she had successfully locked away but as she looked at him she was instantly transported back there. It seemed so long ago in one way, but in another it was as if it was happening all over again.

'I hadn't expected it to be that easy to get you alone,' Edward said as they walked side by side as slowly as they could, towards the ice cream stand that was furthest away. 'It's lucky they're all too lazy to want to go ice cream hunting.'

'Ruby wasn't being lazy; she knew what was happening.'

'What did she know was happening? I need to know because I don't even understand it myself.'

He looked at her curiously as he walked closer to her side so their hands were nearly touching. Nearly, but not quite.

'She just knew something was up, she knows me too well,' Gracie said without moving away, but ensuring there was no contact.

'Yes, something was definitely up; I knew when I saw you. I want you to know I don't make a habit of proposing to random young ladies. This has never happened to me before. Love at first sight? I always thought it was a myth...'

Gracie stopped walking and turned towards him.

'I shouldn't be here with you. I should have told you when we were at the beach...'

'Don't tell me anything I don't want to hear, not right now, please...' he interrupted her.

She looked at him intently. Something told her that he knew what she was going to say, that he'd already seen the ring that she had tried to hide.

'No, I have to tell you. I'm engaged to be married.' Embarrassed she looked down at her feet.

'I know, I saw the ring.'

'I thought you might have and I'm ashamed of myself for trying to hide it. But what you don't know is that I'm getting married on Saturday. This Saturday.' Gracie paused. 'And I shouldn't be walking along here with you; I should be back at Ruby's hotel getting everything ready for the day.'

Edward Woodfield didn't say anything; he just looked a little puzzled. She could see he was trying to absorb the information she'd just given him.

'Is that what you want to do?' he asked.

'We still have a lot of preparations...'

'I don't mean do you want to go home, I meant do you want to get *married* on Saturday – to someone who isn't me?'

'Please don't ask me that, it's not fair.'

'Okay. Well, let's pretend for a few minutes that isn't what's happening. Let's just walk and talk, and get to know each other...'

And they had. Then, when they were nearly back to the spot on the beach, they ducked behind the line of huts and vendor stands blocking them from sight of the others. Edward turned to her.

'Please don't marry someone else, Gracie. I know we've only just met but I feel I know you already. I wouldn't presume to ask you to call your wedding off and elope with me but at least delay it... Please?'

She looked at him and smiled. 'I'm sorry,' was all she said.

He glanced around and then leaned forward, took her face in his hands and kissed her gently on the lips. She didn't pull away, simply savoured the moment with the stranger.

By the time they got back to the group Gracie had just two thoughts in her head.

One was that she could easily fall in love with Edward Woodfield, the complete stranger.

The second was that she had to get right away from him and back to Sean Donnelly, the man she had known for so long and who she was going to marry in a few days' time.

As she and Ruby walked away she could feel Edward's eyes on her but she didn't look back.

'Come on, Ruby, keep up!' she said over her shoulder as she walked away as fast as she could. 'We've got a wedding to go to.' The faster she walked and the further she got away from Edward the easier she was able to breathe and convince herself that she was doing the right thing, even though it didn't feel like it. She wanted to turn around and see if he was watching; she wanted to run straight back to him and see what would happen next but she couldn't do that to Sean so she carried on walking.

'My marriage is over,' Gracie said to Edward. 'He found out something terrible about me and I discovered he was having an affair with my sister. You see?' She looked him in the eye.

'You only know the Gracie who was on the beach than day. That wasn't me. This is me, with more secrets than a carrier pigeon, and I've just had the worst year of my life.'

Once the floodgates were open, Gracie and Edward bared their souls to each other. She was all too aware of the mistakes she had made and was determined not to put herself in that situation ever again. Edward meanwhile told her about the accident and how it had happened on her wedding day. They talked and talked until there was a knock on the door and then Ruby put her head round.

'Witches. Two, ready and waiting.'

Gracie looked at Edward. 'I have to go.'

'I'll wait here...'

'No. It's time for you to go also. Time to go back to Africa and get your life back. We can write, we can be friends and we can wait and see what happens.'

Edward stood up and reached forward to take both her hands. He kissed her slowly on the lips as he had that day on the beach, and then he pulled away.

'This isn't what I want, Gracie. Friends? Pen-pals? No, I don't have to go back. I can work in England...'

'No,' she interrupted him. 'You have to go, go back and do what you love. Write to me with your address and I'll write back. Three years isn't that long.' She laughed.

This time she kissed him on the cheek.

'Goodbye, Edward. Have a safe journey.'

Gracie walked out of the office and went to say goodbye to her mother-in-law.

Ruby accompanied Edward out of the front doors, as if he had been her visitor, while Gracie went over to Rosaleen, who was standing alongside Yolande with her suitcase at her feet. There had been an easy truce brokered between them all after the incident with Fay and Gracie had felt Rosaleen thaw a little.

'Gracie, I want you to change your mind. I want you to come to Ireland with Sean and Fay, and continue with your marriage away from the temptations that are here. We can forget about all this, no one need know anything. They needn't even know where you all are,' she said with a satisfied expression. 'It would be a fresh start for everyone...'

'I'm sorry, I really am you know. I'm so sorry it all happened, apart from Fay of course. But there's no going back now. Sean is sure he's staying with Jennifer and I am with Fay. Did you want to say goodbye to her? She's upstairs with Jeanette...'

The last thing Gracie wanted was to get into another discussion with Sean's mother. She understood her desperate desire for everything to be normal in her son's life and for him to still be her favourite child but she couldn't help her, she just couldn't.

'No. It's too upsetting for me, especially when I don't know if I'll ever be seeing her again.' Rosaleen stopped and looked towards the door. 'Sean! I thought you weren't going to be coming...'

'How could I let you go without saying good-bye?' He smiled the boyish smile that Gracie used to love but which now meant nothing to her.

'And when will I be seeing you?' Rosaleen asked her son as she reached out and stroked his hair affectionately, as if he was still a small boy.

Gracie knew immediately that the woman would forgive her son but it made her smile a little to imagine Rosaleen pitted against Jennifer McCabe.

'Soon, I'll see you all soon,' Sean said but as Gracie watched the exchange she caught him giving his mother a warning look.

'We have to go if you don't want to miss your train,' Johnnie Riordan said as he picked up their cases. 'Are you coming to the station, Sean? There's room if you wish.'

'No. I have to speak to Gracie.'

Again, Gracie caught a look between mother and son. As the car pulled away Gracie stayed inside but she watched Sean wave at his mother and then come back in. 'I need to talk to you. Can we go up to the flat and talk in private?'

THIRTY-THREE

Gracie thought Sean was going to explode with embarrassment when he saw Jeanette in the sitting room of the upstairs flat bouncing Fay up and down on her knee.

'Ooh hello, lover boy...' Jeanette laughed, eyeing him up and down slowly.

'Shut up...'

'Oh sorreee, I thought maybe you were here for the third McCabe sister. You know, all for one and one for all...'

'I wouldn't touch you with a bargepole...' Sean flushed bright scarlet as he looked the other way.

'Oh, I bet you would given half a chance, Romeo, but we're never going to find that out, are we?' Jeanette smirked at him, enjoying his discomfort for a few moments before turning to her sister.

'Do you want me to stay or can I take Fay to the park in her beautiful shiny new pram? I feel so important pushing that round, like a la-di-dah nanny. I could wear my new nurse's uniform and really look the part...'

'It's fabulous, isn't it? The Wheatons really pushed the boat out with that! But yes, you take her to the park – but no uniform! Sean wants to talk to me.'

'I bet he does. Is the lovely Jennifer on the premises? I could go and make small talk with twinnie on the way, show her the baby she didn't manage to do away with...' Jeannie continued, needling Sean.

'Shut up. Haven't you made her life miserable enough, you nasty cow? Anyway she's not there, she doesn't want anything to do with any of you. Accusing her of stealing the baby? How low can you all go?'

'But she did,' Jeanette said, 'and you know she did really, don't you?'

'She said she didn't and I believe her. There was no reason for her to do it and no one has proved anything; it's just your nasty minds, all of you.'

Jeanette looked at Sean open-mouthed and then started laughing. 'She's really got you, hasn't she? Well, give it time and you'll learn, you daft old lump of lard!'

As Jeanette got herself and Fay ready Ruby noticed that Sean didn't even glance at his daughter. Not once.

'Shall we go and sit on the balcony?' Sean asked.

'What? You are joking, aren't you? Just like the old days, sit and have a chat and watch the world go by?' she laughed dryly and shook her head. 'Not a chance, mister, just say what you have to say.'

Sean sat down on the sofa but Gracie remained standing.

'I'm going back to Ireland, just as soon as I can. I can't be working in a café much longer, I want to be a real chef again and I've been offered a job in a restaurant in the city. Mam told me about it...'

'I guessed that from something your mother said and then the strange looks. What has the lovely Jennifer got to say about that?'

Sean paused for a moment before replying, and then the words tumbled out all at once. 'She's coming with me. If you want to divorce me then I'll take all the blame. I'll not deny what happened with Jennifer and I won't mention your secret. You know, about St Angela's, and neither will she, she's promised.'

Gracie stared at the man who was her husband but who now seemed like a stranger. Everything that had happened seemed far removed, and now she found it hard to remember what it was like to be with him, to be pregnant and treated so badly.

She had taken all the blame for their relationship souring, but now she could look back and see that it would all have gone wrong anyway. Jennifer would have seen to that.

'So despite what she did to Fay, your daughter, you're going to go to Ireland and take her with you? You're turning your back on your daughter? I'm so ashamed of you, Sean Donnelly,' Gracie said sadly.

'She didn't do anything to Fay, you know that and we're going to Ireland together because its what my mother wants...'

'No it isn't,' she interrupted. 'Not ten minutes ago your mother was trying to persuade me to go with you, she's disgusted with Jennifer. And you for that matter.'

Sean looked at his wife for a few moments before continuing.

'...and it's what Jennifer wants, a new life away

from here, and I think it's what you want as well if you're honest. Fay is *your* baby, not mine. I'm not saying I'm not the father, I'm not saying that, but you really don't want me in her life...' his voice faded off.

'If I'm honest, what I want would be for none of this to have happened. I would want you and I to still be in our flat, with both our twins alive. I'd want Jeanette and Jennifer to be sisterly again and I'd want my mother not to be so crucified with the pain you and Jennifer have caused her.'

'We don't often get what we truly want,' Sean said sadly. 'And I know that whatever you say, you didn't truly want me, not really. We weren't wrong for each other, we just weren't right enough. We got there out of habit – we courted, we got engaged, we wed, without really thinking about it too deeply.'

'And Fay?'

'I'll come and see her.'

'But you can't be her father, living in a different country.'

'Families survived years apart during the war...'

'All right, Sean, you carry on telling yourself you're doing nothing wrong. You've spent too much time with Jennifer; she doesn't know right from wrong either.'

Gracie shook her head in despair. She wanted to cry but instead she started laughing.

'You are an idiot, Sean. Do you really think she loves you? Honestly!'

'She does love me and I love her. I can't help it and I know you don't want to hear it but I'm so in love with her it hurts...' his voice tailed off as he saw the expression on Gracie's face. 'I'm sorry. Look, I want to ask you something, out of curiosity. What happened to the baby you had at St Angela's? Do you know anything of it?'

'No, nothing, and I never will. The baby was a boy and was adopted from the hospital and that is all I know. I went to live-in at the Palace and that's when we first met. It was 1946, such a long time ago.' She met his gaze and stared. 'You need to be careful, Sean, or you'll end up not knowing anything about your daughter. How sad would that be?'

'I wish you'd told me...'

'I wish you'd told me you were in love with my sister instead of blaming me – but we could keep on talking rubbish like this forever and I don't want to, so if there's nothing else?'

Sean stood up. 'I won't be back then...'

'If that's how you feel, then goodbye.'

Gracie didn't look at him as he left and he didn't look round. He just walked away.

As the door closed Gracie stood stock-still with her arms folded and her eyes dry.

She wanted to be angry but wasn't sure why anymore.

She went out onto the balcony and wasn't surprised to see Jennifer standing on the nearby corner waiting, watching until Sean emerged.

He walked towards her and Gracie could almost feel his excitement as he held his hands out and she ran into his arms. She stepped back to make sure Jennifer couldn't see her if she looked up, she didn't want to give her the satisfaction, but Gracie found she still couldn't look away. She watched them kiss and then walk off hand in hand, shoulder to shoulder.

As she watched them disappear out of sight, she thought back to the night of the engagement, when she and Sean had walked along that same route, holding hands. She had been so excited to be engaged, so happy to have a ring on her finger, but now she could see that was what was wrong.

It had been the engagement and the wedding which she had focused on, without giving enough thought to the marriage or the man. Ruby had tried to warn her but Gracie had been too in love with the idea of being married and having legitimate babies to replace the one that had been taken from her.

For the first time, Gracie removed her wedding and engagement ring. She looked at them in the palm of her hand and thought for a moment about making a grand gesture and throwing them into the sea, but she couldn't. One day she would give them to Fay because despite everything, and whether he ever saw her again or not, Sean would always be her father.

Gracie went back indoors and went through to her bedroom where she kept her jewellery box and carefully put them into one of the compartments. As she started to close the lid she caught sight of the gold signet ring that Edward had given her that day at the beach. She took it out and slid it onto her finger as if she expected it to fit this time but it didn't.

Edward Woodfield.

The reason why she was so wrong to go ahead with her wedding to Sean Donnelly. The man who she had seen that very morning and the man who had once again sent prickles down her spine in a way her husband never had.

Sean was her second best and she could see, with the benefit of hindsight, that she was second best for him. They had loved each other but they weren't *in* love and they should never have gone through with it.

But then she wouldn't have Fay, the light of her life.

She put the ring back and went into the sitting room.

Gracie curled up on the familiar sofa and turned it all over in her head until she was brought out of her trance by Jeanette arriving back. She had Fay in her arms and quickly put her in her crib.

'She is getting a bit heavy to lug up and down those stairs, let's hope they sort the basement out for you a bit sharpish.'

Jeanette looked around.

'I see he's gone then...'

'Yes, he's gone. He and Jennifer are off to Ireland. Seems like it's the real thing between them. Or so he says. Anyway they're going and I suppose one of us should tell Mum and Dad; I'm sure Jennifer won't. Mum will be devastated all over again, regardless of everything she's done and how far she's fallen.'

'You seem happy enough with it, don't you still want to kill Jennifer just a little bit?' Jeanette asked with a grin.

'No, I'm past that now. They're welcome to each other. I feel sad that it all ended like this but better now than in five, ten or whatever years...'

'So shall we go out and celebrate tonight? Ruby won't mind babysitting Fay,' Jeannie said.

'Nice idea but it's too soon and anyway, I need to work my fingers to the bone for a while to pay Rubes back for everything she's done for me. I've disrupted her life and her business a treat!' Gracie paused. 'What a year this has been, eh?'

'It has but now you can look ahead to the future and you know what? I think we're all going to be okay.'

'I hope so,' Gracie said, looking at her daughter. 'I really hope so.'

THIRTY-FOUR

Gracie and Ruby were sitting side by side on the balcony looking out over the water, passing Leonora Wheaton's binoculars back and forth. It had become a bit of a ritual but it was especially poignant at that moment. It was the last night that Gracie and Ruby would be in the flat together. The house next door was nearly ready to open as an annexe to the Thamesview, and Gracie and Fay were going to move into the tiny basement flat there. Meanwhile, Ruby would stay in the top flat alone and get it redecorated before she and Johnnie married.

Although Gracie was looking forward to moving to the more accessible flat, she was also nervous about being on her own with Fay for the first time.

'I can see how Aunt Leonora got hooked on this ship-watching obsession. I could easily be the same, it's strangely hypnotic,' Ruby laughed. 'God, she used to spend hours out here in all weathers trying to guess which ships were going to where from Tilbury.'

'She'd have loved to have gone somewhere on a liner. It's such a shame she never did, a bit of a lesson there for us. You know, life's too short!' Gracie said, looking out across the estuary.

'It's a shame Edward's ship sailed from Liverpool, we could have waved as he went past...'

'Who knows?' Ruby said. 'Next time you might be on one of them, sailing away to Africa! Have you heard from him yet?'

'No, he said the post is erratic but he should be settled back in by now. He seemed to think the warmth would be good for his injuries from the accident. That was a bad crash. I often think he could have been dead and I would never have known. Never ever. I'd just have thought he was still in Africa.'

'Be thankful he's alive and kicking then! Even if he is several thousand miles away.'

'Three years is a long time to be away, it's a pity you couldn't have sorted this out before he went...' Ruby added, holding her hand out for her turn with the binoculars.

'I know, but the timing was all wrong again, so I'll take my chances and hope for the best. Whatever will be will be, and I have Fay so I won't be alone.' Gracie smiled at her friend. 'Anyway, you've waited long enough for Johnnie and now it's all working out for you.'

'I suppose, but we've always been in the same country. Africa is so far away, how did you resist?'

'It was hard but it was the right thing to do for Fay. The dream was wonderful but real life is different and I have to consider Fay. It would have been wrong for me to take her across the world, what with her being so fragile. He offered to stay, you know. He said he'd get a job in England, but how could I stop him being where he wanted to be?'

'Maybe next time he goes you'll be able to go with him. Do you think there's a future for the pair of you?'

'I don't know. He's the right one, I know that, but he's the right one at the wrong time. Not only do I have a child who might have long-term problems, I can never have any more children. If Edward wants children then...'

Gracie's voice faded as she thought about the implications, as she had over and over again. She could see it being the one single thing that would prevent them having a future together.

'He's the eldest son, his family are going to expect him to produce an heir; they're not going to want him wed to a sterile divorcee, are they?'

'What did he actually say when you told him?' Ruby asked. 'Did you tell him all the details?'

'I told him everything, even what I had for breakfast. I don't want to get caught out again, do I?' Gracie said with a smile that didn't reach her eyes. 'He said he didn't mind but who knows?'

Gracie was besotted with her baby Fay and also very protective because of her frailness, but her biggest sadness was the thought that she would never have another baby. First there was Joseph, whose birth was wreathed in sadness because he had to be given up, and then there had been the trauma of losing Phillip, Fay's twin.

'If that's what he said, then he must mean it,' Ruby said.

'But how do I know that? I don't know him, do I? I may think he's Mr Right One but I don't know him at all. We've met twice and shared a few phone calls. That's it.'

Again they passed the binoculars back and forth, until Ruby jumped up.

'I'll be back in a few minutes, there's something I must check on...'

As Ruby left, Fay started crying so Gracie lifted her out of her crib, held her close and rocked her. She would never forget the sheer terror she'd felt during the time Fay was missing. The whole episode had probably only lasted half an hour but it had seemed like a lifetime. It frustrated Gracie that she was so sure it was Jennifer but no one except Ruby and Johnnie believed her.

It had been called a mystery but all Gracie's instincts told her that it was Jennifer's way of tugging Sean back into line and away from his mother. It had been a reckless and wicked thing to do to a tiny baby and Gracie was all too aware that if they hadn't found her in time and the tide had come in, Fay might have been gone forever. She hated her sister for that moment of sheer terror but she knew she could rest easy because Jeanette had found out that Sean and Jennifer really were safely ensconced in Ireland.

It was time to close the door and hope they never came back.

'We're back!' Ruby said as she walked onto the balcony, with Johnnie in tow.

'Now, what are you doing next month, Gracie Grace? On the thirtieth? Not off on your holidays or anything? Not jumping on a ship to Africa? A slow boat to China?'

'Holidays? You're joking, the only holiday I need is what I'm already doing very happily. Working here, looking after Fay and living a peaceful life. It's been so hard lately and now I feel as if a great weight has been lifted.' Gracie paused. 'Sorry, I went off a bit there. End of next month, did you say?'

'Johnnie and I have set the date, we're finally going to tie the knot and be legal...'

'Oh, that is such good news!' Gracie exclaimed. 'Will you have the wedding here?'

'No, not here, and out of respect for Sadie we're not going to have a big fancy do, just a basic ceremony in church with a few close friends and family but we *are* going to have the biggest party afterwards. You up for that?'

'I'll check my diary...' Gracie laughed. 'Oh, I'm so happy for you! I've been waiting for you to set the date. God, I bet George and Babs will be jumping for joy. And Maggie. Oh, this is so exciting, are the boys coming to live here straight away?'

'Not as such,' Johnnie replied. 'They're going to stay with Betty for the time being and come here for the school holidays and then we'll see. Softly, softly. Betty's done so much for them, and for me, that I don't want to upset her. She loves the boys and they're happy so we're going to compromise.'

'Compromise, that's a good word. I'm going to compromise as well. Jeanette and I are going to visit Mum and Dad tomorrow to talk about the Jennifer and Sean thing. They need to know the details, because once again she's just gone off without a word. And we all need to clear the air once and for all.'

'Oh, well good luck then. Do you want to leave Fay here?'

'No, I'm going to take her for her first ride on the bus and meet Jeanette there. It'll let Mum and Dad spend a bit of time with Fay as well.'

'Everything is coming together...' Ruby smiled.

'Yes, at last. It's been a strange old time but hopefully we're going to have peace at the Thamesview from now on.'

'Fingers crossed,' Ruby said with a grin. 'But then again, we do seem to attract trouble, you and I. If it's out there, it'll find us!'

'Are you calling me trouble?' Johnnie asked with a fake frown.

'Yes,' Gracie and Ruby said in unison. 'We all have trouble as a middle name!'

EPILOGUE

Six months later

'Gracie ... telephone...' Ruby shouted from the office.

'Coming...'

Gracie ran through from the kitchen and took the receiver. 'Hello?'

'Hello, is that Gracie? It's Louisa here. Edward Woodfield's sister-in-law?'

Gracie was surprised and cautious. She had had no dealings with Lousia at all and she could think of no reason for her to phone.

'Yes, this is Gracie,' she said, sounding confused.

'I'm thinking you might not have heard from him with the postal system in Africa not really being up to scratch so I'm phoning to tell you that Edward's being flown home. He managed to contract malaria and he's been so poorly. He's been in hospital out there but now he's slightly better he's coming home. I thought you should know. Gracie, it's serious; because he was still slightly weakened from the accident, when he caught the malaria he went down like a ton of bricks...'

'Oh, I see. I'm sorry to hear that. But why are you phoning me?' Gracie asked cautiously. She could feel her heart thumping as she tried to

348

keep her voice calm.

'Darling, I know how Edward feels about you, and I'm sure he would want me to tell you. He's a bit incommunicado himself in hospital in bloody Africa. We didn't find out for a couple of weeks and by then he was over the worst. Honestly, you'd think head office would have had the savvy to telephone us, wouldn't you?'

'How did you know where I was?' Gracie asked. She knew she was sounding stupid but she couldn't think what else to say.

'Oh Gracie, Edward talked about you of course.' Her laugh tinkled down the phone line. 'He told me all about you and his feelings for you, and it's taken me all my willpower not to pop down and look you up.'

'He shouldn't have told you, there's nothing to tell...'

'Well, he did. Anyway, he's still poorly but he's coming home and I can't see him being able to go back for a while. Are you pleased? I know we are. Not that he's sick, of course, but that he's coming home. I'll let you know when he's back here in our clutches; you might want to visit...'

Gracie couldn't think of anything to say so she let Louisa chatter on for a while.

She was bemused by the phone call because it felt as if she was being included in the family situation even though there was nothing of substance between her and Edward. She felt nervous as she thought about him being taken ill so soon into his tour but most of all she felt a wave of elation at the thought that he was coming back and she was going to see him again far

349

sooner than she had expected.

'Ruby?' she shouted at the top of her voice after she'd put the phone down. 'Guess what? Edward is coming home. I don't have to wait three bloody long years! He's coming home.'

The publishers hope that this book has given you enjoyable reading. Large Print Books are especially designed to be as easy to see and hold as possible. If you wish a complete list of our books please ask at your local library or write directly to:

Magna Large Print Books
Magna House, Long Preston,
Skipton, North Yorkshire.
BD23 4ND

This Large Print Book for the partially sighted, who cannot read normal print, is published under the auspices of

THE ULVERSCROFT FOUNDATION